THE KILLER'S DOG

Author Photo: Jonathan MacBride

Book Design: Joel A. Bass

ISBN: 978-1-9324186-0-6

Elixir Press
PO Box 27029
Denver, Colorado 80227

www.ElixirPress.com

Elixir Press is a nonprofit literary organization.

Library of Congress Cataloging-in-Publication Data

Names: Fincke, Gary, author.

Title: The killer's dog / Gary Fincke.

Description: First edition. | Denver Colorado : Elixir Press, [2017]

Identifiers: LCCN 2016007867 | ISBN 9781932418606 (alk. paper)

Classification: LCC PS3556.I457 A6 2017 | DDC 813/.54--dc23

LC record available at https://lccn.loc.gov/2016007867

THE KILLER'S DOG

GARY FINCKE

ELIXIR PRESS

As always,

>for Derek, Shannon, and Aaron,

>and especially for Liz

ACKNOWLEDGEMENTS

Where We Live Now	*Cimarron Review*
Freaks	*Sonora Review*
Smart Boy	*Crazyhorse*
The Killer's Dog	*Cimarron Review*
The Chemistry of Entertainment	*Pleiades*
Gettysburg	*Gargoyle*
Now They're All Strangers	*South Dakota Review*
Somewhere in There, the Truth	*Valparaiso Fiction Review*
Sight Unseen	*Shenandoah*
Are You Still There?	*Santa Monica Review*
Proofreading	*Seattle Review*
Subsidence	*Ascent*

TABLE OF CONTENTS

WHERE WE LIVE NOW

SATURDAY

"Shut that thing up," the prick kid says. He holds his phone at arm's length like he's taking a picture of himself and then slaps it back against his ear.

The loud baby and I are on the other side of the loud TV, way across the room from him. The loud baby is laughing. I wait for him to finish his call, then I go Thelma and Louise on him. I owe somebody's swear jar a fistful of quarters. An older guy I've seen around never takes his eyes off the bass fishing on TV. I really want to put the prick kid's face through the window. A couple of salesmen make a point of coming over, the guy from parts flirts with Lyssa. I'm a regular; the prick kid is just passing through.

The prick kid flips his phone shut and walks to the Michelin display like he has a friend meeting him there to inspect tread patterns, but all he can do is inhale that rubber smell from new tires for a while until Roy, the service manager, says, "Ellen, you're ready to roll." Roy has another invoice beside mine, but he makes silly faces at the loud baby, and I'm paid and carrying her out the door, tires aligned and brakes adjusted for next week's trip to Punxsutawney, before Roy says "Bobby Crowe?" as if the room is packed with strangers.

Ten minutes later, when I tell Edwin the story, he puts his finger to his lips. "The baby will be saying "goddamn" and "go to hell" before she learns to walk." He doesn't repeat "prick" and "asshole," not even in a whisper.

SUNDAY

Right before noon, a commotion starts at the big Presbyterian Church two doors down. An ambulance and the police, all that fuss meaning more than a heart attack. "Whatever it is, we know them," I say.

"Let's hope not well," Edwin says, but that doesn't hold water. I take Lyssa outside with me and let him decide whether or not he'll follow.

The ambulance leaves, but the police stay, going in and out, so I let myself drift their way until Cheryl Walcott, from next door and a churchgoer, comes outside still dressed like she's ready to pray. "In the church," she says before her voice drops to a whisper. "With God watching."

I look at two cops, a scattering of people, all of them a stone's throw from the concrete steps climbing to the main entrance where a yellow crime-scene tape is up, and wait for her to tell me the story.

"He shot her right there in the pew where she sits during the sermon. He marched right down the aisle and fired twice and killed her on the spot, anybody could tell."

"Who?" I finally have to ask, and Cheryl squints at me as if she's just discovered she's mistaken some out-of-towner come to gawk for her neighbor.

"Denise Erhard" she says. "Her ex-husband Clay put two bullets in her before a couple of fellows wrestled him quiet." She looks at me as if she wants me to cover the baby's ears. "In this very town and him a teacher of our little ones to boot."

The church almost shimmers in the overhead, early May sun that is just starting to send the steeple shadow toward Cheryl's Victorian three-story. This time of year the shadow will be over her house before three and over ours less than an hour later. By Memorial Day the shadow will reach us around five like a sundial that says it's time for dinner.

Cheryl looks so much like she wants me to hug her that I say, "Teachers have shot people before."

"What's next then? A doctor? A pastor?"

"Them too."

"A teacher," she says as if she hasn't been listening to either of us. "Me with three girls, the oldest wanting a clarinet."

"You should be thankful he wasn't like one of those lunatics who shoots everybody. You all got to go home with your families," I say, and when Cheryl just stands there, I add, "It's like in those nature films where the lion pulls down the weakest while the rest of the herd thunders away, safe for another day."

Cheryl comes back to life. "Ellen Stark," she says, "somebody else might slap your face for saying that out loud."

While I make sandwiches for lunch, I repeat Cheryl's story, and Edwin reminds me how, when the Erhards had separated a few weeks before Lyssa was born, he'd told me how that meant there were only three other couples in town where both partners had graduated from college, and we knew two of them. "The third," he said, "is a rumor," and I didn't know whether he meant us living together like we did without a license or there was a couple he didn't know. Now, holding his turkey sandwich, he says, "He's not the first. Going to college doesn't keep you from being a killer."

"You sound like one of those profilers you watch on Criminal Minds," I say. "The ones who figure out the reason killers slaughter people."

"Those criminals always kill more than one. They have to establish a pattern."

"What does a woman do to get herself to be the first one shot?"

"There's only the one thing," Edwin says, too certain to be right.

"He's an ex-husband," I say. "There's no sense to that."

"It doesn't matter if they're separated. There's a man out there who's thinking he could have been the one dead and soon to be buried if Clay Erhard had a different way of settling things."

"Well, you can't be an ex-husband," I say, and when he just chews his bite of turkey and bread instead of answering, I watch him and try to imagine how he would kill me if I slept with another man. No gun, of course. Not Edwin, even in our town full of guns. And no blood from a knife. He'd have to smother or strangle me. He'd have to touch me and be close, and then I know all he would do is leave before I say, "I remember from when we were in grade school he wasn't a good-looking man and she was pretty."

Edwin takes another bite and then talks while he's chewing. "You were nine or ten."

"Exactly. Old enough to see that he was an ugly prick."

MONDAY

The newspaper uses the whole front page with the story, including sidebars about the killer and the victim. The reporter spends half a column emphasizing how Clay Erhard isn't some outsider, going on so long I'm half surprised he doesn't say Erhard isn't like some monster in one of those old movies with titles like It Came from Beneath the Sea.

But right there on the front page is the ugly prick in a tuxedo. Like he got to pick which one they print. Like the police let him search the house until he handed it to them and said, "Here, this is how I look."

His bald head and glasses. Dressing up to conduct the grade school band like he's Leonard Bernstein at Carnegie Hall. At least I won't see the like of that when Lyssa is squeaking and honking on something or other for parents who film the show on their phones.

There are a few details Cheryl didn't mention. How Erhard was seen pacing outside before the service. How the minister shouted "No!" just as Erhard leveled his gun. And some she did like how he walked down the middle aisle and fired two shots. How other congregation members grabbed him and held him after the shooting. And some I almost know from living here my whole life: How Denise Erhard was both the organist and choir director. How the ugly prick has taught for more than twenty years at the elementary school. How Denise, fifty-two years old and now dead, taught music at the elementary school in the next district for thirty years. How the church was 180 years old, the oldest thing in town except for an inn turned gift shop on the next block down.

I stop when I get to the part about how the ugly prick will be given a psychological evaluation. "Some lawyer will say he's crazy," I tell Edwin.

"He was at the time," Edwin says like he expects Clay Erhard to dance around murder.

"He doesn't sound crazy," I say. "It says here he called her a filthy bitch."

"They put that in the paper?"

"SueAnne Waltman, the minister's wife, says she heard him plain as day from where she was sitting two rows behind."

"That doesn't mean it gets printed. They should just say he responded with obscenities."

"You sound like you're auditioning for the grade school concert," I say. "I bet he said worse. I bet SueAnne Waltman, a preacher's wife, couldn't bring herself to repeat the real words."

Edwin loops his tie into a perfect knot to remind me he has to go to work half an hour before I do and doesn't have time to argue about the dead, but I read him another quote. "You just feel this tremendous grief and try to process what happened. We are considering closing the church for a month out of respect."

"That's Pastor Waltman," I say as Edwin plants a peck on my forehead. "And here's one from a County Commissioner who lives twenty miles from here: 'This is devastatingly tragic for the community. What a shame this sinister deed took place inside a church.' Who is that guy anyway? He talks like he lives inside some old book."

Edwin sighs. "I bet nobody mentions that if enough have guns, some will use them on others."

"On a wife, you mean?" I say.

"Husbands too," he says, "wives, children" as if he wants me to hate him.

"We don't have guns," he adds, taking that steaming pot off the burner before it boils over.

And then he's out the door before I can tell him that I'd bet Erhard didn't think things were over until he fired his gun. Then he knew he'd closed both sides of his life, the past and the future, each of them useless. That's what he meant to say, at least, though his words printed in the paper were "I had to end it, that's all."

The selfish prick. Thinking like God.

TUESDAY

More of the same on the front page, but room now for a car crash with nobody dead. Still, those two photos of the dead and the living side by side. I look at the ugly prick's picture and think about Jason Fields and the way he looked at me when I told him I was pregnant with Lyssa. Apprehensive. Frightened maybe. And then relaxed just before he said, "We can deal with this" as if he'd just remembered where the jack and spare tire were stored. He even squeezed my shoulders like I was his aunt hosting a reunion dinner.

What he didn't do was ask how I felt.

And what I most remember is the way, a few days later, Jason looked when I said I was keeping the baby and I wasn't there to negotiate. Angry. Like all it took to make him want to shake me was fatherhood.

"That's crazy," he shouted over his shoulder, stomping toward his pickup. "There's no way."

He didn't touch me. I'll give him that. But when he came back around after an hour and I held my ground, I watched him start doing the pick-up-and-go. After he had his stuff stacked in the bed of his truck, he walked to where the woods began, his head down, hunched over, the low sun turning him into a silhouette. He picked up a thick, fallen branch and swung it against the trunk of a tree three times before he dropped it and jogged to the truck. For sure, I kept my eyes on that rusting pickup until it disappeared. "Change locks," I wrote on the to-do list. Right on top where I printed the things that couldn't wait.

I moved in with Edwin two months before Lyssa was born. I'd once upon a time gone out with him for a year before he'd gone off to college and I'd started driving back and forth to the community college for my associate. "I'm willing," he said, sounding like Mr. Barkis in David Copperfield when we read it in ninth grade.

The truth? I was grateful, but I wasn't surprised. I've known Edwin since the first day of kindergarten through when he opened his insurance agency four years ago and then up to the minute he made the offer.

I'd even worked on his teeth, what with me being a dental assistant for five years and Edwin, twice each year, sitting in the chair. He's careful with his teeth. I know that from finding so little plaque it's mostly a polish with him, the curettes and hoes waiting for somebody who comes in after he's got a coat of tartar going deep into his bleeding gums.

But since just before the baby and now, for six more months,

I've kept the books and greeted patients, the baby nearby. Arbogast, the dentist, has promised one year, which seemed generous until the year is nearly expired and a month from now I'll have to trust a sitter and add that expense if I want my old job back, the retired assistant who's filled in already hinting she might quit before the year is up, returning to the front desk because she wants to be off her feet, even if it means twenty-five per cent less pay.

WEDNESDAY

Since Lyssa turned four months old, right about the time winter began to break, Edwin and I take her somewhere on Wednesdays because, as if we need two Sundays in Forestville, everything closes in our town. Selling insurance like he does, Edwin needs to stay in step with the Wednesday close, and Tom Arbogast has had his office closed mid-week at least since when he filled my first cavity.

Outside of town, along Route 6, everything's open all hours seven days a week, so we stop for burgers or pizza before we go to the park or a few miles north to Lake Alice, but I'd thought of Punxsutawney and their famous groundhog Phil last week, and when Edwin said he'd never been, same as me, we made a date.

Punxsutawney, when we get there after ninety minutes, is so plain looking I almost think the whole groundhog thing is a fairy tale concocted by dragging any old groundhog in from some farmer's field. "Phil's hole and all that is right in the middle of town," Edwin says, driving without asking directions. "We've both seen the groundhog's stage a dozen times on television. We'll recognize it when we get there."

A couple of blocks prove him right when they lead to the town square. The place is nearly deserted, which gives us plenty of time to stretch our legs and carry Lyssa, awake after the ride, her diaper changed, toward a carved wooden groundhog that is Edwin's height.

I balance Lyssa and take a picture of him with his hand on the shoulder of his new friend.

"All these years and we've never been," he says.

"Us and a whole lot more," I say, but he's already moving toward the shiny, cartoonish statue of a groundhog in a tuxedo, red bow tie, and top hat who's waving a friendly paw. Lyssa ogles that groundhog's buck teeth, remembering, maybe, the oversized tooth models from Arbogast's. Edwin snaps pictures like we're at the Grand Canyon until three boys, each of them wearing souvenir top hats, come up and surround the cartoon statue to pose for their mother.

Near the souvenir shop a man in a red shirt and top hat is speaking while he holds a gray groundhog that looks drugged. We've missed part of the talk, so I don't know if it's Phil or an understudy. "Phil's favorite meal is dandelion leaves in early spring," the man says.

Edwin looks excited, like he want to hold the real Phil in his hands and ask him whether next winter will be hard. "We need a hook like this to get tourists into Forestville," he says.

"Nobody will care about a cartoon tree," I say, and when Edwin frowns, I add, "A lucky thing, for my money."

Lyssa reaches for Phil with both hands. She laughs. Three women are taking pictures with their phones. Another is talking to somebody on hers, saying "totally fat" and "funny cute." She is wearing a top hat like the ones in the gift shop window and on the heads of the three boys.

Edwin seems dumbstruck. I take Lyssa inside the gift shop and buy her a small, stuffed groundhog. When we come out, Lyssa pushing the groundhog into her mouth as if it's made of candy, I say, "What do you think that guy in the hat says about groundhogs to people he knows?"

I expect Edwin to talk weather forecasts. Instead, he says, "He keeps his mouth shut. Groundhogs are pests."

I think I've missed Phil biting Edwin, but I keep on. "Like a minister when he's socializing," I say.

Edwin looks at me like he's been praying in secret his whole life. He takes another picture of the guy in the top hat. All the way home I have to keep myself from saying that the groundhog's shadow shows or it doesn't. Then it's over. The only complications are the road conditions driving back to Pittsburgh or Erie or wherever people come from to stand in the cold at sunrise.

THURSDAY

Because it's a murder, nobody thinks to make casseroles or fruit-filled breads to drop off at the nearest relative's house. Anyway, there's no immediate family who live in town, so there's nothing to do but show up for the viewing, murmuring condolences to strangers with hugs that seem selfish as if something has been earned through simply surviving.

Edwin says he can't close early, but Sally Arbogast, Tom's daughter just home from college, offers to sit in for me at the desk and keep an eye on Lyssa when I leave at three o'clock and promise to return by 4:30. I walk the six blocks back to the church by myself, thirty-four houses until ours, and with each one I pass I pretend I can know people by the houses they live in. I want to think that siding and shutters and the spotted or spotless windows explain how the owners act, but the houses refuse to add anything to what I already know about the people who live there. Even ours looks like the start of some Penn and Teller trick, like it has a false front that says "ordinary" that will vanish while my gaze is drawn away by clever patter or gesture.

The door to the sanctuary is still yellow-taped. They have Denise in an open casket in what looks to be a social room downstairs. I notice her hair is styled like in the newspaper photo. And I notice how much weight she carried, enough, I think, for Edwin to be wrong about dying for sex. With her being childless, it's just two sisters and her mother receiving the sorry's. The old woman is in a chair with a high back, the daughters standing on either side like slaves. If there are friends of the ugly prick filing by, I bet they've been sworn to silence by their wives.

I sit on a folding chair like everyone else. Moved to the basement, even the funeral itself can't shake the anger and fear from its grief. I examine the men for copycats. I watch the women for helplessness. As if Denise Erhard was victim zero, as if by attending her burial a plague would begin the way it does when those tribal women I've read about wash the body of an Ebola victim.

Cheryl catches up with me on the way out. She walks with me toward Arbogast's because she says she needs some air. "So close," she says. "There will never be a way to feel safe again."

"Local let us down. I'll give you that," I say.

"That's Ralph Sauers across the street mowing his lawn. He's only a block away, and he could be as crazy as Clay Erhard. Buddy Fields getting his mail next door to Ralph could be angry enough to do something crazy."

"You should have more faith in human kindness," I say, and it sounds like I've been staying up late reading.

"The town must be having bad dreams," she says. "Everywhere somebody must be waking up sweating."

It's like listening to a fortune teller. No matter how silly, Cheryl sounds confident, her voice as assured as a news anchor. "I have something to ask you," she says. "We have to do more than a few loaves of zucchini bread," and by the time we get to the office Cheryl has made a push for me to hit up a big chunk of Forestville to donate to a scholarship in Denise's name.

When I tell her I'll canvas fifty houses for contributions, she smiles as if she believes a few thousand dollars might pay for a resurrection. "Saturday morning," she says. "You can have Arbor and all those tree streets where there's the most money. Take that adorable baby. She'll make you our best money raiser."

FRIDAY

The paper comes after both of us have left in the morning, so I don't see it until after five-thirty when I get home late from Arbogast's because I had work to catch up on. The funeral is on page one with a photo of pall bearers carrying the casket a few minutes after Cheryl followed me. From now on, I think, everything will be about that ugly prick crying crazy.

Edwin is in the living room eating Cheerios like a boy come home from grade school wanting a snack. He eats nothing but the old fashioned plain kind for breakfast every day except Sunday when I make omelets that he orders by opening the refrigerator and picking three things for me to chop and slice before sprinkling them over the whipped, thickening eggs. "Hungry?" I say, but he scoops up the rest of the cereal and drinks the milk from the bowl before he says anything.

"It feels like we've lived here forever," Edwin says.

"You're tired of having me around?" I say and add a laugh.

"I mean all the time in Forestville."

"Twenty-eight years," I say.

"That's every day of our lives. That's the same as forever."

"That's not much of an eternity."

Edwin looks at me as if he's seeing all the ways I could be somebody he's disappointed in. He puts the bowl down on the coffee table and tells me the best guess for my age when I die is eighty-three, and I notice he has his actuarial tables open on the floor beside the couch. "Fifty-five more years," I say.

"On average," he adds, "but every time you go off and run alone like you do you lose a fraction of those years. It's like smoking. Or gaining weight."

"And here I am ready to change into sweats and do just that," I say.

"Whether you run by yourself isn't a question anybody asks in my business, but maybe they should. A woman running alone is a threat to herself. The danger outweighs the benefits. The numbers say you'll run into the devil out there some day."

"It's still too cold for him," I say. "And anyway he was in church last week, so everybody recognizes him."

Ten minutes later I hand him the baby. "There's no more reason to be afraid now than a week ago," I say.

Lyssa starts to whimper. If she begins to cry, Edwin will hand her back and expect me to stay inside. "Logic doesn't live here," he says, but Lyssa settles.

"What?"

"There aren't any words for where we live now."

I don't tell him how foolish this sounds, but I say, "Where does a music teacher keep a gun?" Forcing a shrug. Adding "In a house like this, where?" as I open my arms, palms up to lift an answer from him.

"No kids," Edwin says, "so there's a spare room turned into an office."

"A desk, a computer, and a gun in the closet."

"We don't know."

"Maybe up high so she never even saw it. His secret waiting to be told."

"And her secret, too," Edwin says, angry now. Like I'm accusing him of having a hiding place.

"Or not," I say, and close the door behind me. I walk the three blocks north to where the houses thin before I start to jog. In 100 yards, by the time I reach the dirt road that winds up to Lake Alice, I'm loose enough to stride where it's not muddy. Edwin tells me to go to the high school and run on the track, but he should worry about the young girls who are parked with boys in trucks once the road is passable. Fourteen, even thirteen—I recognize some from their appointments though they pay no attention to me. I recognize the trucks too, some of them driven by young men already out of high school.

I try to do a mile, but it's mostly uphill going out, so I stop before the steepest part and walk, catching my breath. At the crest, before the road winds down to the lake a mile farther on, I can see the steeple of the Presbyterian Church through a space where the trees make way for the creek that feeds the lake. Nothing else of Forestville shows. Other towns have a courthouse or a bank for the building that can be seen from a mile away. We have a church where a woman gets murdered during the sermon. Earlier today, seven different patients told me it's staying open, that the tape is coming down and there's a service on Sunday

SATURDAY

Some of the women on Arbor and Hemlock and Spruce invite me inside when they see the baby. I never go farther than just into the living rooms because sitting down will keep me from doing the thirty houses I think can be handled in the three hours I give myself with Lyssa riding on my back in the carrier.

I finish twenty-three houses in two hours, four of them with no answer, and then I tell myself twenty-five and done until next Saturday because Lyssa is squirming and so am I.

House twenty-four, at the end of Hemlock where the forest begins its run all the way to the county park a quarter mile away, is Fred Vogel, a widower who lives alone. He comes outside like he needs to keep me away from his house and stares as if he doesn't recognize me. He frowns. His lips are tight, and he works his mouth as if he's turning over a melting sourball with his tongue. "Your little one looks like a papoose back there behind you."

"It keeps my hands free."

"You've seen pictures, right? Squaws with their young on their backs."

"She seems to like it."

"My Ethel, God rest, always held ours in her arms. She wanted to know how they were doing every minute."

"Times change," I say and regret it at once because Fred squints and looks me up and down like a side of beef.

"You hear them?" he says, not taking his eyes off me. "The birds?"

"Sure," I say.

"I love hearing English in the morning from my backyard birds. I remember you now. You've lived here all your life so you know what I mean. It's good to know they're like citizens, ones that were born here like the ones before them and the ones going back to when Ethel would take our daughters out in the yard and tell them the names from bluebird to swallow, all of them chattering without any damn accents." His mouth flexes. The sun lifts above the tree line and this small-town prick and I are caught in its light.

I mean my nod to be neutral, but I see Vogel's glance move to where I've left footprints not quite vanished from when I cut across from the neighbor's yard to save a few steps. When a siren opens full-throated on the nearby county road, I try to translate its accident. Squalled from among the bright new leaves, the cries of those birds who chirp in English sound nervous. "Just because a man's a damned fool doesn't make me want to give money that will get handed to somebody I might not know," Vogel says and goes back inside.

I take a breath and cross the street to stand on the lush lawn that surrounds the Harshbargers' who have given me a check for fifty dollars. Lyssa is so quiet I unstrap the carrier and work the thing off my back, lifting it up in front of my face. She opens her eyes and looks at me, her hands reaching, as always, for my glasses, and I lean in close to feel her breath on my face, letting her tug the glasses loose. We are standing on thick grass. When she drops them, there will be no chance they can break, but the future seems so empty and bleak I think that if I look at Lyssa she'll read such fear in my eyes that she'll be tugged toward it as if the future possesses the gravity of Jupiter.

SUNDAY

Instead of making omelets, I go to the service at the church. All these twenty-eight years, most of the last one living two doors away, and I've never been in the sanctuary. The pews have cushions, something I've never imagined because the Lutheran I did until I was fourteen only had padding on the kneelers. Right away I see that Lyssa is the only child under six in the church. As if the young are checked at the door like coats

The second pew on the right is roped off the way I've seen them reserved for funerals and weddings. On either end there are two wooden posts painted white with a white velvet cord hanging loose between them. Because it's the only completely empty pew, I sit in the one right behind it. There are so many people behind me that I sense, for a moment, how Clay Erhard might have believed that someone would stop him as he walked up the aisle or that all those steps would give him time to change his mind, something to have faith in right up until he pointed the gun and fired.

Although no one is there to play the organ, there is singing, but I rock Lyssa to the hymns' rhythms, and she seems to nod off. But when the church goes quiet, the minister begins to speak, asserting that the church will never close, not ever as long as there are those who seek its comfort. "Think of what science has shown us," he says.

"Tarantulas leave behind footprints of silk."

A ripple of appreciation goes through the congregation, and Lyssa stirs in my arms as the minister launches into his sermon, reading Bible verses that make it seem like Easter. "Respond," he says. "Relieve. Restore. Rejoice." So much like a slogan I half expect him to add "resurrect." When his voice swells with volume and then pauses for a moment for a practiced effect, Lyssa fusses as if she expects my voice, but I let myself disappear. She begins to cry.

Lyssa stretches herself and screams. Pastor Waltman doesn't resume. He looks my way as if he can't go on unless I carry the loud baby outside or someone slides into the pew beside me and asks do you need help, can you carry your child, can you stand and walk, can you please, please, please allow us to worship in peace?

The loud baby cries as if Pastor Waltman has been describing hell. She is so loud the congregation expects an apology, maybe, when I get up and go. Pastor Waltman is smiling at me, calm. A shepherd, I think, holy and purposeful, showing everyone I am the woman who has forgotten how to be a mother.

There are murmurs behind me. I reach into my purse and find the small, stuffed groundhog, but the loud baby turns her head as if she wants to see what all the whispers are about behind us. When she cries again, she could be telling all of them to shut up. But then I decide she is trying to get them all to cry and scream.

FREAKS

The summer I was about to turn fourteen my sister went headless. She was just out of high school, four years older than I was. "We're perfectly apart," she'd said since she'd entered junior high. "When you start junior high, I'll be out of there. When you're ready for high school, I'll be gone."

She'd met a guy the summer before, and it turned out they'd kept in touch. "A carnie," she said, "Ok?" the third time I asked. "It was when his show was in Beaver Falls for five days in July." And after I let it slip to our father at dinner, she told him, "I know what you're thinking, but they're not all bad people."

Dad looked grim. He kept his eyes on Susan until she glanced at me and said that the carnie, whose name was Ronnie Czak, had got her hired as Justina, the headless girl. "All I have to do is sit there," she said. "I'm supposed to have been decapitated in a car crash and saved by a doctor who knows how to keep my body alive while he's waiting for a head to attach."

"It's not your head I'm worried about," Dad said.

Two days later Dad was looking out the window at a man standing beside a powder blue Impala that was creased along the passenger side as if it had sideswiped an iron fist. "A man parks at the far end of the driveway and doesn't come to the door isn't a good thing," he said.

"Ronnie knows how you feel," Susan said. She was holding a small duffel bag that was sized for an overnight trip, but she'd already tossed a big suitcase into the back seat of the Impala.

Dad was holding a drink like he always did after work. "Even more reason," he said.

"It's just a job," Susan said. "It's people shopping. It's no different than standing behind a counter in a department store."

For a moment, when our father moved away from the window, he looked like who I imagined him to be, a man brave enough to stand in the doorway and take my sister's fists and feet until she exhausted herself and gave up. "Who do you think you are?" he said. He stood in her way, but so far from the door she could walk around him at more than arm's length. When she opened the door he didn't turn. "You think you're all grown up now?" he said, but he was facing me and his voice trembled.

My sister left the door open so Dad, for a few seconds, must have thought she was hesitating. "Think about it," he said, his voice sounding more confident. His hands tugged at his shirt as if he were smoothing it before he turned to confront her.

I watched him take three deep breaths before I said, "She's gone, Dad."

His hands fluttered back to his shirt and then dropped to his side. "Close the door then," he said. "The house will be full of flies."

I didn't move. I wanted him to run after her or slam the door or even slap me for disobeying, but instead he looked so pitiful I was afraid he'd sit on the floor and cry. With the door open, the light in the room seemed to shimmer as if we were near water. The sound of tires on gravel churned into the house and then spun away. I turned back into the hall and walked to my room. A minute passed before I heard the front door shut and the sound of the bolt sliding into place. I heard the refrigerator open and ice cubes dropping into a glass. When the television came on, women's voices talking among themselves, I closed my door and turned on the radio, keeping it soft but pulling it onto the bed and laying it beside my head on the pillow.

20

That summer living with my father was all silence. We ate frozen pizzas and tv dinners and hot dogs. My father made me drink milk and orange juice with each meal so, he said, I'd get all the vitamins I needed.

He drank steady each night, but mostly it just put him to sleep with the television on, and every morning he was up and gone to work. He managed a Hickory Farms franchise at the mall. Whenever Susan would make fun of his job, holding her nose as if the raunchiest of the cheeses was sitting open in the living room, he'd say the same thing: "There's a future in the cheese business. They're building malls everywhere, and each one needs a Hickory Farms."

"And that greasy beef stick, too," Susan would say.

"Really," he said, "people come back for more cheese. It's habit forming."

""That's because it's ordinary," Susan said. "That's because they don't know any better."

For a while boys called for my sister during the day, and a few girls rang her up as well, but when word got around that she was traveling all summer, the phone hardly ever rang, never at night, because my sister, when she called, always did it in the morning, to let me know where she was without having my father know she was checking in.

Susan traveled all over Western Pennsylvania and Eastern Ohio and Northern West Virginia, what everybody who lived in those places called the tri-state area—Youngstown, Wheeling, Uniontown, Steubenville. Johnstown, Akron, Altoona—a new place every week, sometimes two places if one was a small, three-day venue like Harmarville.

We lived an hour's drive from Harmarville, about four miles from where Susan and I had grown up as kids, just far enough to be in a different school district in a house that didn't have a street address. RR#4 it said on the envelopes that arrived in the mail. There were empty fields our father called meadows on either side of the two-story house that had been built in 1954, the year I was born, when every other new house was a one-story ranch, Developers were coming, our father said, but we could hope it would take them a while longer. We'd moved right after I finished fourth grade, and three years later our mother had died. Thirty-four years old with breast cancer. The odds were so low she said she'd told herself it couldn't be true until it was too late to do anything about it.

So I had to ride my bike if I wanted to do anything with other boys, but the truth is I didn't do that very often, and nobody rode out to see me. "It's up to you to get along," Dad said from the day we moved in, but I still felt like a stranger at school.

The best thing was that there was a separate garage, and I kept the grass mowed so I could pitch a tennis ball against the side of it or loft the ball off the angled roof and chase down the fly balls that arced off the ricochet. I had a four team league. The players had names, and I kept statistics for all of them, keeping track in my head until the end of a half inning before I filled in a scorecard. "You'll throw your arm out," Dad kept saying, but that summer, with Susan gone, he seemed glad I had my league going again. "As long as you tend to the yard and don't make a mess in the house."

Mostly the weather was so good that I only spent an hour a day in the house, but the second day that it rained, this time all morning and into the afternoon, I ended up in Susan's room.

I pretended I was there to just look around because I was bored, but after a minute I walked to the wall that held the only full length mirror in the house. It was Mom's old one, and Susan, after Mom died, had nailed it up flush to the wall. Even then I was taller than Susan, which made it simple to see myself headless by pushing up on my toes until I was positioned exactly right for seeing myself cut off at the neck.

I stared at myself, but it didn't seem anything like being real. I

22

didn't feel headless at all. I backed away and looked into Susan's open closet where she'd left all of her dresses, taking just skirts with her to the carnival. I picked one with a scooped neckline and walked to the mirror, closing my eyes as I placed myself where I'd stood earlier. I held that dress in front of me and stood on my toes again, trying to remember exactly the height I needed before I opened them to see myself headless again.

I was Justina, the lace at the neckline the last visible thing before I disappeared. I held my breath for half a minute, staring, and then I heard a noise outside on the porch roof that made me duck away from the mirror. A squirrel, I thought, but I hung the dress up on its hanger and didn't go to the window to check. Instead, I walked to my room and looked out from there. The porch roof was clear; the field on our side of the house was empty, but I leaned out and looked up at the house roof, blinking into the rain.

* * * * * *

Mid-morning, the day after the carnival played Harmarville, the blue Impala pulled up to the house, and Susan stepped out of the passenger side I watched her walk up to the porch before Ronnie Czak got out of the car, looking younger than he had a few weeks before because it looked as if he'd shaved five minutes before they'd arrived.

"Dad's at the store, right?" Susan said, looking past where I stood in the doorway.

"Yeah."

I thought Ronnie had shaved that morning to please Susan, and it made me happy. His old-fashioned, slick-backed hair wasn't as important as his face, smooth-shaven with just the thin sideburns. What I noticed, though, was he had two missing teeth, one on top and one on the bottom, right and left of center, not jack-o-lantern bad, but far enough apart that I thought decay, not a fight. In a few years, I thought, Ronnie Czak would have the mouth of an old man. He'd be hissing his sentences.

"I have some stuff to get," Susan said, "but we can stay for a while as long as Dad's gone for good."

"Help yourself," I said, as if it mattered, and she disappeared up the stairs.

After we were alone on the porch for a few minutes, Ronnie offered me a cigarette that I turned down. He shook his head and lit up. "A boy your age don't smoke makes him look he might be in the pink army. I bet you don't drink either. Maybe you don't even think about pussy."

"I think about it," I said, and took one of the cigarettes, a Camel, and let him light it for me. I held it in my mouth and puffed a few times before he frowned. "You got to inhale or it's just a burning thing in your mouth. You might as well have a dick stuck in there."

When I choked after inhaling, Ronnie clapped me on the back and laughed. "That's the stuff," he said, and he looked across one of the meadows for a minute as if he was thinking about something deep and meaningful.

Finally, he turned back to face me. "Your sister's a pistol," he said, and that phrase, something my father always said, made him look like he would never change, like he'd combed his hair in a D-A when he was fourteen, and it had stayed that way for ten or twelve years on its way to forever. I was going to be fourteen at the end of August. It made me stop and think.

"Your sister says you're a reader."

"Sometimes."

"What about the rest of the times?"

"I don't know."

"You ever look at your sister and think about what she looks like underneath?"

24

"No."

"You don't have to lie to me. I'm not your father." He walked off the porch and started into the meadow to my right as if he'd seen something to check out close up.

My sister came out on the porch and watched him for a few seconds. "It's a good job," she said, still looking into the field. "Ronnie made sure we're a single-O."

"What's that?"

"One admission for one attraction. It's not just a bunch of stuff like a cheesy museum people walk through. People pay just to see me."

Ronnie turned around and started back toward us. "He talk about me?" Susan said.

"A little," I said, the truth, and that made her smile though all he'd said was, "She's a piece of work." and "She makes Ronnie, Jr. want to stand up and shout. No offense her being your sister."

"I'll be back in the morning tomorrow," she said. "Ronnie's got stuff to do in Pittsburgh for a day before we're off to Meadville." Later, when they left, I watched them walk toward the powder blue Impala. The crease hadn't been repaired, but what I paid attention to was how Ronnie Czak had his hand under her shirt as they walked.

* * * * * *

"What sort of business?" I said the next morning as we rode our bikes toward town. "Serious business," she said. "He's a grown man." We were on our way to our grandmother's house. It had been just over two years since she'd died, outliving our mother by twenty months. Susan didn't have a key, but she said she knew how to get inside by working an old cellar window up.

"You sure?" I said.

"Real sure," she answered at once, and I thought she'd been

there more than once since the house had been closed up. "This is a big house," she said after we crawled inside. "Grandma lived here all by herself for almost two years after Grand Dad died."

The place was so empty her voices echoed, but when we reached Grandma's old bedroom there was a mattress on the floor, and all around it were empty beer cans and cigarette butts. Further away there was a black comb with missing teeth and one blue sock. "It's hard to believe anyone we knew ever lived here," I said.

"There must be somebody who thinks that way about every place in the world."

"As long as it's wrecked."

"It's not wrecked," she said. "It's just messy," though just then I noticed a used rubber dangling from an empty Colt 45 malt liquor can. It could have been stuck there by anybody, but I was suddenly sure my sister had been fucked on that mattress, maybe even the day before by Ronnie Czak, who wouldn't face my father or pay for a motel. I could feel it.

I went back downstairs before she saw me staring at the limp rubber and opened one of the kitchen cupboards. There were a few cans of vegetables and Vienna sausage, stuff that thieves wouldn't touch—and honey. Susan, who'd followed me, opened the jar and said, "Honey never spoils."

The jar was nearly full. It looked hard and grainy and dark. "That's impossible," I said. "Everything spoils."

"Go ahead," she said, "You can eat it right now Eat some. Don't be such a baby. All you have to do is put your tongue to it. You don't have to take a big bite or anything."

She pushed the open jar toward my face, but I backed away. "Lick it, and I'll tell you how I lose my head," she said. I let my tongue touch it, but even though there was something close to sweetness, it was more like licking sandpaper than tasting anything. "We could heat it," Susan said. "We could at least put it in the sun, and you could even enjoy it because it would soften." She was talking as if I didn't know how to look something up in an encyclopedia, but I said, "It tasted fine. I believe you," because I wanted to know how she got to be headless.

"Ok," she said, screwing the top back on, but leaving the jar sit on the table as if she expected to sit there later and spread it on bread. "There's these mirrors they have that are stuck together with hinges. If you get just the right angle and point them toward the audience, my head disappears and you see all that other stuff instead. It's not that hard. You just have to know how to set it up and then keep your head in the same place."

I couldn't see what she was describing. Not at all. "If it was easy, there would be headless people everywhere," I said.

"Well," Susan said, "that's part of the problem. The trick's been around for a while, so now there's a girl who turns into a gorilla. It's mirrors, too, and a guy in a gorilla suit, but Ronnie says people like it better because it scares them more. The gorilla charges the crowd and a lot of them turn and run. People love being scared."

"It would scare me if I saw you being headless."

"That's sweet of you, but if I turned into a gorilla you wouldn't have to know me to be scared."

She started upstairs again, waving me on. "Come on," she said. "This will be cool."

"What?"

"Remember the attic," she said, waiting for me to reach the first landing.

"Yeah."

"Come on then," she said, starting up the next flight of stairs to the third floor where the attic had been converted to bedrooms years ago. "You know what Dad did once?" she said when I joined her at the top. "He saved me on the roof up here."

"I never heard that."

"Look how far down it is." I glanced toward the window without following her, but I knew how high we were. "I was supposed to be taking a nap," she went on. "Imagine falling off of this. I bet Dad was half drunk when he saved me. It was a Saturday afternoon, so he'd probably had a few under his belt already."

I didn't know what to say. I thought she was making it up to see what I was willing to believe about our father. Susan crawled out the window and scrambled toward the edge before she turned and swung her arms toward me. "Wuss boy, come on out—have a drink with your sister."

"No thanks," I said, but I moved to the window, my breath slowing when she sat down at the edge.

She pulled a flask from her purse. It was silver and thin, the kind of thing somebody gives you as a gift if they know your habits. "Mom had me at eighteen and Grandma married Grand Dad at eighteen," she said, her voice growing louder instead of her turning to face me. "Can you imagine? If I was them, I'd be married to somebody by October." When she took a drink from the flask and laughed, I thought of Ronnie Czak in a tuxedo and shuddered.

"Hey," she said then, her voice softening as she swiveled enough to look at me. "Isn't it funny how she never touched the stuff and Grand Dad was a drinker, and even though he was like twelve years older than Grandma, he only died three years before her so he outlived her in a way."

"Like Dad, right?" I said, swinging up so I sat on the window sill.

She shook her head. "You ever coming out here?"

"I don't know."

She shifted her legs so she could lean my way as she talked. "Mom took a drink of my vodka once," she said. "I was sitting on the back porch and it must have looked like soda with the ice cubes and everything in the glass, and she always had that dry mouth of hers. She asked for a sip and what could I do but let her have some? She made a face and then she said, 'Thank you.'"

"So she knew you were drinking in high school?"

"She didn't say anything, but I started the summer before freshman year, the same as you are right now. Mom was probably sick already when she had that sip." She unscrewed the cap from the flask, but she didn't drink. "Here, wuss boy, have a drink. You've been a teenager for almost a year now. Live a little. Don't worry, it's mixed with ginger ale."

"No, thanks," I said again, terrified when she turned away, threw her head back, and drank from the flask.

* * * * * *

"Tell Dad I'm ok," Susan said before she left. "It's just Meadville this week. He knows where that is. And next week's even closer—Beaver Falls."

"That's where you met Ronnie."

"Fifteen miles from where you're standing," she said.

My father already knew about Beaver Falls. "Get yourself in the car," he said ten days later, so I knew we were going to the carnival, and he didn't want her to know.

The carnival was set up in the parking lot of a big discount store that had closed a few years before. You could still see the lines for the spaces as we walked toward the entrance, and you needed not to look at the huge boarded over windows and graffiti covered walls if you wanted to believe in the magic of the midway.

"You keep your eye out for this fellow Czak," Dad said. "I'll bet he's not far off." It was the first time he'd mentioned Ronnie since the Impala had driven away. My father had seen Ronnie just that one time, and from far away, so I'd thought about pointing out a man who looked more like somebody my father might approve of, somebody in a dress shirt, somebody clean shaven. Now, though, he said Ronnie was a sorry sight, even from a distance, for a man who dressed himself in a sleeveless shirt. "Like Big Klu," he said, "only he doesn't have the muscle for it."

I didn't ask who Big Klu was, and my father, like always, didn't tell me. If I wanted to know, I'd find out for myself is what he always said. "You need more than a tough guy's haircut and a cigarette in your mouth for shirts like that," he said, and I was glad I hadn't seen anybody half way to respectable and been tempted to lie.

Kept Alive through the Miracle of Science

I knew Dad had seen the sign because he picked up the pace. He didn't say a word, but he handed over two quarters, and we slipped inside. Sure enough, there was a girl with no head. I felt sick looking at her with all those tubes coming out of her throat. They arched up from between her shoulders, a thick one in the middle like a fat artery and eight more curling off it like spider's legs.

A man who was supposed to be a doctor was hovering over her, fiddling with one of the tubes as if Justina might be in distress. He was dressed like he'd just stepped out of an operating room in light blue scrubs, a surgical mask dangling below his chin, thin transparent gloves on his hands. I knew it was Ronnie's voice that was coming through a speaker, but I didn't tell my father. Anyway, it sounded recorded so Ronnie could have been anywhere. Justina had been rushed to a hospital, bleeding badly, the voice told us. She'd been given transfusions while a famous doctor was called, the one who knew how to keep a body alive while a search went on for a new head to replace Justina's disfigured, brain-damaged one. It had been months now, and yet here she was, the doctor still hoping.

Ronnie's voice went on like that, but I was staring at Justina's outfit, a halter top that showed cleavage and a skirt that didn't reach her knees. I'd seen my sister dressed like that, but without a head, Justina looked like a girl I'd think about until I had to lock the bathroom door and stroke myself.

30

A few murmurs rolled up when Justina moved her hand. "She's not a dummy," someone said. "She's real." I glanced at Dad to see how he was taking it, but he was looking at the other customers, maybe a dozen of them standing around and staring, all of them men.

When we left the trailer, my father walked up to the pitch man. "That Justina you have sitting in there," Dad said. "She's my daughter."

I stood there thinking of Dad examining Justina's body to be sure she was Susan, what parts of her made him certain, but the pitch man nodded as if a headless girl was easy to identify. "You keep that to yourself and I'll pass it along, you understand?"

"This boy is her brother."

"He can keep a shut mouth too then," the pitch man said, and we waited while he asked the four men who were bunched together nearby to hold on just a minute or two. "You put some distance between us while you're waiting. Go over there by French fries and funnel cake, you understand? She'll be by presently."

The pitch man waved the customers away and reached under the set of two stairs that led to the trailer entrance. He fumbled for a second because he was watching us retreat, but then he pulled out a card that he tacked on the door.

Justina is Resting, the sign said. **She'll Return at** _____ **P.M.** He chalked in a 3. My watch said 2:48.

"You'll never see a headless boy at the carnival," my father said, picking at the French fries he'd given me money for. "You're old enough to get my drift." When I didn't answer, he added, "Right?"

"Right," I said.

Just before three o'clock, my sister came up from behind us. She was wearing shorts and a white blouse buttoned almost to her throat. "Hey there," she said to me. For a moment she sized up Dad's expression. "Hi Dad," she said. "I'm ok. See?"

Nobody around us seemed to notice her. "There's another girl," she said, standing among a crowd without anybody knowing she was Justina, who they'd paid to see half an hour ago. All she had to do was change clothes and give everyone a look at her face.

"I asked about your schedule. You have days off in a few weeks. Come see us."

"You asked?" Susan began, but then she and I both saw Ronnie walking our way, and he was almost to us before he recognized me and stopped. "That's the Czak fellow," my father said to me.

There was nothing to do but say "Yes," but Ronnie, after a few seconds, put on a smile, stepped forward, and stuck out his hand toward my father as if he'd known him for years. "Susan's father, correct?" he said.

My father didn't answer. He didn't move either one of his hands, though I could see them curl into fists just before I blurted, "Dad of the Headless Girl."

Ronnie laughed. "Good one," he said, but he had his eye on my father's hands. "Dad's daughter is a good actress," he said. "She should be in a movie. They'd show the wreck and all to make it exciting."

"And a second wreck to get her a new head," I said, but my father put a hand on my shoulder and squeezed.

"She has all her parts," he said.

"Dad," Susan said, but the word didn't seem to reach him.

"You watch yourself now," he said to Ronnie, his hand tightening on my shoulder. "You getting my drift?"

Ronnie nodded. "I keep an eye out," he said.

"I bet you do."

I stretched up and whispered to my father that I had to use the men's room. "You know how," he said, not looking at me, but his grip softened and I was glad to be away from him, circling back a minute later to pay with a quarter of my own money to see the three p.m. Justina show. The pitch man didn't act as if he recognized me.

Inside there was another girl who looked just like my sister from the neck down—the halter top, the short skirt. With Susan outside, I could stare at this girl's breasts and imagine what they would look like if her top slipped down. A headless girl wouldn't know, would she, if her breasts were bare? Didn't you need a brain to tell you your body was naked?

Fifteen minutes later Ronnie was gone, and I told Dad and Susan that I'd stopped to watch men who swung a sledge hammer as hard as they could to try and drive a piece of metal up to where it would ring a bell. "No problem," Dad said, "as long as you didn't throw your money away and take a swing."

"I didn't," I said, but I didn't tell Dad then or in the car on the way home that Susan and Ronnie had stopped by ten days before. What I said was the question I thought would most please my father: "Why would Susan like that guy?"

"Because she doesn't know him," he said without taking his eyes off the road, "but she'll learn."

* * * * * *

Half way through August, as if the newspaper ads for back-to-school sales made him remember the change that was coming for me, Dad said, "What do you plan to do with high school?" We were standing on the porch, and he had his drink in a blue plastic tumbler that made it look like an empty aquarium. For all I knew, except for the two ice cubes, all of the liquid was gin, not just the three fingers he usually measured when I watched.

"I haven't thought about it," I said, which was honest.

He held up the tumbler as if he'd noticed the odd color and was worried. "I planned on graduating when I started. You get my drift?"

"I'll graduate. School's not hard."

"Sure you will. I mean after."

"I don't know."

Dad took a long swallow, and I couldn't help eyeing the level when he finished, gauging how close to half of it he'd taken in one gulp. "You like that circus we went to?" he said. "The freaks?"

"I didn't see any freaks."

"You saw the signs for them. You couldn't miss them—fat, short, hairy, missing one thing or another that everybody else has."

"I guess."

I knew my father didn't expect college out of me, that it was steady work and decency he wanted. All I had to do was maintain a job with regular hours that had responsibility attached to it. But when he took another drink, just a sip this time, I knew he wanted a name for whatever ambition I might have so he could compare it to what my sister was doing.

"Freaks," he said again. "Fuck."

I held my breath as if he'd drawn a gun. He took another sip and held his eyes on me over the lip of the glass. "Guess again," he said at last, and went inside, the screen door hanging ajar like it always did unless you reached back and pulled it shut.

* * * * * *

One morning in late August, when I walked into the kitchen in only my boxers, Susan was at the table eating breakfast. "Hey there," I said, turning back for a pair of shorts and a t-shirt. I thought she was home on break again or the shows were over. School was starting in a week. But she and our father, when I returned, were so quiet I started to evaluate the way my sister looked. She was wearing blue jeans and a tight, sleeveless t-shirt. She'd cut her hair short and looked so much like Ronnie Czak I was surprised she didn't have a tattoo on her arm. Nobody, I decided, would be interested in a headless girl wearing a t shirt and jeans. "Dad and I watched the riot last night," I said, pouring some Cheerios into a bowl.

34

"What riot?" Susan said, and Dad, without saying a word, pushed back his chair, stood up, and walked outside as if he always drank his coffee on the porch.

"In Chicago," I said, keeping my eyes on Susan. "At the convention."

"I haven't been keeping up." She glanced at the screen door, but Dad had moved out of sight. "Since when does Dad follow the news?"

"Since you left."

"What's he think? I'm going to be on it?"

I poured milk on the Cheerios, and when I heard her chair move, I said, "Did you see Rosemary's Baby?"

"A movie? No, I haven't kept up with that either."

She didn't stand up, but to keep her at the table I started in on telling her about how this woman was about to give birth to Satan's baby.

"You could show that baby and make a million dollars," she said. "People would pay big money to see it. "Dad watch that with you, too?"

"No."

"You went by yourself?"

"Dad dropped me off and told me to be standing out in front in exactly two hours."

"Some movies are longer than two hours."

"Maybe, but he said I'd have to walk the five miles if I was late, just check the time and I'd know to get a move on."

"Where's he go? Down to the cheese store?"

"No," I said, but Susan was touching the sides of her head and then the back as if she was feeling for lost hair. I worked on my Cheerios for a while so as not to watch her, and I was almost finished before she said, "I quit the show."

"Just like that?"

Her hands were back on the table where they belonged. "They can make do with one Justina," she said. "They can say she's been sick. That makes it better anyway. Scarier."

"What would a headless person be sick with?"

"Lots of things. Look at yourself. There's a lot of stuff inside us that's not in our heads."

I walked my bowl to the sink and ran water in it before I turned it upside down on the dish rack. From behind me I heard Susan say, "Ronnie said he wanted Justina, but my face was always there. You know what I mean. He tried to work out the mirrors, but the trick doesn't work close up."

"I'm sorry," I said, my hand resting on the bowl as if I needed to keep it from rolling away.

"Yeah."

That afternoon in late June, I'd finally crawled out on the roof. "There's my brother," Susan had said, and she'd passed the flask to me. As soon as I'd taken a drink, she'd clapped her hands. "You know what I wish?" she'd said.

"What?" I'd tried not to look down to where a cement wall ran along the tiny front yard.

"That I'd been a couple of years older that afternoon I walked out here so I could remember being out here."

"We're here now. You can see what it's like."

"That's not what I mean. I've been out here a few times. You know, since the house has been empty. I mean what it was like to be saved. Knowing when those hands reached out that somebody was terrified that I would fall."

After I finally lifted my hand from the bowl, I turned away from the sink, but Dad was coming back inside, and Susan hurried past me on her way to the stairs. Dad rinsed his cup out, standing beside me, but not saying a word. For a half a minute we stood like that, so quiet, so still, that we couldn't miss hearing Susan moving around above us. It sounded as if she was pacing, and I thought it must be hard getting your head back after all those weeks. Like getting out of bed after the flu. You think you can just go do whatever, and your legs go wobbly.

What would my sister think, looking in the mirror in her room and examining every part of her face? Who was she now that those tubes and wires had disappeared? She might even run her fingers over herself like the blind.

SMART BOY

When smart boys are on television or in the newspaper, they always want to build rockets or cure cancer. Things that only smart people can do. They even look smart. Like they could never dribble a basketball without staring at it or hit a baseball even if it was underhanded to them. Like sissies.

My son Jason is a smart boy, so I see one every day. And though he's bigger than those other smart boys so he doesn't look like Little Lord Fauntleroy, he doesn't try to play sports, so there's still all that to worry about.

What's different, and not to the good, is he's not interested in science and such. I'd welcome a chemistry set or a microscope in the house because this smart boy of mine just loves puzzles, the kind they give you to solve on IQ tests to measure how fast your brain works.

He loves taking tests is all. Getting the highest score. It doesn't matter what subject. I tell him there's no job called test-taker waiting for anybody, and he shrugs like he's not smart at all. My wife Alice shakes her head and says, "There's plenty of time for that yet."

He's in fifth grade already, so I'm not so sure. Right this minute, instead of getting excited about the Pirates and how the baseball season starts in less than three weeks, he's talking about doing a fifty mile hike like the President has people doing.

Or trying to do, because you just know most of those hikers quit long before they get that far. Fifty miles is an hour in the car going north on Route 8 from where we live near Pittsburgh. Butler, the biggest town along the way, is a drive, and it's only about half way. I point out Grove City on a map so Jason can see where he has to get to if we followed the main road north like nobody would want to for all the traffic, and he says he can't wait to start because it's something nobody else in his class will ever do. "It's just walking, Dad," he says. "All you have to do is not stop."

"That Kennedy and his big talk," I tell Alice when Jason is in his room. "He thinks we're going to the moon just because he says so."

"He got us through Cuba," she says. "We didn't all go up in a puff of smoke."

"You want the boy to fail?"

"It might be good for him."

I nod, but her mouth is pinched the way it gets when I put my elbows on the dinner table. "It would be better if he failed something at school."

Her lips part as if she needs to suck in a big breath. "That's a terrible thing to say," she says, leaving extra space between each word.

"It would make him normal. He might have a friend."

"By being less than himself?"

"By being more."

Her lips clench again. "You don't make sense," she hisses, and I know I'll have to put up with this talk until Jason finds another puzzle to work on.

A man who works with me at the machine shop has a retarded son, a Down Syndrome boy who is sixteen. He's grown large. Become frightening somehow. When that boy had been as old as Jason is now, I'd wondered how a father could deal with such difference, and now I fight feeling the burden of my own son's intelligence.

It seems shameful to think fathering a smart boy is difficult. Selfish. Weak. Alice, when I asked her how she felt once, thought I was joking. "That's not funny," she said. "I've thanked God a thousand times for his blessing."

Her tone said whatever fault there was lay with me, so I let it go, but I'm right about this Kennedy thing. What's more, Alice says I'm the one who has to walk alongside Jason, as if she wants me to be there when the impossible happens.

I remember how this whole thing started. There was Kennedy just mentioning some old Marine test, and before you know it there were crowds of people bunched up on a Sunday morning like it's Easter and sunrise is the most important time of day. Somebody from the newspaper takes their picture as they start out, but that's the last we hear of it because the paper isn't interested in how many drop out after a couple of hours, not even to ten miles.

For starters, you barely have enough daylight in late March like it is. If they don't quit, most are going to end up in the dark. And there's no way that's going to happen for almost everybody. Figure on midnight. Figure cold this time of year. Rain. Snow even. And walking where there's traffic that doesn't give two hoots about hikers where they don't belong.

Foolishness. They might as well be stuffing themselves in phone booths or swallowing goldfish or seeing how long they can keep a hula hoop circling around their bodies. Everybody forgets that the Marines are supposed to do the fifty miles in twenty hours, but they have three days to do it.

But Jason keeps up with it, and I think it's connected to these tests he's taking this week to see whether skipping a grade is a thing to consider. Those experts act like maybe he won't score high enough, but I know what question is coming to Alice and me. Sixth grade, he'd miss. Jump right into the new junior high school so he wouldn't be seen by his old classmates every day in another room like he was special. There are eight grade schools in our district. Instead of being some freak, his showing up for seventh grade would make him, for most, somebody from a school that the others didn't attend.

"Give us a chance to thoroughly evaluate," they said at our pre-test appointment, but all of us in that room knew Jason would pass. Those experts claimed to have it all worked out even though they should have noticed in first grade when the change would have been easier. He's a big boy, they say now. He's not going to get picked on like some who are smart.

Alice knows better, but she thinks he'll be happier away from kids who have made up their minds about him. "I know he's been in fights," she says, even though Jason has never said a word to either of us about them.

"Fights with older boys will hurt him worse," I say.

"If the other boys are older, they'll pick on him less."

There's no reasoning with her about thinking she's Mary the mother who can interpret the smallest gesture. "He's not Jesus," I say. "He doesn't have to be martyred." And she cries and then turns to stone, not speaking for two days while the test and the deadline for saying yes or no rushes at us.

Alice and I always take Jason when we go out. I don't drink, so there's that not to worry about, and Alice can do without. Mostly, we go to movies and the things the church puts on. Alice sings in the choir, and there's like-minded among the others for pot luck dinners and such.

It's when we go to what the others call parties that there's trouble. Every group, even the choir, has those who think fun comes from a bottle. Alice likes to dance when she's had her drink. I'll hold her and let her lean into me. There's no other children at these affairs, but Jason would entertain himself regardless. It's when the music's fast that there's worry to have.

This last time Alice did The Twist with another woman. She's seen the Kennedys or people just like them doing it on the news. "Your father's a stick-in-the-mud," Alice said. "A party pooper," and

Jason laughed like he'd heard something funny.

"It's like you have a spring inside you and it broke," I said. "I hate you acting the fool."

"It's not acting the fool. It's called fun."

I let it go in front of Jason, but after we got home, the boy in his room, I said, "Forty-eight years old and dancing like a high school girl showing herself off."

"Like an adult," she said. "Like people who are famous."

"Next thing you know you'll be acting like them for other things."

"Other things?" For a few seconds Alice acted like she didn't know straight away what I meant, but then she unbuttoned her blouse and let herself show. "You mean intercourse?" she said. When I didn't answer, she slipped the blouse off and moved close. "If that's what you mean, say the word, Max."

"You know what I mean."

She slid her skirt off and stepped out of it. "If you don't say it, I'll say worse, and you know how that sounds."

I looked toward the window over her left shoulder where I half expected to see a face. "Intercourse," I said.

"See?" she said. "Lightning didn't strike." She picked up her skirt and carried it to the closet to hang up. "You know you have to go with him when he takes his hike," she said. "He might make it. I heard there are Boy Scouts who've finished. He's as old as they are."

"Those Boy Scouts aren't like Jason, you can bet on that."

"Maybe he'll out walk you."

"I can last all day on my feet," I said. "It's what I've done all my life. It's the boy who will fail."

"If he makes the fifty miles, you have to let him skip," she said, as if finishing is a man's job.

"He could fail the test."

Alice smiled as she tossed her blouse into the hamper. "Now who's acting the fool?"

I feel my son examining me. While we eat dinner. While we sit in our pew at church.

My father isn't a smart man is what he's thinking.

Fathers always disappoint their sons, falling from perfection, but Jason isn't disappointed, he's curious. He wants to know what I'm thinking the way he wants to know how a dog or a cat thinks about its life.

"You're imagining it," Alice says, the boy is in his room with the radio playing like it always does on Sunday afternoon.

"I know what I know," I say.

"He doesn't look at you like that. You're not being tested," Alice declares, but when I shake my head, she goes on: "All right, then, maybe it's good for you. You'll sit up straight when you eat instead of hunched over like you do. You'll sing the hymns instead of mouthing the words. Those things never hurt anybody."

"I've heard all that before."

"What if it was the opposite and he'd never learn? Tell me you'd like having him stay the same forever."

"There's other than two choices."

"That's for before. Now there's what you have."

"It's more than manners and singing. You know that."

She softens then. "Yes," she says. "For him there's always more. He can't help it, but you don't have to be great. Ordinary is fine if you handle it as best you can."

When I don't answer, she seems satisfied, but I'm relieved when she doesn't try to hug me because I think I might knock her away with the back of my hand.

"Do you want to hear a joke?" Jason says at dinner.

"Leprosy isn't allowed at this table," Alice says, reminding him about last year's jokes.

"Neither are morons," I say, going back another year.

"It's about an elephant."

I shake my head, but Alice says, "All right" the way she does too often.

"Why did the elephant cross the road?" Jason asks her.

"To get to the other side?"

He laughs. "It was the chicken's day off."

Alice groans, but Jason keeps on. "Why do elephants drink so much?"

Alice looks like she's really concentrating, but after a few seconds she says, "They're thirsty?"

"To try and forget."

Now Alice smiles. "That's sort of funny," she says, but I'm glad when Jason goes back to his roast beef because I've heard elephant jokes at work even, another fad like the fifty mile hike. Only there the answers are always about sex. "What did the elephant say to the nude man? "Cute, but can you breathe through it?"

And that's the best of that bunch. The rest are crude. Given the size of an elephant, you can imagine what else gets said. And yet people laugh.

It takes until dessert for Jason to let us know the tests are over and done with. Like he wants cake in front of him before he says anything. Something sweet, Alice bringing more milk out for the pitcher in case we need it to wash down the sticky icing. "The tests were fun," he says, and Alice leaves the pitcher unfilled as if she can't listen to this and use her hands at the same time. "It was the best day of school all year."

"What did they ask you?" she says.

"They asked how many 9s there are between 1 and 100. 'Twenty,' I said. That's an easy one to do in your head."

"Really?" Alice says, and she looks as pleased as if he's come home with news about making a friend.

"Then they asked if I could figure out the equal number of

quarters, dimes and nickels it takes to have nine dollars and sixty cents."

"Did you get to use pencil and paper?" Alice asks, and Jason shakes his head.

"I didn't ask. I just gave them the answers. That one was twenty-four. It's not hard either."

"Was there one that made you stop and think?" Alice says, and when Jason nods, I sit up straighter to listen.

"If you have a five gallon bucket and a three gallon bucket, how do you get exactly four gallons?" Jason repeats.

"I heard that one once," Alice says. "I could never figure it out."

"The trick is it sounds complicated when it isn't, so I didn't get the answer right away like I did for the others. They said, 'Take your time,' and then I knew it was Fill the 5 and dump into the 3, dump out the 3 and pour the 2 into it. Fill the 5 and dump 1 gallon into the 3 and you have 4 gallons left. See?"

Alice stares at her cake as if the answer is written in the icing. I'm finished with dessert, and the two of them haven't taken a bite. "These are better than elephant jokes," Jason says "You want to hear the one about the trains traveling at different speeds or driving a car and always turning left?"

"That's ok," I say, but I can't resist pouring milk from the bottle into the empty pitcher on the table to see if I can guess how much is a glass full. "What are you doing there, Max?" Alice says. "Don't make a mess."

When I pour the milk from the pitcher, I'm so close I try to squeeze all of it into the glass, but a few streaks run down the side as Alice frowns. "Look at that," I say. "It's like that problem."

"No, it's not, Dad," Jason says. "It's just guessing."

Alice reaches across the table with her napkin and daubs at the ring of milk. "What else did they do besides ask you riddles?" she says.

"They asked me to name the planets. Who couldn't do that?"

"There's nine, aren't there?" Alice says.

"I told them about the solar system I built out of snow in our yard during Christmas vacation. I made it to scale. Jupiter was a big snowball and the sun was huge. I had to go into the Rompolski's back yard for Pluto. I couldn't see it when I went back to where Earth was."

"So Pluto's the farthest thing away from us?" Alice says while I drink all that milk straight down without taking a breath.

"Planet. But I made another star, too. I made a snowball like our sun at the end of our street and thought about who might live near that one where you couldn't see any of the stuff in our back yard."

Here's a story: A few weeks ago I saw Jason outside with a group of boys. They were in the Rompolski's yard, so I couldn't be certain, but they looked to be older. Not surprising, since Jason has stopped playing with boys his age, choosing to do things alone. "Good," I thought, watching them, but a moment later I turned uneasy. The three older boys formed a loose triangle around Jason, nothing like a game or a way of talking to each other. I leaned forward until my forehead touched the window pane, and I recoiled from the sudden cold, standing up straight, one hand gripping the crank that would open the lower half of the window so I could shout to scare off those boys.

I hesitated, but it was already happening, one boy stepping forward and driving his fist into Jason's stomach. My son doubled over, clutching himself, and the other boys walked off, not looking back, not even when my son vomited on the sidewalk.

Macaroni soup, I thought, the lunch that Jason had eaten left-over a half hour before. That casserole dish is what my wife calls the kind of goulash she makes with macaroni and ground beef and tomatoes and onions and water. Jason stayed bent over, and I knew he was examining the puddle of puke while he fought to get his breath back.

When he looked over toward the house, I stepped back, afraid that he'd seen me in the window. I went to the couch and opened a section of newspaper I'd read at breakfast. When Jason walked in a minute later, I glanced over the top of the paper, but he passed without speaking, going directly to the bathroom.

I said nothing to him, or later, after my wife came home from shopping, to her. It was as if I'd seen my son masturbating. I knew one more shameful thing about him that I have to live with.

You have only one child and there's no margin for mistakes. It's working without safety glasses, counting on fortune. That Down syndrome father has that boy by himself, the mother gone to better odds. Alice and I, we came to Jason late, surprised, and we've never clicked again.

When they call us with the results of the skip-a-grade test, they say Jason's scored so high that there's no doubt he can make the move and still get straight As, and I remember that fight I witnessed when Alice says, "Now we have to decide for real."

"My no has always been for real," I tell her.

"So one of us needs to be convinced," she says.

"Does the boy know?"

"I haven't told him. He could break the tie, you know."

"Only if you let him," I say and go down the hall to his room where he's sitting on his bed surrounded by sheets of loose paper covered with lists of song titles, what he's been doing for months now, keeping track of the songs they play on the radio.

"'Watermelon Man'?" I say, noticing that title on the closest paper. "Is that what's on the radio these days?"

"Yes. It was new last week, but it's gone up every day."

"Who decides?"

"It's Pittsburgh sales and requests during the week. On Sunday it's from all over the country."

I pick up the paper and start to scan it. "Is 'The Twist' on here?"

"A long time ago." He tugs the paper from my hand as if all those names were code for military secrets.

"If you got a high score on those tests you took, would you want to skip?"

His face lights up, and my heart sinks, but he reaches for the radio and turns up the volume. "Here's my favorite song, Dad," he says. "'Killer Joe.'"

I listen for a few seconds. "They sound like kids."

"They are kids. They're the Rocky Fellers." He adds the title to the list at #8. "It moved up again."

"Good," I say. "Just turn it down when it's over," and I go back to Alice to let her know how the rise of "Killer Joe" is more important to Jason than skipping a grade.

"When was 'The Twist' a hit?" I ask Alice.

"1960," she says at once. "All summer it was on the radio."

"That can't be right. Jason would have been eight. He didn't even have a radio then."

"It came back a second time. It was #1 again last winter. That's when all those people you say you hate started dancing like kids."

When Jason comes down the hall for dinner, Alice congratulates him, but he doesn't ask whether he's skipping. He wants to know his score. "I asked Mrs. Atkinson, but she didn't tell me," he says. All she did was say, "I imagine you did quite well."

"Your teacher shouldn't be telling you your score. That's private."

"Could I skip two grades? Was I that high?"

"I don't know," Alice says, and though the testers had said nothing about two grades, I think it's true.

Jason is beaming. "What if I got everything perfect?"

"I don't think that's necessary."

"Maybe nobody's ever answered every question right. Maybe I'm the first one ever."

"Maybe."

"'He's So Fine' is still #1," he says to me. "Twenty-four days in a row. I thought you'd want to know."

"'Killer Joe' sounds like it will get to #1. Let me know when that happens," I say.

After he leaves the table, I tell Alice that I'll take her bet—if Jason finishes fifty miles, he can skip, and then I never want to hear about it being a good or bad idea ever again. Fifty miles is forever, and even Kennedy must know that, not strolling down Pennsylvania Avenue toward Virginia and wherever the road would take him.

I know what school taught me—that life was a matter of luck. Who your parents were. Where you lived. Jason didn't know how smart he was until he went to school. There, in first grade, before September ended, he understood that half the students were stupid and most of the rest were unremarkable. It was impossible to keep his secret; once the other kids knew it, he was alone.

It took a few more years before he knew Alice and me were just as ordinary as the kids in his class. All we had as advantage was being grown up. "And being kind," Alice kept saying.

How had this happened? It was the same question that fellow at work must have asked while he watched his boy fall by the wayside. I looked up heredity in the encyclopedia we bought one volume at a time at the grocery store, and all I learned was it was about the laws of chance, like flipping a coin to see who was smart and who was dumb. Jason would love all that business. He'd be in his room with a penny counting the heads and tails. And he'd be making one of those charts with the Xs and the Ys, branching them out until it went all the way back to Adam and Eve and there wasn't room enough in the house for all those ancestors.

This afternoon, when I come home from work, Jason is waiting in the living room. "I walked around the track at the high school," he says. "It's a quarter mile, and it took me 475 steps. I wanted to be sure, so I did three more laps, and I'm glad I did because it took 1920, an average of 480. So it's 96,000 steps I'll need to take to finish fifty miles."

"There's hills," I say. "There's getting tired. Maybe you'll end up having to take 100,000 or even more."

"We'll find out, won't we?"

Alice is standing in the doorway. Before she can add anything, I say, "Let's you and me drive out twenty-five miles and find out how far we have to go before we turn around and head for home."

I'm counting on this making Alice and Jason happy at the same time, but he says, "No, it has to be fifty different miles."

"That's a hundred miles of driving," I say.

It sounds like a perfect argument, but Alice says, "Go ahead, you two. We can eat dinner late," and we end up driving north while Jason follows the odometer carefully

I use back roads, but Jason doesn't seem to care until we drive through Mars and I say, "Wouldn't it be fun to tell people you're from Mars?"

"No," he says, keeping his eyes on the odometer. "They'd all make fun of you." A half minute later he says "24,000 to here," so I know Mars is almost one fourth of the way.

Fifty miles puts us just past Harrisville. "Stop right here," Jason says, and he gets out and begins to gather stones from just off the road's shoulder. In a minute he has a mound formed where the weeds thin.

"I know it will be dark when we get here," he says. "Mom will be in the car right back there at the ice cream stand. It's three tenths of a mile. We'll know how close we are when we pass her. Then we can start looking for these stones, and we'll know exactly where to stop."

Alice has me stop off at the grocery after work on Friday to get steaks. "For the boy," she says. "Sirloin, for once. Not the cube steak. It will help."

Frank Wainscott, the man with the Down Syndrome boy, waves when he sees me by the meat counter. "I cook on Saturday," he says. "I make something we've never eaten before because this is the one time Gina, my girl friend, comes over. There's a million recipes. You can't live long enough to use them up."

His voice is different than it sounds at work, and I wonder if he's been drinking already, whether that's something he does as soon as he punches out. Whether drink is part of the special meal, a different bottle of something from the liquor store that I walked through once, years ago, in order to know what it was like in there with all that foolishness.

I look in his basket, and I don't recognize any of it. "Fettuccini," he says, as if I've asked. "Scallops. You ever have scallops? And these here little grape tomatoes are something special."

"I bet."

"The boy eats with us, if that's what you're wondering, but he gets macaroni and cheese. He loves it, so there's no problem with any of that."

After he moves on, I walk to where the boxes of spaghetti are stacked.

I count three different brands and two kinds of lasagna noodles and macaroni. Off to the side there's that one brand of fettuccini. And one brand of linguini, something else for Frank Wainscott to cook up some Saturday when he gets bored with his scallops and those marbles he calls tomatoes.

Twenty minutes later I walk in on Alice lifting a liquor bottle from a paper bag, the radio playing so loud from Jason's room I know she never asks him to keep the door closed when I'm not home. "That's a first," I say.

"What?" she says, as if she doesn't know what while she puts the bottle under the sink like it's dishwashing detergent.

"Bringing it into the house."

"It's not a sin to enjoy a drink every now and then," she says, just as the music from Jason's room shuts off like he's begun to listen to us. "Jesus drank wine, you know."

"It was different back then."

"That's what you think," she says, but she's looking toward the doorway as if she's listening for Jason sneaking down the hall to eavesdrop. "I'll start the steak," she says. "You go talk to your son and leave me to have one drink without you acting like prohibition ought to come back to save us from ourselves."

"One," I say, and she takes the package from my hand.

It turns out the countdown Jason listens to is already over. "It's after six, Dad," Jason says. "You're way off schedule."

"Your mother had me stop at the store," I say, and though the bed is covered with a scattering of song title pages, the paper he has in his hand has a string of numbers going sideways across the page. "Do you know what Pi is, Dad?" he says.

"Geometry," I say. "I know something about that. The short version is 3.14."

He seems pleased that I recognize it. He stands up and hands the paper to me, and I read, "3.14159265358979323846."

"What are you going to do with all these numbers?

"Keep figuring out more and writing them down."

"Why?" I ask, and Jason reaches for the paper as if my question means I might tear it up and throw it away.

"To see how many I can do."

"There's people who have figured this out to hundred of places, and it's never stopped yet."

Jason looks at the numbers so carefully I'm afraid he's memorizing them. "What if I'm the one who goes out so far that I find out

53

where it ends?" he says, and he drops back onto the bed with the page held up to his face like a magazine. All those numbers stretched across the page might add up to the distance to heaven except for the decimal point making everything smaller and smaller until nobody could possibly care.

The sky is the dark blue that it gets just before the sun comes up when we set out Saturday morning. There's frost, but it's clear with no wind, about as nice a day as you can count on for the end of March. For the first fifteen minutes, we don't talk, but Jason calls out every hundred steps he takes, so I know, when he says "Two thousand," that we've made at least a mile.

"How many miles do you think people walk during their lives?" Jason says.

"A lot."

"You have to guess."

"Twenty thousand."

"Sixty-five thousand," he says

"How many walked fifty of those miles at one time?"

"Hardly any. That's why this is fun."

"Ok then. We're not going to worry about everybody else," I say. "Fifty miles is fifty miles."

Jason takes a breath and says, "Twenty-one hundred."

We're four thousand steps into the walk, the sky bright now, when I hear a car slowing as it comes up on us. I brace myself for shouted words, but then my heart races when I see it's Alice in the Impala, and she's parking fifty feet in front of us.

Jason doesn't recognize the car until Alice steps out. "It's Mom," he says, and he picks up his pace just as she lifts the Polaroid and snaps a picture. "Got you," she says, and Jason waves as she stares at the developing photo as we pass by. "See you boys tonight," she says, and when I don't hear the car door close, I know she's taking a second snapshot from behind.

"Forty-one hundred," Jason says.

"Your mother isn't smart about some things," I say, not breaking stride.

"What things?"

"Things she'll have to live with," I say, but he doesn't answer, concentrating on the shoulder of the road where we're walking.

It takes us three hours to reach what Jason says is ten miles because he's taken 19,600 steps. For the last two miles he's been limping, and I know he has blisters forming, that we're probably half a mile short of the ten mile mark. He's stopped calling out his steps by the hundred, speaking only when he gets to another thousand, his jacket unzipped, the gloves he was wearing at sunrise stuffed in my pockets so they don't get lost.

"21,000," he says, and then silence settles in around us.

Twenty minutes more and Jason is hiking on tip toes, an odd gait that promises nothing but the end of walking. He seems bewildered. He looks like the apprentice at the machine shop who ruined a fitting last week. Like somebody who has to apologize.

"Nobody's here," I say. "We can stop."

I expect him to shout "no" or maybe cry, but instead he says, "How do we get home?"

"Your mother picks us up. We have to call her, but it will be a while yet till we find a phone." There's a guard rail running beside us, and Jason sits on one of the posts and takes off both shoes. "We can't stop here," I say.

"In a minute, Dad. We're almost to Mars. It's only a thousand more steps. We're right on top of it."

I don't say anything about that number, but it's uphill here, a curve a hundred yards ahead that keeps things so well concealed you could believe Mars was just over the crest. "It's not much of a rise," I say. "You can't just sit beside the road by yourself."

"Mom will be sad when we call."

"Your mother knows fifty miles is forever," I say. "The Marines get three days to do it."

Jason stands and steps out onto the asphalt. "I can walk if I don't put my shoes back on," he says. "I can make it to Mars."

"You'll ruin your socks," I say and begin to think about how heavy he is for carrying.

Jason sits back down and gingerly pushes his feet into his shoes. When he stands again, he grimaces, but then he begins to walk, taking tiny, shuffling steps. "We can mark the spot in Mars where we call from," I say. "We can come back tomorrow after church and start from there."

"That's such a stupid name for a town. It's like a little kid named it," he says, and then nothing at all, not even a number by the thousand until, ten minutes later, he says, "I think my feet are bleeding."

There's another rise in the road that I think might be the last one before Mars. "Go ahead and walk in your socks then. Your mother won't care if you ruin a pair of socks."

He carries the shoes and walks. After he says "24,000," he stops and looks around. "Where are we?" he asks.

"We're real close now," I say. "It takes more steps in your stocking feet."

He lifts one foot and runs his hand along its underside, feeling, I'm sure, to see if the sock is worn through. "If I don't skip a grade," he says, "kids will think I failed that test."

Something like terror rises through me the way cold seeps up when you stand on ice. Like I might scream when Jason comes home from seventh grade and runs to his room to crawl under the covers. I watch him test the other sock and wait for him to say he can't take one more step, but he starts forward and says, "Won't they?"

"Only if you told somebody what you were doing."

"Who would I tell?" he says, and it's all I can do not to hug him.

"There's a gas station," I say. "Up ahead there. See?"

He squints as if it's hard to make out. He needs glasses, I think. The gas station is half a mile away, maybe farther, and for all I know it may be out of business on a road like this that's been replaced by a four lane highway traveling in the same direction less than a mile from where we're walking.

Five minutes go by, and the station still looks distant. We're walking so slowly I think it will be ten more minutes. There's a phone booth set off by itself. I can make it out now, but Jason has his head down, staring at the asphalt as if it's booby-trapped. I decide to wait for him to notice the phone booth for himself. He'll look up before too long. It's impossible not to.

THE KILLER'S DOG

When she knocks on his locked screen door, Frank Fawcett's sister, who hasn't had a dog since the two of them were teenagers, stands beside a full-sized German Shepherd on a chain leash. "Dog-sitting," Maureen says, and he's glad to see she has the leash wrapped around her wrist.

"For how long?" Fawcett says through the screen's fine mesh.

"Maybe a while. Can I bring him inside? I bet you think he's a beast to hold, but this chain is just for show."

Fawcett has a dog-hating wife who Maureen knows is at work at the mall, so he understands she expects him to give in. "Only in the kitchen," he says, going ahead to drag chairs in front of the door to the living room.

"You don't have to worry," Maureen says, "He's a whole lot less messy than you are," and as if to prove that, she tells the dog to sit, then lie down, and it obeys like it's being paid.

"So who's too sick to keep their dog?"

"Sick's not the problem." Maureen looks at the dog as if she expects it to answer for its owner. "Hutch is in jail."

"Hutch?" Fawcett says reflexively, but he recognizes the name because within the past week two bodies have been found buried on Hutch's property, alleged drug dealers missing for nearly three weeks when they were dug up. "You'll have the dog until it dies then."

"He might get off with a light sentence. The dead people were scum. It was self-defense."

"He buried them."

"Wouldn't you?" Maureen says. "No matter how it happened, dead people are hard to explain." She glances at the window, and for a moment Fawcett imagines somebody evil following her, somebody obsessed with revenge and settling on Maureen as a surrogate, but she doesn't appear nervous when she turns toward him again. "Maybe you remember meeting Hutch a couple of weeks ago at Cindy's party?"

"Fourth of July?"

"That's the one."

"He'd already killed them by then, right?"

"Yeah. It looks that way."

"Jesus, Maureen. Don't tell me you're best friends or something worse with this guy."

"Friends is all," she says, but Fawcett wonders if it's a lie coming so easy, that if he asks around he'll learn more about his sister than he can live with. "Nobody else has room like I do, or they already have dogs of their own." She drops the leash, but the dog doesn't move. "His name is Marlow. I've heard there was a detective in some old movie with that name. Hutch must have thought that was ironic or something. You know, sorting out the good and the bad."

"He's never said?"

"Nobody asks Hutch why he does what he does."

"I hope you're wrong about the detective. If Hutch got that name from reading Conrad, that would be way more interesting."

"Conrad? Whatever. Your one year in college made you just smart enough to think you could be on Jeopardy! or something."

"Everybody knows Heart of Darkness."

"Now you're just being an asshole."

"It's just reading. You went to college longer than I did."

"I went to a school that showed you how to do a job. That's not college."

Maureen is thirty-one, her next birthday a month away. She'd gone back to school at twenty-eight, declaring to Fawcett that she had to be somebody else by the time she turned thirty. It had sounded like a judgment when she'd announced that at his 30th birthday party because he'd worked at McDonald's for six years by then, a manager since he was twenty-eight without any possibility of change, unless he resigned, from that day on. Now, she glances at her watch and says, "Hey, it's five. Turn on the news. I've been keeping up with Hutch and you should too."

Fawcett doesn't tell her he knows Hutch has been on the news nearly every night for six days, four of those days the lead story. There are rumors of more bodies buried on his property. Indications there might be a national serial killer story in the making, though so far there's been nothing confirmed except the familiar story of a drug deal gone bad.

"See?" Maureen says after the newscaster says nothing is new in the double homicide case. "Such bullshit. People just want the story to be worse so they have something to talk about. They wish he'd killed twenty people as long as none of them were friends or family."

As soon as Fawcett powers down the television, Maureen tells him she wants him to learn something about Marlow. "All we have to do is walk a couple of blocks," she says. "And don't worry, your neighbors won't recognize the dog and start calling 911."

A half block down the sidewalk, when Marlow drifts in front of her, she yanks the leash until the dog retreats and falls in beside her. "Hutch gave explicit directions. The dog never leads. If you let it walk in front of you, it thinks it's the master."

"Makes sense," Fawcett says, imagining Hutch choking the dog until it understood the advantages of obedience.

"Remember when we had Blaze and she was always dragging us along, sniffing at everything?"

"We were kids."

"Mom and Dad should have trained her. We had her for twelve years, and I never heard any of this." The dog turns its head toward a power-line pole, and Fawcett watches as she tugs the leash like she's inscribing an exclamation point on the air and the dog faces forward, leaving the temptation of scents behind.

At the corner, the light red, she says "Sit," and Marlow drops its hind legs like they've turned to sponge. "See? Isn't this great?"

"Elise will appreciate that the dog didn't leave a trace."

"She'll find a single hair on her carpet and think she'll have to hire somebody to steam clean it."

"You're only looking on the dark side."

"You should have kids. You should have a real house." After they cross, she turns and lets the light go red again, saying "Sit" as if Fawcett needs his opinion of the dog reinforced. Marlow sits. "Hey," Maureen says as they cross again and head toward Fawcett's house, "HIV Positive is playing at FloodPlain Saturday night. If I see Elise there with you, I'll admit I'm wrong about how uptight she is."

"She's on late shift through Saturday."

"HIV Positive has gotten huge since your last time. Once upon a time you were the guy telling everybody to get tickets."

"That was two years ago. Anyway, it hasn't been that long since I went."

"Yes, it has. Get your ass in gear or else I'll start thinking she's trained you to sit like a dog."

Even though the band plays five shows a week within a two-hour drive, Fawcett hasn't seen HIV Positive for more than three months. The last time he went, he thought something had moved on, the style of music maybe, the nature of the venue falling on hard times in a part of town college students and white collar workers avoided. A singer in an orange prison jumpsuit was something, maybe, you could only get excited about once or twice. "OK," he says. "I'll give it one more shot. If the dog can sit through an entire set, I'll buy all your drinks."

62

"Maureen stopped in," Fawcett says at once when Elise comes home at 10:30. He's already in bed, thumbing through a copy of People, which Elise says she subscribes to for her job. "Because I need to keep up with celebrities," she's told him. "So I can make small talk with customers." His alarm, for the fifth night in a row, is set for five a.m. because he has the early shift, overseeing four hours each of Egg McMuffins and Double Cheeseburgers.

"She the same as always?" Elise says, an edge in her voice.

"Actually, she was different."

"How's that?"

"She's been changing for years," Fawcett says, deciding to omit the dog. "Ever since nursing school."

"You keep saying that and pretty soon you'll believe it."

"I made spaghetti if you're hungry."

Fawcett sees Elise soften. She drops down on the bed, kicking off her shoes, and flicks at the People with her fingers. "Now we have things to talk about, right?" she says. "Thanks for the spaghetti, but I ate Arby's on my break. I wished for a steak with each bite of my regular roast beef."

"One more day of the sunrise shift."

"And one more day of nights. We'll go out next week. We'll have a meal without any buns involved."

When Fawcett comes home late the following afternoon, Elise is already gone. There isn't a note, nothing about how, with a few hours to inspect, she's noticed dog hair, so maybe there had only been the two thin strands he'd found and walked outside after Maureen left. Hutch was such a perfectionist, maybe the dog waited until it was outside before it shook loose a cluster of hair. He has time to take a nap before he showers and heads out to show Maureen he still has stamina.

As always, when he first gets to FloodPlain, Fawcett's first beer goes down fast, and he buys a second before stepping away from the bar, but already he feels bloated, as if he's guzzled a super-sized soda at work. Fifteen minutes later, the beer in its plastic bottle going warm in his hand, he knows he is going to watch this show sober, but not without the bottle because it seems impossible to stand among the crowd with empty hands. Like a chaperone, he thinks. Like some high school teacher watching half-buzzed students grope each other at a post-football dance. And despite Maureen's enthusiasm, the crowd is nowhere near capacity, and there are even groups of men using both pool tables, their girlfriends sitting on chairs watching them instead of working to find a great place from which to watch the band.

When he's jostled from behind, Fawcett doesn't turn and complain. When he's shoved again, hard enough that he has to take a step to catch his balance, he braces himself and keeps his eyes forward, ashamed. For a moment, as he waits for a third shove, the one that will shout "Fuck you" in his ear, he thinks about leaving, then puts that choice away because he would be more easily beaten outside.

The shove doesn't come. Those shoulders turn into accidents. And when he shuffles his feet enough to shift sideways and inspect for trouble, there isn't anybody within six feet of him. He sees Maureen near the stage, a beer in each hand. The man beside her, tall and burly in a leather jacket despite the club's heat, is holding a phone to his right ear, one finger pressed to his left, and Fawcett decides they are together even before the man closes the phone and Maureen passes him one of the beers. Fawcett watches her for two minutes, but she doesn't turn around and check the crowd.

The room goes dark then, sequenced red and blue lights flashing across the stage while feedback from a guitar being passed near an amp rises and falls like the voice a killer alien might have as it lunges from its space ship. Fawcett brings the beer to his lips to keep from retreating. It tastes like saliva, warm and frothy, like the remnants of an unwanted kiss. It's a relief when the singer, stepping through a roiling cloud of smoke, yells, "How the fuck are you?" and everybody in front of Fawcett roars as he begins to scream. Even now, with his head shaved instead of sporting the blond Mohawk he'd displayed at the show three months ago, the singer, this time in a blood-red jump suit, seems so familiar, the performance feels likes it's being beamed onto an enormous screen from a DVD.

Fawcett moves up, getting far enough into the crowd so he's among the two hundred or so who seem to be into the show, holding up their phones to take pictures or record something to put up on YouTube. "You can't slack off anymore," a woman in matching black leather pants and halter top beside him shouts his way. "You never know what's going to be posted, so every song matters."

He tries to believe that, but the other third of the audience isn't paying much attention. And when the singer drops to his knees and moans out the chorus, Fawcett wonders if anybody in the audience is thinking James Brown and expecting somebody to step out with a cape to wrap around the imaginary prisoner of love.

When the song ends and the singer pauses to drink from a plastic milk carton, the woman leans closer and says, "Everybody's been telling me your sister's great with Marlow. Hutch sends his appreciation."

Keeping his eyes from her cleavage, Fawcett looks at her face more closely, but a name doesn't surface and he opts for "The dog sure does listen."

She looks annoyed for a moment before she smiles. "For sure, Hutch is the original Dog Whisperer."

Hutch's girlfriend—Fawcett recognizes her now. Jackie something. A woman eager to display her extraordinary abs. On stage the singer is running through so much patter that Fawcett decides he's already drunk, that if there is beer in that milk jug, a second set might never happen. "Hutch has a lawyer who knows his shit," she shouts as the music begins again. "A deal's going to get done. We'll all be together again before you know it."

He can't remember her last name, but Fawcett recalls every word of his first conversation with Jackie, the girlfriend. "Seriously. You work at McDonald's?" she'd said when they met at the Fourth of July party.

"Yeah."

"A grown white man?"

"I'm the manager."

"That's better. For a second there I thought you were retarded."

He'd imagined how she'd talk to somebody she knew. To Hutch maybe. When they were in bed together, that dog told to sit beside the bed because it made being fucked more exciting. Everything about her was so exaggerated—her clothes, her makeup, her body—he thought she'd be scarier than Hutch with a gun in her hands. Hutch would put a bullet into his brain; Jackie would shoot him in the groin and then maybe give him the stigmata before she dropped him with one to the chest.

He sees Maureen turn and wave after the fourth song, but by the seventh, Fawcett, needing a break from the din, lets his bottle drop to the floor and moves to the side door where a bouncer says, "You leave, you're gone for good."

While the singer roars, "Fuck me, I'm fucked up anyway," Fawcett nods and exits.

Outside, the music muted enough that he can hear the high-pitched ringing in his ears, Fawcett stands near three women who are smoking. They're laughing at something already said among them, and then they inhale in near unison before one of them speaks, nodding toward him, her words smothered by the shrill whistle of his tinnitus, and they laugh again.

He makes a handgun from a finger and his thumb and points it their way, squinting down the length of the barrel as if he wants them to raise their hands. They stiffen and stare, uncertain for a moment, and then the woman who talked raises a middle finger. Fawcett remembers other hand gestures, their pantomime of contempt or longing. Instead of employing one, he drops his gun and waves before walking toward his car. Halfway there he turns, and he sees that the women are re-entering through the side door.

A few days later, when he meets Maureen for lunch, Fawcett is relieved the dog isn't sitting beside her. "There's a crate," she says. "Jesus, Marlow's not a seeing-eye or something."

"I thought maybe you could say, 'Lie down all day' and Marlow wouldn't move."

"You know what, Frank? You're not a funny guy, but I'm going to ask Hutch if I can keep Marlow."

"If he's convicted, you won't have to ask."

"So he's comfortable. It's no different than working with patients. I'll still ask. It's the right thing."

Maureen has been a nurse for nearly two years, which right now, seems obscene, even if she is the kind of nurse that is more like a secretary, filling in forms while the patient keeps a thermometer under his tongue. She knows the heights and weights of hundreds of people she sees on the street. She knows what medications they take and how often. She knows which patients the GP she works for has referred to specialists because they have something way worse than the flu or a strep throat.

Worst of all, she knows his private statistics. It means that at least once a year he has to listen while she takes his blood pressure, telling him "140 over 85, a little high" and adding "slow down on all the chips and bean dip" as if he's a boy running at the public swimming pool.

"Hutch doesn't believe in doctors," she'd said when he'd asked her if he was that GP's patient like practically everybody else he knew.

Just like she denied ever seeing Hutch at the fitness center where she worked before she'd decided to go back to school. "I would remember Hutch being there, trust me. I remember too much about those days. I was about sick of fitness. There's enough vanity there to sink the Titanic."

"Darwin at work in the 21st century," Fawcett had said.

"Whatever. Those shits used to look at me like I should beg them for it."

"If you worked the counter at McDonald's you'd get the same scummy eyeball, only it would come from lardasses waiting for Big-Macs and fries."

"But they'd be doing the wishing instead of thinking it was me fantasizing."

Now, though, she wants him to know she has Hutch photos on her iPhone. "Here," she says, "check these out. He's in three of them."

In the third one Fawcett is in the frame with Hutch, who is smiling as if he welcomes Maureen taking his picture. "You want me to believe he's normal, right? That he's that close to me and yet I'm safe as can be?" He doesn't add that those pictures make him suspect there's more to her having that dog than being willing.

"Look at you," she says. "You look like a stick man standing beside Hutch."

She's so accurate, he doesn't answer, but as Fawcett examines the pictures, he understands that the photograph of Hutch he's seen on the news doesn't show the thin, manicured sideburns that seem to float on the sides of Hutch's face, that the televised photo isn't as current as his sister's. He pulls a fourth photo up and Hutch disappears. "So now you remember?" she says.

"I always remembered. This is just the rerun."

"That other guy—go ahead and back up and look again. See him there on the other side of Hutch. He's a prison guard."

"John, right?"

"Yeah. John. You remember everything then? They're best buddies from way back. And here Hutch is under his lock and key until the trial at least. It's like a movie or something."

"Next you'll tell me there's going to be a prison break."

"Really, you should stop with all this worrying. You're not on his radar. You're not into drugs; you don't even drink the hard stuff. A beer drinker who goes home early would be way down the list of people he'd want to get back at if he was on the street."

Fawcett scrolls through ten more photos without seeing himself. "It looks like that's the only one I'm in."

"What did I just say? You'd be in more if you hadn't left before it got dark."

"Elise wanted to watch fireworks at the park."

"She dropped you off and picked you up like she was your mother."

As if Maureen has sent him, the next day John eats lunch at a McDonald's table. "What's the point?" Fawcett thinks, but he waits until John is nearly finished with his Big Mac before he pours himself a large soda and wanders over to where John sits by himself. "Hey there," he says, "I'm Maureen's brother, remember me?" and when John smiles, Fawcett sits down. "I saw you yesterday, too, in Maureen's pictures from Cindy Viker's Fourth of July party."

"Do I look wasted in all of them?"

That has to be scripted, Fawcett decides, and keeps on. "You do; Hutch doesn't."

This time John takes his time to answer, polishing off the Big Mac and wiping his mouth with a napkin first. "Hutch had things on his mind right about then."

"I bet he did," Fawcett says.

John eyes him for a moment and then relaxes. "Hey, if you're wired up about Marlow living with your sister, relax. There's no strings attached to that shit. The only reason she has the dog is because she's been out to Hutch's enough to be family."

"So there's no place like home?"

"She's not into drugs, if that's what worries you. Hutch wouldn't have junkies and shit driving up like he was running an ATM for whatever gets some fool high."

"Maureen thinks you're funny."

"Then I wish she was my sister," John says, and Fawcett watches him pick up Big Mac lettuce shards off his tray and eat them. "Seriously, man, she's got her shit together, and no rudeness intended, I'm out of here. I have to guard more than a bunch of burger flippers."

"You never can tell," Fawcett says as John slides his garbage into a bin, but when John leaves without turning around, Fawcett slurps down the rest of his soda so fast he feels chilled, a headache beginning to form behind his eyes. If anybody is timing, he has six minutes left on his break, so he walks to the employees' entrance to get some natural air. As always, the ground near the door is littered with cigarette butts. Worse, there's a glare from the sun that makes his headache flare, and he lets the door swing nearly shut again, breathing in the warm, humid outside air through a space so narrow he feels like he's drowning.

He's ready to retreat, but he notices two couples standing between their cars, and something about how focused they are on each other nudges him to suspect he might be witnessing a drug transaction, that the couples, all four of them with the pallor of indoor living, even in August, work in pairs to make their dealings safer. He keeps one foot wedged in the door and leans back, watching as they exchange McDonald's bags as if they've had their orders mixed up, silently together, then dividing again.

Anything is available, Fawcett thinks. Nothing else moves in the lot, nothing in the two backyards behind it, a set of swings in one that he's never seen a child using all summer, a deflated small plastic pool near the back door filled with a jumble of toys, including a tricycle and a fat plastic bat for swatting whiffle balls. Somebody has gathered the toys and consolidated them like a half dozen unpaid loans, but the pile hasn't been touched since April. It's as if a child has died in that house, as if some terrible exhaustion has set in on the parents. The toys had lain scattered all winter, covered completely or partially by snow, resurfacing during warm spells before being covered again.

The cars drive off, leaving only the ones parked by his employees. Fawcett props the door open with an unopened box of napkins and walks to where a grease-stained KFC bag lies between where the cars have been parked. It is full of bones. Because there is no sign of ants, he knows one of those couples has dumped it. He flings it into the dumpster.

He counts to fifty, and when nothing else moves he lets the door swing shut before he gives into the impulse to get in his car and leave.

Each time the double-murder story comes on, the station shows the same photographs behind the news anchor, Hutch over the right shoulder, the dead man and woman over the left while the anchor begins with a summary of the case. Fawcett expects that routine, but for once Elise is watching with him, and she's impatient. "It's like they think nobody has watched the news for two weeks giving this recap of the grave and how long they think the bodies were in it," she says.

"I guess," Fawcett says, although Elise sitting there makes him recognize that the report needs only three or four new sentences to be featured, that regardless of what he hears, he still keeps his eyes on the photo of Hutch, the executioner, and the indecipherable tattoo on the side of his thick, defensive lineman's neck. Absolutely, Hutch had to have been stunned that the husband and wife tried to steal from him, that they believed him somehow vulnerable to the threat of a gun in his own house. That such a realization drove a fury through him.

"That vicious bastard was at that party I dragged you away from," Elise says. "Your sister, too."

"Yes, he was," Fawcett says, and something about her tone makes him want to tell her about Marlow, how well-trained he is. He takes a breath, deciding.

"You know what I think," Elise says. "No woman would be friends with somebody like Hutch. They'd either avoid him or fuck him."

"Can you hear yourself?" Fawcett says.

"Loud and clear. What part don't you believe?"

The news has switched to weather before Fawcett, without saying another word, gets up and goes to his computer.

Fawcett follows the MapQuest directions he's printed out and parks a hundred yards away from where he sees the driveway to Hutch's house begin. He keeps an eye on the house as he cuts through the woods because nobody could be inside except someone who would see him as an enemy. Six acres Hutch owns, the newspaper has said, and the state game lands bordering this side assure Fawcett nobody lives anywhere close behind him, something that makes him uneasy as soon as he's farther into the woods than anybody stopping to take a piss.

The house, even though he's seen it on the news, surprises him. The wooden siding is newly stained, and so is the deck that runs the length of the back side of the house. And though he can't see inside from a hundred feet away, he appreciates the meticulous landscaping that surrounds the house. The way a forest of rhododendron gives way to a strip of azalea and finally to a variety of ferns and a low swatch of unfamiliar thick green leaves that provide ground cover to the edge of a stream a few strides from where he stands. Even in August, with three weeks of neglect, it looks like something to photograph. Something, he suddenly thinks, that reminds him of an enormous, poisonous flower. Something that would be less threatening if the deck was collapsed, the door off its hinges, the house surrounded by a field of burdock and milkweed.

He turns his back to the house and moves farther into the forest where yellow crime-scene tape flutters like an obscene flag. The earth is still piled in a mound beside an open hole as if somebody might need to lower himself and look for additional clues. When he leans over to look, Fawcett feels lightheaded.

He spends fifteen minutes examining the ground where he walks, his steps as short and slow as those of his grandfather, who uses two canes as if he were skiing. He remembers the cemetery where he has visited his mother's grave for fifteen years, how, after a year or two, the earth mounded over the freshest burials settles and the grass blends, and he is able to cross those plots without feeling disgusted with himself. Hutch, the newspaper had reported, has lived here for six years. If he had buried others three or four years ago, the sites could be anywhere.

When Fawcett finally gives up the search, he's so far behind the house and so disoriented, he can't be certain it's the one that belongs to Hutch. He tries to make out his car, but the road has disappeared. He stares at the ground near where a rash of thorn-covered bushes clusters into a dense thicket. For a moment he believes that he can make out the shape of a grave, the feeling so strong, he lays a hand to the earth, imagining the bones beneath it. He rakes at the soil as if he might distinguish how recently it was disturbed, and then jerks his hand away when he hears a dog bark.

Hutch out on bail, he imagines crazily. The merciless and his well-trained dog. Or his sister, he thinks next, though he remembers that Marlow never barked while she visited.

The dog barks a second time, and though he can't make out whether it's closer now, Fawcett feels the sweat of his foolish panic in his armpits, and when he skids a few steps, turns and searches, the sweat comes from his scalp when the car isn't visible

There's a third choice, he tells himself—a neighbor on the opposite side, somebody living on a large plot of land like Hutch. Everybody in an area like this would own a dog. Maybe two. All of them big.

A buzzing begins in his ears, something like the tinnitus that stayed with him for two days after only forty-five minutes of HIV Positive. The sound makes him want to stick a finger into each ear and dig. As if he's just sat through a double feature without leaving his seat, heaviness sets in behind his eyes. He feels unsteady. A year ago an earthquake struck 200 miles from here, the first in over forty years, and he'd been fascinated, listening to things he owned rattling on shelves and tables, feeling the house vibrate as if a road crew was blasting away rock from a nearby cliff to widen the highway.

Now he just feels sick, nausea amplified by the certainty that if he's confronted he'll beg and plead, not even capable of fleeing. It's just you being an idiot, he tells himself, but he positions himself behind a tree as if he can sense a sniper somewhere nearby. The dog sounds closer when he hears it again, and he tries to reason with himself. The dog doesn't belong on Hutch's property any more than he does. There's no reason for it to come after him. He backs up three steps, looking through the trees, and though he sees nothing and the dog doesn't bark again, Fawcett keeps retreating as if the dog has gone mute in order to stalk him.

He's backed up twenty paces before he pauses to search for the road again, and this time he picks out the car. He doesn't look back as he walks toward it, keeping his eyes on the Prius and wishing he'd driven his SUV instead of this weak, effeminate thing, telling himself one more minute, then thirty seconds more, then ten and ducking early as he scrambles to open the door and push the start button, hearing nothing as always but having to trust that the car is running.

He drives to Maureen's, but instead of telling her about being at Hutch's, he tells her about talking to John. "You mentioned Hutch to John?" she says. "You know that John works for him, don't you?"

"He deals?" Fawcett says, looking at Marlow as if the dog might be ready to snitch.

"Like me, I mean. Now that Hutch is inside, John does favors for him."

"Sort of on spec?"

"You're all the time so judgmental. He's not unlocking the doors or anything."

"I don't care what he's doing. It's him saying you're family and me thinking that doesn't mean you're anybody's sister."

"You're in asshole mode again. No wonder you don't have any friends."

Fawcett grabs her shoulders and twists her to face him. "It's not being an asshole to ask that question." He feels her try to free herself, and his fingers dig into her, insisting, but he's controlled enough to remember Marlow, who stays sitting, his head cocked as if he expects something.

She winces when his fingers find bone and says "OK," but he holds his grip until she seems to get chilled, shivering a bit and starting in with "If you have to know this, I'll tell you."

His hands open and lie across her shoulders the way he remembers his high school coach's did before he sent him into a game. "Expect success," that coach had always said, at 6'7" always looking down at Fawcett.

"Hutch and I were together for a while but not long."

"How long is not long?"

"Two months, maybe less. It was like something you'd do

at summer camp and move on. He was intense." She looks away, searching the room until her eyes rest on Marlow. "And it turns out I'm not."

"Good."

"Hutch said he didn't want me, but he trusted me." She looks into his eyes again, and he holds them. "He said I'm rare."

"How long ago?"

"Two years. Right before I got the job at Dr. McElroy's."

"Why don't I know this?"

"Who am I with now?"

"No idea."

"That's why," she says, and steps back as if she's unlocked herself, moving toward her bedroom.

She's already to the door before he thinks to say, "Have I ever seen the new guy?" but only the dog looks back as if it's forgotten something before she pulls it shut and he hears the lock click.

The next morning, his day off, Fawcett shows up at 8:30 when he knows she's getting ready for work. "Peace," he says.

"What's that mean? If it's an intervention, hurry up. I have to leave."

"How about I give Marlow a day off from the crate?"

Though it's forced, Maureen laughs out loud. "Go ahead. Take him for the day. You look like you need yourself some company that doesn't talk."

"That sounds correct. I should paste a star on you."

"Fuck's sake, Frank. You talk like that to the dog and he'll forget who you are."

"He doesn't know me."

"Right now he remembers who you were yesterday, and pretty soon he'll decide that was somebody he could learn to hate."

"That what you've decided?"

"I'm moving in that direction, Frank. Living with self-righteousness is a disease. Pretty soon you won't be able to treat it."

"Give me the leash and a couple of Milk-Bones. If Marlow rips my throat out in the car, you can tell everybody you were right."

Fawcett drives to the riverfront walk, two miles of narrow park that runs along the flood wall. Twice he yanks the leash, and the dog falls back the same way it did for Maureen. There's a pleasure in knowing that people passing him must think he's trained that dog. Hutch has made it as perfect as a dog could be, so compliant that Fawcett can imagine Marlow witnessing the killings, sitting as Hutch dug a grave large enough for two bodies. What it had taken to make a dog sit in spite of excitement or curiosity or fear.

When two attractive women approach, Fawcett pauses and says "Sit," as if he needs to insure their safety as they pass.

Marlow sits and he lets the chain leash go slack. When the women get within what might be striking distance, the dog doesn't move. "Wow," one of the women says. "How does that ever happen?" She kneels in front of Marlow, her skirt tight against her thighs, and rubs him under his chin. "You're such a good dog," she says as if she could fall in love with obedience.

The other woman, her blouse cut low enough to distract Fawcett, begins to apologize. "Janelle is so into German Shepherds," she says, but Fawcett has already returned his eyes to the kneeling woman, imagining what she will say after they move on, starting with superlatives for Marlow's behavior that might spill over into praise for his owner.

He watches them walk away and waits for the woman who hadn't knelt to look back, a sign the kneeling woman has mentioned him. When neither turns, Fawcett wonders what command for "attack" Hutch has taught the dog. Whether Marlow has learned another command that overrides anything said in anger or fear. For now, Marlow stands beside him for another half a minute until the women are so far away they could turn around for any number of reasons than evaluating a man and his dog.

THE CHEMISTRY OF ENTERTAINMENT

One night in late September, the year I turned fifteen, my father was robbed at gunpoint of sixty-seven dollars. My father owned a magazine and newspaper store. Along with the magazines, he sold candy and beef jerky and junk food in the single room he'd bought from my mother's uncle when he married her in 1955 and now, twenty-two years later, he was barely hanging on. The store looked exactly like it had since I could remember, and there were pictures to show it had looked the same when my mother's uncle ran it during World War II and the years right after.

"Sixty-seven dollars," my mother said. "With all the stores in town, that idiot picked us? Any fool would take one look and know there's not much to be had." I didn't argue, but I knew that thief had chosen my father's store because there weren't any cameras or any kind of security, and the chances of a customer coming in were slim. And I remember the date exactly because it was the same week Nick Ressler became a legend by doing a Gene Simmons imitation for his process speech right after Janelle Fidler showed everybody in our sophomore English class how to type without looking at her fingers.

By 1977 Kiss had been around for what seemed like forever, so all of us had seen somebody blow fire like Simmons, the band's front man. Nick, though, was addicted. Every time there was a party, you could count on him becoming a dragon when a Kiss record got played, but nobody had done it in front of a teacher during class.

Janelle Fidler, for the process speech Mr. Stallings required us to give, demonstrated a typing lesson on a manual typewriter, one with thin keys that seemed always about to jam, clicking out a page of words in two minutes without looking at the keyboard. "I can do eighty, sometimes, ninety words a minute," she said, passing the page to Mr. Stallings so he could inspect it for errors. "It's not much different than playing the piano. I would have given a piano lesson, but I couldn't fit it through the door." For a moment, she smiled, acting as if talking in front of the room was easy, and then she explained where to position your fingers and why the letters were arranged the way they were to lessen the chance of the keys jamming. "The typewriter is one of the world's most useful tools," she said, without reading from a note card. "Everyone should own one, whether a traditional one like this model or the best-selling IBM Selectric, which features a pivoting type ball in order to eliminate the jamming of keys." She was fifteen, the same as I was, but she sounded like a teacher.

After Janelle sat down, Nick announced the title of his speech as "How to be a Dragon," and I could see most of the class sitting up and leaning forward. Mr. Stallings didn't look like he knew what was coming. It was hard to believe he'd never heard of Kiss, but even after Nick said something about how he'd learned to be a dragon from watching a rock show in Buffalo, Mr. Stallings just sat behind his desk making marks in his notebook as if every word was sacred.

Nick turned his back, then pivoted and blew fire, spewing lighter fluid through a sudden, lifted flame from his lighter. He'd mastered that trick so well he stood there unharmed to cheers from everybody but Mr. Stallings and Janelle Fidler. After we quieted down, Nick put the lighter in his pocket and said, "That's it. Flame on, flame off. That's how it's done."

Mr. Stallings put his pen down. "Don't sit down yet, Mr. Ressler. This is supposed to last three to five minutes."

"That's all there is," Nick said. "You just spit the lighter fluid out and light it as it flies past."

"That seems dangerous."

"No, it's not," Nick said. He started to push his hands into his pockets, but there was the lighter in one and the thin lighter fluid can in the other, and only his fingers fit, leaving him with his thumbs out like a kid playing cowboy.

"Have people harmed themselves doing that?"

"If they were stupid."

"You could have looked that up and added it to your speech. Someone may have died."

"If they were really stupid."

'Well, Mr. Ressler, that gets you to three minutes. Sit down."

I could tell that most of the class was thinking Legendary or Classic, the words lying unspoken on everybody's tongue like a slow-melting lozenge that would take minutes to dissolve, but it was my turn.

When I walked up to explain the intricacies of tying the Windsor knot, I was so nervous I looped the ends of the tie incorrectly and had to start over. The class laughed, but I noticed that Janelle didn't, and my second try produced a perfect knot. "Men need to know how to properly knot a tie," I said. "It's essential for looking professional," a line I'd copied from a book on dressing for success. "Just like this," I added, "the wide part reaches the top of the belt and the tip hangs slightly across it."

I owned two ties and one white shirt my mother washed every Monday after I wore it to church. On Tuesday she ironed it and hung it in my closet beside the gray sport coat I put on every Sunday after I correctly knotted one or the other of those ties."All those colored shirts with the designs on them are for school," she repeated about once a month, acting as if I'd forget. "On Sundays, you leave them where they belong."

Even with the mistake, I was standing there wearing my perfect

Windsor knot in a minute and a half, but I turned over my note card and started in on the list of other knots I'd written down so I'd be sure to reach three minutes. "The four-in-hand," I said, "is asymmetrical and narrower. It works best with thicker material."

I spewed out the history of that knot, the eras of its popularity, but when I paused, I saw Mr. Stallings glance at his watch. "The Pratt knot," I started back in, "starts with the tie inside out."

"Really, Mr. Yordy?" Mr. Stallings said. "You're not fooling us with that one, are you?"

"No," I said, though I hadn't looked at the diagram in the book I'd copied from.

"Well then," he said, but I was at three and a half minutes, and the bell was about to ring. "We'll trust you until further notice."

I could have filled the rest of the five minutes with quotes from Successful Dressing, but I was glad I didn't get to my emergency stuff, how, the year before, my mother was the person who'd showed me the Windsor knot. She'd told me before church that I needed to leave my "redneck knot" behind unless I wanted to announce I wasn't able to work with my brain. She took me into the bathroom and made me look at my buttoned collar until the thin knot became a birthmark. "It's about how you're seen," she said. "You should know that my father thought I was making a mistake marrying a man who couldn't make a decent knot in a tie."

I didn't say anything. "Your father," she went on, "won't change, but you can," as she untied that knot and handed me each arrowed end of the cheap paisley-designed cloth. "Ready?" she said. "Ready?" as if we were about to run through fire. "Over. Like this, and then under," and I followed her hands at my throat until she finished and tugged that knot up close to my collar, changing my face into one that belonged to a boy who understood the difference knots can make, one more thing to announce aloud like the Nicene Creed instead of reading it from the hymnal like the ignorant who couldn't manage remembering a simple pledge to God. "Now," she'd said, untying that knot, "show me," and I did, hands twisting like someone who would grow up thoughtful. "Now no father will tell his daughter that about you," she said, smiling, and I walked the Windsor Knot to where my father was waiting in his white shirt, his neck flushed from the tight collar buttoned to keep his simple knot in place.

When I got home that afternoon, the paisley tie pressed inside my notebook, my mother told me the police figured there was about no chance of catching the thief because my father was such a terrible witness. "He told the cops he saw the man's face but didn't remember anything except he was white and clean shaven. Can you imagine how helpful that was in this town? The guy didn't even bother with a mask. Like he knew your father wouldn't notice anything."

"The guy had a gun, Mom. Dad was probably looking at that the whole time."

"That's where you're wrong," she said. "When your father told the police about the gun, they asked him if the robber showed it, and he said 'Not exactly.'"

"But Dad said."

"You know what Dad said?" My mother raised her arms like a minister offering a benediction before she said, triumphantly, "'The man told me he had a gun, and I believed him.' I wanted to leave the room right then and there."

"You get an A for tying that stupid knot?" Nick said the next day.

"Yeah."

"Fuck you and old Stallings too."

"I looked up all that stuff about its history," I said. "I added things. That's how you get an A."

"We were supposed to show how to do something, not give a report. I bet Fidler got an A too, typing while Stallings got a chance to stare at her tits." He punched me on the shoulder. "And you, too, right?"

"Whatever you say."

"You know what I say? I say your old man should sell Hustler and Penthouse," the same as admitting he jerked off as much as I did. "You'd get rich selling to kids. Like beer. Nobody cares about what's legal. That just means it's boring. And just think, you'd get to check every issue out for free and wish Fidler had tits like any of those fuckables."

Nick was right about one thing. For the past six months, I'd dreamed about Janelle Fidler while I danced with myself to songs on the radio in my room. I kept the door locked because early in the summer my mother had opened it in the middle of me slow dancing to James Taylor's remake of "Handy Man." Embarrassed, I'd slammed the door shut in her face. She'd never brought it up, surprising me, but it had made me start thinking about what else she knew about what a fifteen year-old boy did in private. If so, she would know how excited I became imagining Janelle's body, how I used up Kleenex as if I had a chronic cold. Maybe that door slamming had told her it was better not to interrupt anything I might be doing with the door closed.

But It wasn't as if I was making the whole thing up the way guys did with centerfolds. Janelle and I went on a few dates. I danced with her and held her hand, and finally, after our third time out, I kissed her after we walked home from the movies.

But when school started, I found out she'd started going out with a senior named Carlton Bellows. "You're so young, Michael," Janelle had said the first week of class when she turned me down. "You'd never know we were in the same grade."

I felt panicked. I started to sweat and needed to piss, but she went on.

"You're afraid to touch me. It would be cute if we were in eighth grade instead of being sophomores."

"It's respect," I said, my voice squeaking.

"No, it's not," she said, and then she seemed to soften. "At least you didn't pretend to know anything. Being transparent counts for something."

I knew transparent from junior high science—transparent, translucent, opaque—easy answers on a test about light and how it passes through things— but the word sounded terrible, like she was naming a disease. "When you're a senior, there will be a girl who's smart in tenth grade, and by then you'll know enough to be interesting to her."

"So how do I learn?"

She stared into my eyes. "There are plenty of dumb girls, Michael," she said, which turned out to be the last things besides "Hi, there" that she ever said to me. I looked down, trying to muster up another sentence to keep her there, but she used that moment to turn around and begin to walk, and I didn't have the nerve to raise my voice and call her back.

I let it go like I did everything. By then I'd become a kid who looked down when I answered, my words balanced on the cusp of being unheard. "What?" my mother would say. "What was that?" and I'd raise my voice slightly, changing the words from "Honest to God, Mom" to "Honestly, I don't know."

My father, if he'd been a mumbler, was now all silence. There had been a time when I'd thought it was a manly thing to be. Stoical, I'd thought, when I'd learned the word for a vocabulary test in seventh grade, but now it just made me afraid of becoming that way myself.

One thing I did after Janelle moved on to Carlton Bellows was stop riding my bike. "I can walk," I told my mother, but I knew I'd stopped because Janelle wasn't interested in anybody who was riding a bike. They were all boys or old men. The bike was hanging from two hooks in the garage as if it was already winter when nobody who lived near Buffalo could ride.

"Does this have anything to do with that pretty girl you took to DarienLake in July?" my mother said.

"I don't know," I said, mumbling

"What? You have to look at people when you talk."

"Who knows?" I said.

"Michael," my mother said. "It's just that I want you to stand up for yourself. It's good to aim high."

For once, I kept my eyes level. "It means I'm never happy."

"If you aimed low and hit the mark, would you be happy?"

"Not anymore."

"Well," she said. "There you have it."

I knew who Carlton Bellows was. He was going to the University of Chicago because he'd won the science fair from our region of the state and then came in second at the national science fair in Chicago, which earned him a full scholarship offer on the spot. When Nick Ressler found out I'd been dumped for Bellows, he said, "All that chemistry and shit Bellows knows. He should figure out a way to set somebody on fire without getting hurt. Can you imagine a rock band like that? Kiss would be out of business."

"But you still have to make good songs," I said.

"That's your problem. No imagination. Once you see the band on fire, the songs are twice as good. Maybe Fidler was right to shoot you down. Haven't you ever done anything cool?"

"I don't know," I said, not mumbling, but still the same as admitting he was right.

"Too bad you weren't working when your old man's place was robbed. Having a gun stuck in your face would make you the coolest guy in school."

That afternoon the school held an assembly to give out academic awards for the year before. I got to stand next to Janelle for having an average during my freshman year of 3.75 or higher. There were thirty-eight other students on stage, some of them guys or girls I didn't think were smart at all. While we were all standing there, the principal called out Carlton Bellows' name, and he came up alone to receive a plaque and a savings bond before the principal announced his scholarship. Janelle whispered "Yes" and clapped, and I wished I'd received a 3.74 so I could sit in the auditorium and not move my hands

"You looked like you wanted to cop a feel up there," Nick said as we filed out of the auditorium.

"You know what?" I said. "Here's something you should have said in your speech so you'd get an A. There are guys in carnivals and places like that who can turn a blowtorch on themselves without getting hurt."

Nick looked skeptical. "Inhaling?" he said. "You're making this shit up. I'd believe you more if you said you fucked Fidler."

"Nobody can inhale. It just looks that way, so everybody thinks he's doing something impossible, not like Kiss that everybody can do. They snuff the flame with their mouths. The trick is the tongue's insulation and holding your breath."

"Like an acolyte," Nick said, which must have made me look so surprised he added, "I did that shit for a year when I was twelve. Put out candles with a little bell thing."

"You're allowed to sound smart," I said, and Nick shrugged, about as close as he was going to get to admitting he agreed about the importance of breath control in the chemistry of entertainment.

"I should have shown Stallings how to get high."

"Teachers know about marijuana, even Stallings."

"Can you imagine him toking up? Wearing a tie and those short sleeve white shirts he lives in. Trying to read Shakespeare while he's buzzed."

"He might."

"And he might give me an A, but that's not what I meant. I should have done huffing for him. A can of Dust-Off—he wouldn't have known what I was doing. You think any teachers get high like that?"

"No."

"That's their loss then. It's cheap and quick."

I stayed quiet too long and Nick smiled. "You don't know what I'm talking about, do you?"

"Drugs," I said, as if that might be convincing.

"Yeah. Right. Drugs. You don't have to lie. There's nobody else here."

I shrugged in a way that I could deny was a confession if Nick turned out to be an asshole. "Get yourself a can of Dust-Off and pretend you're a typewriter. That's all I'm saying." He laughed. "No, don't do that. I'll show you what's up so you don't fuck yourself over."

"Ok," I said, but I was sure he was lying.

When I got home I gave the honors certificate signed by the principal to my mother. "Another one of these," she said. "That's good," and she put it in a drawer.

Saturday, after dinner, I walked into town by myself. It was just over a mile and a half, not that far unless you were by yourself like I was and had nothing to do but think about how terrible it would be to turn around and go back home to watch television. A half hour of walking, but then I began to worry about the crowd outside the theater, who would notice I'd walked in like some bum who nobody would pick up as he hitchhiked.

So it was a good thing I'd gotten the time of the movie wrong, that it had already started, the street outside deserted. That theater, with its single screen, had about as much chance of surviving as my father's store, but right then it was showing Exorcist II, and I was happy to walk in fifteen minutes late because the place was dark and nobody could see me slip into the first aisle seat that was empty.

I could tell that the audience was mostly high school kids because there was a lot of talking out loud and even, after a while, shouting at the screen, boys laughing at Linda Blair, asking her to spin her head around and throw up pea soup like she had in the first Exorcist.

"Show the devil your tits," some guy yelled, and nobody told him to shut up. I could hear snap tops being pulled. Paper bags rustling. I recognized Richard Burton and remembered how my mother had told me he was so handsome and such a great actor, but now he was just an old priest in a terrible movie, and there were people leaving before the end, walking back the aisle talking out loud like it didn't matter if anyone else could hear the dialogue.

I didn't care either until I heard Janelle's voice. In the light from a bright scene, I saw her and Bellows coming up the aisle, his arm around her shoulders, her blouse made of some material that reflected the movie's flickering light. When she was close, I looked down, so all I could see was the bottom of her flared pants until she passed and I turned to stare at how those pants tightened over the backs of her thighs as she leaned against Carlton Bellows. I knew there was a party they were probably going to, and I knew you had to be a senior or come with one if you expected to be allowed in.

The movie dragged on for a few more minutes but nothing about it improved for Burton or Blair, even with a swarm of locusts thrown in as something the devil would conjure up in 1977 when there were way worse things to worry about. I hurried out before the last scene ended, nearly tripping over the feet of somebody who laughed as I stumbled.

My father's store was two blocks away. It was just past nine o'clock, but he stayed open until 9:30 on Saturday, mimicking the business hours of the stores at the mall north of town near the thruway exit. The store, I was happy to see, was empty. There was a new sign posted above the checkout counter that said: We Do Not Keep More Than $20 In The Register. I was sure it was the police department's idea, somebody from the station telling him to post it like it was some sort of bulletproof glass. But I thought that a robber who would risk prison for $67 would risk it for $20.

"No friends tonight?" my father said.

"Later," I said, and my father nodded like he knew that meant "None at all."

"Not much going on here," he said, turning back to the morning newspaper as if he'd just gotten around to reading it.

I wanted to ask him if anybody ever bought a Saturday morning paper after nine o'clock at night, but instead I picked up two Milky Ways and handed him a dollar. "Your money's no good here," he said.

"Go ahead and give me my change," I said. "I want to pay."

His face tightened then, and he glanced toward the front window as if he expected to see somebody waiting outside. "Your mother send you? She tell you to start chipping in to make ends meet?"

"No, Dad."

He looked at the window again before he rang up the sale and dropped a few nickels and dimes on the counter. "Your mother thinks I'm a lost cause," he said.

"No, she doesn't."

He smiled. "Saturday night's for lying, isn't it?" he said. "You enjoy those candy bars and tell your mother I haven't broken anything today and don't intend to in the next twenty minutes."

"She doesn't hate you, Dad."

"All I can do is try."

"I guess."

He was animated now, pacing behind the counter, but he seemed to be acting like somebody else, and his words sounded like slogans. "There's plenty who don't," he said. "More than plenty."

I took a back road home. Two miles of walking, but none of it facing headlights of cars that might be full of kids who'd notice me, and no chance of my father pulling off and offering me a ride. I ate both candy bars and stuffed the wrappers in my pocket, and when I saw my father's car in the driveway, the lights on in three rooms, I sat on the swings in a neighbor's yard two houses away and waited another half hour so I could walk in acting like I'd been somewhere and know both of them would be more interested in getting ready for bed than asking me questions.

Sunday morning, just after I knotted my tie for church, my mother was waiting outside my door. "Michael," she said. "Michael."

"What?"

She swallowed and started again. "Janelle is dead," she said, and when I looked at her blankly, she added, "Your Janelle. It sounds like she was doing drugs, something I never heard of."

"She wouldn't do drugs."

"The man on the news used the word 'huffing.' He said she and some others were inhaling typewriter cleaner at a party."

I undid my tie and unbuttoned my shirt. With my mother still standing there I hung it up again and slid my pants off, hanging them up as well. My mother didn't turn her head, but she said, "You can stay home this once."

Standing there in my briefs, I didn't know what to do next, and neither did she. Maybe ten seconds passed before my father appeared in the doorway. "What's going on?" he said.

My mother stepped toward me, kissed my forehead, and turned. "Just get in the car," she said. "Just get in the goddamned car."

I found another news broadcast after they left. I sat there in my briefs and listened as a doctor was interviewed. The chemical name for the active ingredient, she said, was toluene, and she named other products that contained it—nail polish remover, aerosol sprays, deodorant, hair spray. The newscaster asked why anyone would inhale something so dangerous. "It makes the users drowsy," she said. "It makes them dizzy and causes loss of inhibition. But the effects don't last very long and there is the possibility, however small, of cardiac arrest or asphyxiation."

Janelle had used the stuff Nick Ressler had joked about, stuff you spray on typewriter keys to clean them. Anybody could buy a can, but my mother used a brush. I'd worked it among the keys once or twice when I was bored. Mostly, I'd never cared about dirt unless something got stuck on the key ball. I shut off the television, walked to the spare room, and sat in front of the Selectric. There were little bits of stuff caught among the keys—a strand of hair, dandruff, dust. I blew on the keyboard, and the hair and some tiny white specks scattered.

The typewriter cleaner was just air, I thought, but something had to make it spray harder than my lungs. I imagined Carlton Bellows explaining the chemistry to Janelle, and then I imagined her doing her own homework before trying it. I had to believe that. If someone like Janelle Fidler could kill herself by accident, there wasn't any hope for me.

I was dressed when my mother and father came home. "Good," my mother said, but she excused me from lunch when I said I wasn't hungry, and she waited an hour more for me to find her by the television, my father minding the store from one to six to duplicate the mall's Sunday hours.

"She was too smart to do that, Mom. She was the smartest girl in my class."

"She's still fifteen," my mother said, "no matter how smart she is. God, Michael, I've been thinking about her mother all day."

I'd met Janelle's mother once. Labor Day weekend, the last time I'd gone out with Janelle, she'd driven Janelle and me to a dance at the country club where, it turned out, she was the chaperone. She was dressed as if she'd forgotten the dance was for "under 18"—a black dress that I imagined she wore to dances when teenagers were home watching television.

Later in the evening was when Janelle told me about Carlton Bellows, how she felt bad but wanted to be honest, that she'd asked me because of a promise to her mother "to be fair." "My mother said I owed you."

I felt myself choking, every answer I wanted to say out loud strangled.

"I like you, Michael. That's why I'm telling you this. So you're not fooled into thinking the wrong things." I looked down, cursing myself. "Ok?" she said.

"Ok," I said, taking her hand, pulling her close, and beginning to dance. She didn't say anything else. She let me press against her, and desperate for something to say, I managed, "You and your Mom are almost dressed like twins."

Janelle pulled back and looked at me. "You mean the style? There are a ton of differences."

"The color, I guess." I'd wanted so much to speak, but now I felt lost.

"The colors are different, Michael. Black and navy blue aren't the same at all. Do they look the same to you?"

"Almost," I said. I wished immediately that I hadn't. I should have laughed. I should have pulled away and admired her dress and said something like "I prefer navy blue." Anything but such a lame denial, as if I'd been caught in a lie.

She dropped my hand, and I hurried to say, "School starts in three days."

"Yes, it does," she said.

"I know hardly anybody feels this way, but I'm looking forward to going back."

"School is for what you need to do; the rest is for what you want."

"Carlton tell you that?" I said, sounding like I was eight years old.

"My father told me that, Michael."

Her mother, when she came looking to drive us home, said, "You two looked like you were having a good time," and I wondered if she lied so often she didn't recognize the habit.

"By now everyone has heard about the accident," Mr. Stallings said on Monday. "Today we'll just read silently, and tomorrow many of you, I imagine, will be excused to attend the service."

Mr. Stallings had a stack of Scholastic Magazines that he passed out once or twice a month for us to read "independently" before writing summaries of the story we chose, so everyone knew what to do when he passed them back each row. Everybody was quiet, but hardly anybody opened their copy, and Mr. Stallings just sat at his desk, the only teacher all day who didn't invite us "to talk it out."

After the bell rang, everybody placed their magazine on the corner of his desk and filed out, but Mr. Stallings called out to Nick and me to wait for a moment. "Do you know anything about this breathing from aerosol dispensers?" Mr. Stallings said.

"As much as you do," Nick said.

"What kind of answer is that?"

"Only that you'd be crazy to do it."

"You don't have to be so flippant. I was just trying to learn."

Nick swung away from Mr. Stallings, but then he pivoted and faced him again. "Why don't you ask Mikey? He's the Janelle Fidler expert. He might have the inside dope."

Mr. Stallings turned toward me, puzzled. "Is that so?"

"Not really."

When Nick was gone, I drifted back as if I'd forgotten something. "Nick doesn't do huffing. That's the truth," I said, though all I had to go on was he wasn't like Carlton Bellows.

"Ok."

"Nobody I know does huffing. Not one person."

"Except Janelle."

"Not her either until that one time."

"Maybe that's so."

"It is. Only idiots do huffing. Retards. Burn outs." I could hear myself breathing between words.

"Waste products," Mr. Stallings said, and the phrase, coming from his mouth, made me swallow hard and hate him. I waited for Mr. Stallings to say there are exceptions to every rule and wasn't Carlton Bellows the smartest boy in the senior class? But Mr. Stallings didn't say anything else. He opened his grade book and looked down as if there was something important on the page where the names had a series of check marks and minus signs and percentages trailing across the page, all of them adding up to one of five capital letters.

"You look sharp," my mother said as she drove me to the church, but I pretended to be lost in thought, staring out the side window, and she didn't say anything else except "I'll be parked right here in an hour" as I got out.

As I sat down by myself in the back, I saw Carlton Bellows sitting with what had to be his parents. Word had it that he'd told Janelle huffing wasn't as safe as drinking, but I didn't believe it. I'd listened to Carlton Bellows when he acted like there was such a thing as a teaching assistant in ninth grade science, giving advice at our lab stations because the teacher, Miss Smolcic, adored him so much she let him. The word came from his friends who'd been there, and when they said he'd warned her when the can was passed around, trying to stop her, I was sure what he'd done was list the effects and the dangers like the tv doctor, reciting from a menu of expectations as if something like that had ever prevented anybody from putting themselves at risk. I wondered if Bellows would lose his scholarship, whether a place like the University of Chicago would even find out about this. Or maybe he would go to jail. Janelle had been right. I didn't know anything except what somebody taught me like a teacher. All those things people knew because they'd tried them were a mystery.

I'd never seen Carlton Bellows wearing a tie, but now I could see he had a perfect Windsor knot. When Janelle's mother was escorted by the funeral director to the front row, Bellows turned his head. I thought of Nick's full-body rock star fire effect, how Bellows would look inside those flames—not like the monk in the famous photograph from Vietnam in our history book, but waving his arms and running like a fool who didn't know enough to drop and roll.

Mrs. Fidler's dress was black, and for a moment I thought it was the one from the dance, but of course it wasn't, the sleeves long, the hem a few inches lower. Mr. Fidler followed behind in a dark suit that fit so well I knew that it had been tailored.

Afterwards, in the car and without my asking, my mother said, "We never know everything about anybody. If we did, we couldn't stand each other."

"Dad?" I said. "Me?"

"Everybody," she said without hesitating, "but that doesn't mean we can't love each other."

I wondered what things were buried in the house—objects, letters, keepsakes. I thought of how Janelle had been dressed the night she died. How her body looked in the shimmering blouse and flared pants I'd seen her in as she and Bellows had walked out of the theater twenty minutes before Exorcist II had ended, nearly brushing my arm as she passed. And how it would have looked lying there after. Already I had a secret, aroused by the dead, and though I told myself to turn on the light and think of something else, I felt my penis stiffen in the dark. It was all I could do to keep my hands off myself, keeping them behind my head to maintain some small part of self-respect.

NOW THEY'RE ALL STRANGERS

While they ate dinner, the Cajun chicken sandwiches and black beans Doug Troup made once every two weeks, his wife began telling him how one of her students had been molested by her mother's boyfriend.

"So to hell with that guy," Doug said. Nadeen taught fifth grade. The girl had to be ten or eleven. "That's it for him."

Tomorrow was Thanksgiving, and Doug hoped this was Nadeen's last miserable school story until after their sons came back to spend the long weekend. She scraped bits of seasoning off the meat, sprinkling her plate with red and black pepper, cumin, paprika, and garlic. "They didn't press charges," she said.

Doug took a bite of his sandwich and chewed it slowly. He felt like sopping up the seasoning on Nadeen's plate with his bun. "So maybe he didn't do it? Maybe the girl just hates him?"

"He did it all right. The mother told me, not Tracy. She wanted me to know why her daughter's been absent so much and not doing her homework. 'Timmer,' she calls him. They spent this past weekend at his house."

"Timmer?" Doug said.

"You know what she told me," Nadeen said. "'I still have feelings for him.' How does a mother say that?"

"The fuck."

"Her daughter, Doug. And she knows and says that? They drive to Timmer's every weekend. It's not like he barges in on them. She puts that child in her car and drives there knowing."

"Fucked up, for sure," Doug said.

Nadeen looked at a magazine lying on the side of the table where they stacked the mail each afternoon. Allure, it said on the cover. "No Fear Tanning," a title promised. "Thighs to Die For." A sample copy had shown up in the mail that afternoon. He thought she might open it and start reading about the "Ten Ways to Surprise your Man in Bed," the third teaser that ran beside a model in low riding jeans that were unsnapped. "There should be a phrase worse than 'fucked up' to say," Nadeen said. "Fucked up isn't good enough anymore. This isn't fucked up—it's worse."

"If the world gets any worse, somebody will think of something," he said.

Nadeen grimaced. "If the world gets any worse, that child will be dead."

"Yes," Doug thought, but when he opened his mouth it came out, "What can you do?" a phrase that sounded so horrible he hurried to add, "Sorry, I just found out I've got this thing to do in Tampa in a couple of weeks, this building under construction that has a possible sway problem."

"I heard what you said, Doug. I hope you heard it, too."

"Once every fourteen years, on average," he pushed on, "Tampa has hurricane-force winds that push the limit of what this building has been designed for."

"You did this before, Doug. In Charleston. You went down there and convinced them to reinforce the building. You told me all about it. The wind has to come from exactly the right angle, too. It's not just speed."

"You should be an engineer. You pay attention to everything."

Nadeen finally seemed satisfied with her sandwich, taking a small bite. Anyone else would simply say she hated Cajun chicken, that she'd rather fast than eat one more mouthful, but he knew she was waiting for him to prepare hers differently without her asking, that he was supposed to make lemon-pepper chicken for her because he'd noticed, since he'd started to share cooking these last six weeks, the care she took with cleaning off the spices. "There was a man, once, who wouldn't walk past the CitiCorp Building in New York," Doug said. "He was the engineer who discovered it was unsafe, that it hadn't been built according to specs, bolts instead of welds. He knew its limits."

"What did he do about it?"

"He blew the whistle. It was fixed before hurricane season."

"And then he walked past it?"

"No. He still went out of his way. It wasn't the danger. He couldn't get over the idea that such a mistake could be made."

"Buildings aren't people, Doug. You don't mourn a building."

"CitiCorp is fifty-nine stories. You know how many other buildings there are in this country that are taller than 500 feet?"

"You think you can prevent catastrophe," she said.

"No, just make it less likely."

"You think you can make the chance so minute you'd be more likely to win the lottery."

"Yes," he said. "That's what I can do. Lengthening the odds so far people stop worrying."

"That's where you're wrong. Nobody in a tall building ever worried until the crazy men in planes showed up."

Dough stared at the wreckage of dinner on her plate. "That can't take us anywhere besides despair."

Nadeen took an even smaller bite. "Do you think somebody like Timmer should be killed?" she said before chewing.

"For raping a child?"

"Yes."

Doug hesitated. The terrorists had thought people should be

killed for living in a prosperous country. Their daughter Andrea had worked for a brokerage firm on the 77th floor of the south tower. When she'd gotten the job, he'd smiled at her address—it had seemed charmed. Andrea had survived by walking down the stairs among hundreds of people who weren't panicked because they thought they were evacuating a buiding where all of the disaster had happened to people a few floors above them. She had stepped outside so close to the time of collapse she'd been less than two blocks away when the tower had fallen. "I've said this before," he finally said, "the towers held up well, considering."

"They didn't hold up at all," Nadeen said. "They fell the fuck down."

"She walked away."

"No, she didn't."

"Any skyscraper would have fallen."

"You have to say that. That's the sort of logic that lets somebody like Timmer keep breathing."

"What can you do?" Doug said for the second time in minutes. And when Nadeen pushed her plate into the center of the table with half a sandwich still sitting among a puddle of beans, he added, "Go out and kill him?"

"I thought you wanted certainty."

"There's no such thing," he said.

"But you do what you can."

"Yes."

"Exactly." She seemed triumphant. "How do you suppose Timmer talks to that girl? What does he say when she walks into his house on Friday night? 'Hi there, princess'?"

"Four hundred and sixty-nine," Doug said.

"What?"

"That's' how many buildings there are in the United States that are more than five hundred feet tall. That's how many targets are on the lunatics' radar." Nadeen picked up her plate, and for a moment Doug thought she was estimating the mess it would make if she threw it. "You know how many blocks they planned on evacuating if CitiCorp was in danger of collapsing?"

Nadeen stood, still balancing the plate in both hands. "Ten," Doug said. "Just to be safe."

And when she said nothing, carrying the plate to the garbage can and scraping everything off inside, he said, "And you know who supervised the repair of the CitiCorp Building? The man who designed the World Trade Center towers."

Doug had thought that after the first anniversary of the attack, after the media dropped the subject, there would be a lessening of his wife's anger. Andrea had problems, but she had lived, after all.

Only once during the first year had he said aloud, "Thank God all of our children didn't work there." Nadeen had given him a look that froze his tongue, but those words surfaced in his thoughts nearly every day, and there was nothing to do but acknowledge the truth of it to himself. Now, more than a year later, Andrea had yet to work. She'd abandoned her apartment after missing two months' rent and moved in with a man named Kevin who was a waiter, he said, while he waited for his career as a singer-songwriter to take off.

Kevin was the same man she'd broken up with three months before the towers had collapsed. He'd been playing free shows for tips then and was still doing them once or twice a week, lugging his acoustic guitar to a coffee shop or bar and performing an hour's worth of mournful songs, several of which about Doug's daughter leaving him.

They were good songs, Kevin said. There was no sense in not playing them just because she was back. Doug wondered how mournful Kevin's new songs were if they were about a young woman so traumatized she refused all transportation and didn't go into any public places that held more than thirty people because she was sure a suicide bomber was inevitable.

For a year, when they stopped in for the occasional dinner, their sons Alex and Daniel had talked about the Trade Center and their sister, how they'd each visited her three times in New York, trying to convince Andrea to leave the city. They'd both brought back stories of spending weekends inside Kevn's apartment, going outside only for breakfast, and then so early there was only one tiny restaurant open in the neighborhood. "Terrorists need a crowd," she told them over omelets.

Now, at the end of the Thanksgiving weekend they'd spent in the house, his sons' talk was about themselves. They were both in graduate school—music and business. Neither had a girl friend steady enough to bring home. For three days they'd gotten up in the afternoon and started in on 30-packs of beer they'd stacked in the garage to keep cool. On Thursday and Friday nights they'd gone out around eleven o'clock, looking for old friends in local bars, but by Saturday, after dinner, they seemed to have lost momentum, drinking slowly, the music less loud in the basement while they shot pool with Doug.

He watched the long, slender fingers of his son the pianist curl around the cue stick, and when Alex left himself an impossible shot, his son muttered "Fuck."

"Neither of you see the geometry of the table," Doug said.

"Geometry is what I copied from my girlfriend in tenth grade," Alex said, trying a banked combination shot and leaving the table open when it failed.

Doug finished the game by running six balls and nudged the cue ball back up the table for the break. "This is about as much fun as watching those towel heads on television," Alex said as he racked while Doug nodded at Nadeen coming down the stairs.

Daniel laughed. "It could be worse," he said. "It could be the dots." Both boys, especially when they were drinking, had fallen into the easy use of slurs that covered the Middle and the Near East from the Mediterranean to the Himalayas. They used these names now, Doug thought, the way they used to say "gayness" when they were in high school. The Middle East had replaced homosexuality as the most readily slurred, and he understood they used this language even when Nadeen was nearby because they knew their mother, who had preached to them daily about prejudice while they were growing up, wouldn't lecture them now. "All that education," Doug said, "and this is how you talk."

"How's that?" Nadine said, not smiling.

"Let's just play," Daniel said.

Nadeen always volunteered for two games, partnered with each son. "Ok, Mom, let's take them out," Daniel said before he turned toward Doug. "If you weren't our father, you'd say it too."

Nadeen shot as if she were playing some sort of adaptive 8-ball, using the bridge whenever the cue ball was half the length of the table away or lay within six inches of another ball. She refused to lean over the table. Doug thought she was being modest, that it was some habit born years ago when to lean over a pool table would invite boys to look down her blouse.

During the second game, partnered with Alex, she used the bridge on three consecutive shots, making all of them. Daniel laughed. "The one-armed man is still on the loose."

"Go ahead and talk, sand-monkey," Alex said. "She's running the table."

Nadeen didn't look up. She used the bridge again, finally missing, and Doug hesitated, realizing he was surprised when Nadeen didn't curse as she put the bridge away.

As he finished off another wide-open table, Nadeen began to retell the Timmer story, hurrying toward, "What would you do if you were this girl's brothers?"

"Castrate him," Daniel said, and Alex nodded as Doug tapped in the eight ball. "The hypothetical vigilantes," he said.

Alex looked right at Doug. "Definitely cut off his balls," he said.

Nadeen shook her head. "These aren't the times for Bible talk," she said. "Those people back then were so ignorant they thought the world was as simple as an eye for an eye."

Daniel rolled the cue ball with his hand, sending it against the rail hard enough to ricochet through four banks before it spun off one of the three balls still lying on the table. "I get it," he said. "Take him out."

Doug swept the balls into the pocket nearest him. "Thinking like a terrorist," he said.

Alex snorted. "Mom's right. The line gets drawn somewhere, and this guy Timmer is on the other side."

"A line like that isn't easy to locate," Doug said.

"Yes, it is. Just think of what absolutely should never happen again," Alex said.

"Fucking a little girl," Daniel said.

"Yes."

"The Trade Center."

"Unacceptable."

Doug shook his head, but Alex kept on. "Andrea's as fucked up as the dead, Dad. Those towel-heads murdered her spirit."

"She can recover."

"It's been over a year."

Nadeen looked triumphant. "Sure," she said, "and just think, that eleven year-old girl will be just fine eventually."

In late September, once the anniversary had passed, Doug had driven the three hundred miles to New York with determination. "Come home," he had said to his daughter. "You'll get a job in no time."

"Because I'm a survivor?" Andrea had said. "You think this is the Holocaust or something. That people will hire me because I'm somebody who walked down the stairs?"

"You worked in New York City. Surely you can work in Phillipstown."

"I'll work here when I'm ready."

Kevin had tried to pay for dinner, which, for the three of them, was over $100. The restaurant was so small, half of the two dozen customers ate, like them, at three tables on the sidewalk. Andrea had chosen the restaurant because the seating was ideal despite the traffic three steps from their food. "This is perfect," she'd said. "This is where I want to eat the next time you come to New York."

"She's twenty-seven," Nadeen had said when Doug came home empty handed. "She's been on her own for five years. What are you going to do—kidnap her?"

A week later, Nadeen had started going to a women's health club where all the workouts, according to the pamphlet she showed him, were designed for the female body. The machines she used, Nadeen said, were simple and tension-driven. She described how an attendant adjusted them as she and the other women circled the room, moving through eight different machines that defined different muscles and accelerated her heart.

She was thinner now, with more energy, and Doug was beginning to believe the owners, whom he'd seen as quacks, were on to something. For two months she had gone three days a week and every Saturday. She never missed, not even when it snowed heavily the week after Thanksgiving and he figured the place for closed. "The owner lives upstairs," Nadeen explained. "Of course she was open. She was a little surprised to see me, but she was playing the music, and I thought she expected other women."

He'd fallen into the habit of watching television while she was gone, often for more than two hours because, she said, she sometimes enjoyed drinking coffee afterwards with other exercisers. He kept his post Trade Center vow of not drinking during the evening, but now he ate ice cream or gorged on potato chips. Nadeen had begun squeezing his new spare tire in early November. "They should open a men's exercise place," she said, "so you'd have some place to go."

"I can do sit ups right here in the living room. I can do push ups while you're gone."

"Sure you can, Doug. And I can use the stationary bike I put in Daniel's old room when he left for school."

Now, watching the snow still accumulating in the driveway, his trip to Tampa less than a week away, he made an exercise resolution, and for one week, beginning the day after the snow storm, he followed through seven night in a row, including the evenings she was home and could watch. "See," Nadeen said, standing over him on the seventh night. "Self-discipline."

Doug grunted through his count to fifty-three, getting to his age in sit ups. "Our sons are next," he said. "They can put down their beer and clean up their mouths."

Nadeen stepped across his chest so she straddled him. "You know why the boys talk like that?"

"They think anger gives them an excuse."

"People talk like that when they need to do something."

"People talk like that when they stop thinking. Jesus, you're a teacher."

"It's because I'm a teacher. I deal with people. You deal with buildings. They aren't malicious."

"I make sure of that."

"Yes," Nadeen said. "Isn't it easy. After the boys, you can cure our daughter." She sighed like she was looking down at him over the bars of a crib. "People used to know their enemies. They lived in the next town or just down the street. Now they're all strangers."

"There's enough scumbags close by to go around. Just read the paper."

Nadeen sighed again. "Timmer's never been in the paper. He's an alien. He might as well be from the Middle East."

From below her, he could look up her skirt, follow her toned thighs to the dark blue of her silk panties. She seemed so at ease in her posture he suddenly thought she was seeing someone, walking away from those machines into the arms of a man who was excited by a woman working out in a warm-up suit.

The following night, instead of turning on the television after he finished his workout, he parked across the street from the club. He switched off the CD player and sat in silence as if he expected to hear the chatter of the women. After a few minutes, he felt as if he was waiting for the women inside to undress, that the exercising stations were props for a kind of fetish pornography, every push and pull full of sexual innuendo. Doug cursed himself and gripped the key, restarting the car, so awkwardly nervous he nearly clipped the left taillight of the car in front of him as he pulled from the curb. Nearly two hours passed before Nadeen swung into the driveway.

Two nights later he parked a block away in a spot from where he could watch the club's entrance without being seen, arriving so late he only had to wait ten minutes for her to finish and leave. Nadeen and two other women walked out together, took six steps, and entered the doughnut shop next door. She and the others drank what he took for coffee, and by their gestures he was sure none of them had ordered doughnuts. He checked his watch. Thirty minutes it took for them to finish their drinks, none of them, after that, touching their cups again for fifteen more minutes. If Nadeen was unfaithful, she wasn't in a hurry, Doug nearly said aloud as he started the car. He drove home and did sit ups, going past fifty-three to sixty, and then, fantasizing he would die at the age of the number where he stopped, he struggled to seventy before he cramped and lay curled on his side, cursing his three score and ten.

In Tampa, two days later, Doug flipped on the turn signal of his rental car to enter the underground parking garage, but then, as he slowed, the arrow blinking left, he looked in the mirror, saw no one behind him, and accelerated, nudging the signal arm back to off. He shuddered a moment, beginning to search for a parking space along the street, considering, after two blocks, turning back and trying the garage under the high rise again.

He didn't turn. Two blocks later he found a space and filled the meter to its four-hour limit. The walk would clear his head, he thought. He was in Tampa, warm and sunny in early December. There were reasons enough to account for not parking in the garage.

The office where his appointment was scheduled was located on the twenty-first floor. When the elevator door opened in the ground-floor lobby, Doug hesitated, allowing six people to push past him before he took a breath and stepped inside. Don't be irrational, he told himself, and he rose with the other passengers, surprised when 21 was the first stop, all the rest going to higher floors.

The meeting was in a room that faced east. A set of drapes was pulled shut against a morning sun that would be angled directly into the room. "We open them after lunch," somebody explained. "It's the hangover room. You have a morning meeting here, and you feel like you stayed out all night."

He smiled, thankful. He could get through this. The building under construction, where someone would surely take him in a few hours, was a mile closer to the shore line, far more exposed than the one he was sitting in, but there wasn't enough wind forecast to sway a house of straw. After he passed out his report, all of his howling statistics turned back into numbers.

He moved the rental into the parking garage. When he went out that night, Doug ordered Mexican, enchiladas smothered in enough cheese to stop a young man's heart. He washed them down with six beers and felt his short run of workouts sag over his belt like yeast-driven dough. He ate a double order of chicken wings the following night and finished his stay in Tampa with a dinner of three-meat pizza and eight beers, celebrating to himself the agreement that the corporation occupying 75% of the new office space had struck to subsidize the necessary repair.

"Timmer's gone," Nadeen said while he unpacked the following evening.

"How's that?" he said, and without answering she followed him upstairs where they stored their suitcases in Andrea's old bedroom closet as if she wanted him to be completely finished with the trip before she explained.

"It looks like he's left town. Tracy told me. Over a week now and not a word."

"Lucky Tracy."

"Yes."

"Somebody like that always comes back."

"Not always," Nadeen said. "Sometimes the world gets lucky."

"Yes," Doug said, and thought immediately that she would know he wasn't going to ask her anything that suggested Timmer might be injured or dead. There was no end to this, he thought. Unless Timmer came back he was going to believe his wife capable of conspiracy or worse.

Three years earlier, Doug had made an office out of his daughter's room. Now he stepped past the large desk that accommodated blueprints as well as a computer to stand in the window that faced away from the back of the house. Because the house had been built into a slope, it was like a third story, and when he opened the window and leaned through the space, the fall, because of the brick patio beneath him, seemed life threatening.

He heard Nadeen settle into the padded chair he'd bought for himself. A small plane was circling to land at the nearby airport. Its engine sputtered once, and he had to force himself not to duck back into the room and shut the window as he imagined it stalling and tumbling into the side of his house. And then the sound went smooth again, and the plane dipped out of view.

His weakness surprised him. It came to him that his weight was a kind of re-engineering, adding pounds to keep himself from tumbling, and he told himself "how ludicrous," that the world was a literal place and nothing he could imagine was better or worse than what he could verify by taking care with numbers.

Doug turned and waved his arm toward the old prints of Andrea's that still hung on the walls. "Her problem is trauma," he said. "It's like a broken leg. It's not a cancer or some craziness she has in her genes."

"The engineer," Nadeen started, and then she stopped like a teacher who was looking for someone else to call on.

"It's not engineering. It's common sense. You stay off a leg for a while and then you rehab the muscles until you're good as new." He wasn't going to stop because Nadeen didn't believe in anyone's will power than her own. "Getting out of New York is what she needs to do while she works her strength back."

Nadeen shook her head. "That leg of hers is shattered, Doug. It doesn't take an engineer to know she can't put her weight on it."

The next night, Nadeen gone to exercising, Doug sat with Alex near the basement stereo, neither of them, for once, holding a beer while they talked to each other. Sober, Alex seldom offered more than one sentence at a time. He was capable of an hour of silence, even in a car listening to CDs of heavy rock music that never employed a piano. "You don't write specs in your spare time," he'd say, as if that explained why a jazz pianist would never play a CD that sounded anything like what he practiced six hours a day.

Now, five minutes into Doug's fumbling about Timmer's disappearance, Alex said, "What do you want to hear, Dad? Whether Mom asked us to kill Timmer what's-his-name? Have you lost your mind? We're not assassins. Mom's not a Mafia Don."

All of Doug's logic collapsed. Of course it was ridiculous. Everything, from ethnic slurs to revenge scenarios, was just talk, and yet he kept paying attention to Alex's tone, the way he sat in his chair.

Alex walked to the stereo, pushed a button, and the CD slid out. "Mom wants him to be dead, all right," he said. "That's not in question, but I think she's just hoping for lightning to strike. Isn't that what we all hope for when some asshole does something we can't stand?"

Alex slid another CD in, and to Doug's surprise, the guitars were acoustic and melodic, soft enough so that when Alex said, "Mom said some men can't find hope in themselves so they find victims instead," Doug heard every word before the song erupted with amplification, and he shook his head as if the volume kept him from asking whether Nadeen had been talking about Timmer or the terrorists.

That weekend, on the way to the grocery store and the shopping they always did together, Nadeen, without looking at Doug, said, "You've quit, haven't you?"

"Quit what?"

"Exercising."

Doug sucked his stomach in, then let it go. "I missed a couple of days."

"You quit."

"I need something more than sit ups to stabilize myself."

"Stabilize?" Nadeen said. "You're not one of your skyscrapers."

"We all have our P-Delta moments," Doug said.

Nadeen stared through the windshield as if the early evening traffic had suddenly thickened. "What's that, an engineer's metaphor?"

"It's the moment when a building reaches its point of instability. All tall buildings sway in the wind, but some are more limber than others."

Nadeen kept her eyes on the road. "You're trying to make them sound human."

"I'm just saying that some buildings sway more than others, but approaching P-Delta is rare."

Nadeen smacked the steering wheel with the palm of her right hand. "Rare isn't good enough," she said. "Not when you're standing inside that building. Not when you know somebody standing in there."

Doug waited until she turned into the road that led to the grocery store. "Rare is rare, not just uncommon. But there was a time during Hurricane Alicia in 1983 that brought a skyscraper very close to instability."

"You mean collapsing?"

"Yes. They stiffened the frame so there wouldn't be a next time."

"You mean they didn't know until after it happened, right?" She looked over at him. "What do you think, Doug. I'm sleeping with another man?"

"I don't know what I'm thinking. You don't look like yourself. It makes me think anything's possible."

"I'm the same, Doug. It's the way you're looking that makes things different. All I did was hear a fat woman who felt sorry for herself because her daughter's had a tough time, and I told that sorry bitch to shut the fuck up."

"Those terrorists let something loose into the world," Doug said. "The common denominator is lower than it used to be."

"It's always been like that," Nadeen said. "It's because you drive thirty miles to work in an office with educated people. You don't live here, Doug. Our house is a motel where you sleep and eat."

As they swung into the parking lot, an arc of red and green lights blinked on their right. "That's the entrance to the cemetery people are complaining about," Nadeen said. "That's where they decorated it with Santa Claus and the elves and eight tiny reindeer while you were out of town."

"And people pay to drive through?" Doug could see the glow of colored lights rising behind the grocery store. While Nadeen parked, two cars slowed and settled by a makeshift tollbooth.

"It's early," Nadeen said. "They'll be more when we come out."

"I hope not."

"It's for charity."

"Santa Claus standing on a grave. What kind of charity is that? Rudolph smiling among the tombstones?"

For ten minutes Doug followed Nadeen through three aisles, letting her choose produce and canned goods. Frozen foods and snacks were the only sections he was looking forward to. "Mrs. Troup," he heard as they paused by the pasta display, and Nadeen turned. She started to talk to a woman and a young girl who stepped back and sideways, placing herself half behind her mother in such a way Doug decided she was the girl Timmer had violated.

Her coat was open, and Doug could see she had the beginnings of breasts. He cursed himself, looked away, then glanced back at her legs before he drifted down the aisle past the whole spectrum of pasta products—linguini, fettuccini, angel hair, lasagna noodles—examining the boxes as if they were an exercise prescribed by a sex therapist.

Doug turned into the next aisle, pet foods, and told himself that if he walked slowly his wife would be finished with the woman by the time he arrived at the end, that Nadeen would gesture him alongside as she passed because they hadn't had an animal in the house for five years.

He evaluated six sizes of rawhide bones, eight varieties of meat treats before she reappeared. "That girl was a joy to have," Nadeen said.

"Was?"

Nadeen turned into paper products, reached for a box of tissues. "What did you think, a girl that looks like that is in fifth grade?"

"She looked frightened."

Nadeen turned. "You thought she was Tracy? I had that girl two years ago. Tracy looks like a little girl compared to her." She pushed the cart forward again. "You'll be interested in this. You know what that mother told me?"

Doug remembered the girl's body, the way her coat opened like an invitation. "What?" he said.

"Timmer got himself a good beating last night."

"I thought he was gone." Doug felt something he imagined was joy.

"He came back two days ago. I didn't think you wanted to hear about him."

"I'm glad to hear this."

"It was just one guy giving him the beating. It was about a woman in a bar, nothing to do with Tracy."

There were only three cars in the toll booth line when they came out. "Maybe people have some sense," Doug said. "Maybe somebody's stupid plan can fail."

"Let's go through," Nadeen said. "Let's give ten dollars to the hospital fund." She was already turning into the line.

"This can't be anything but horrible," Doug said. "They made a cartoon out of remembrance."

"It's not so bad. Most people like it."

114

"Who do we know who's buried here?"

"Sarah Kelly. Breast cancer. She taught third grade until last year. Frank Torok, the suicide from the end of our street."

"You always know these thngs."

"Rachel James," Nadeen said, "and Ruth Grafton. You should pay more attention."

She handed over ten dollars and started along the narrow cemetery lane. Doug repeated the names, telling himself he'd remember them tomorrow as Nadeen stopped the car beside a fat Mr. and Mrs. Santa Claus. "You drive," she said. "Just go slow. I want to look."

He slid over. She sank into the passenger seat. They passed elves and angels, a red and white striped North Pole, before Doug slowed for a grinning snowman and four smiling children. "I'll have to admit," he said, "Andrea would like this one. For sure. She loved Frosty and all the little kids following him."

"In the song," Nadeen said, "Frosty followed them home."

"Really?"

"You just don't listen."

"I'm surprised someone doesn't want to ban it then, say it sends a bad message to kids."

He turned into a service road and drove across the center of the cemetery. "I want to loop around and take a look at that snowman again," he said. "I want to see if he's following them or they're following him."

"They'll think we're cheap. People who want to go through twice."

"People think what they think," Doug said, and he looked over at Nadeen. "Our daughter isn't buried yet. She can recover."

"All those people aren't buried anywhere, Doug. Bits and pieces of them are in a dump somewhere. In among tons of fucking trash."

Doug let her talk. Sooner or later she'd exhaust this like she always did. He could ride it out. But when he approached Frosty and the children again, he realized they were in a circle around him, that whoever had set up this display hadn't thought for a second about the lyrics to the song.

Just before Christmas Doug and Nadeen went to New York together. They walked with Kevin and Andrea to a restaurant that had six tables and a counter. "They filmed a music video here," Kevin said. "Lenny Kravitz."

Andrea stood just inside the doorway as if she was waiting for a hostess, but Doug suspected she was examining the room for Middle Eastern faces. He counted twenty-six customers, thinking "capacity," a number low enough to allow her to sit down.

So far he hadn't said one word to her about leaving New York, and after they ate, Kevin walked them past the apartment Lenny Kravitz had entered in the video. He pointed to the window where Kravitz had lip-synched less than a mile from the Trade Center site.

Kevin's apartment was two blocks farther south in Little Italy, the street they followed so narrow the skyline Doug could see didn't seem as altered as it had earlier from Kevin's third floor apartment. "We watched the Macy's parade on television," Andrea said. "I thought there would be a bomb. All those children and all those cartoon balloons. What a mess it was going to be."

"But it turned out ok," Doug said. "There wasn't a bomb."

"Yes," she said, and he felt a surge of hope. "They're waiting until we feel good again. That's what they do—wait until we think the world is a good place to be."

116

GETTYSBURG

The cannonball came right through the side of the house. Like I was in a cartoon, the ball rolling across the floor

I thought something like that was supposed to explode like a grenade, but there it quietly sat like a misplaced toy. I was thinking of touching it when the front door opened without a knock or a ring of the bell and my neighbor Abner Kincaid stood there saying "I'm sorry" three times like he expected to wish that hole in my wall sealed up and the siding restored without a scratch.

"The fuck you say," I said, one time only, regretting I hadn't just gone after him with whatever was handy, a fork, my coffee mug, even the ball on the kitchen floor.

Kincaid grew up in South Carolina, which I don't hold against him, but these past seventeen years he's been a re-enactor. He grows sideburns and a mustache every summer, sometimes a full beard, so he can drive to Gettysburg and die as a Confederate soldier, complete with one of his old rifles and a sword by his side. He's got a whole shitload of paraphernalia. If there were re-enactments for the Middle Ages, he has a cross bow; if there was one for the first war of the Bronze Age, he has a spear that looks to have spent a few centuries in a cave. All he'd need would be some animal furs to wrap himself in before he got run through by a triumphant Cro-Magnon.

Though not for long, Kincaid's wife Cynthia gets to be a widow every summer. He stays dead as long as an hour some years, cut down by the first volley as he rushes across one of those fields somebody's kept safe from developers. There was even a year, he's told me, when he got to surrender, and there's no telling which fate makes him more excited, him with his hands held high or sprawled out in the field with his eyes staring at the sky while planes pass overhead.

One thing for certain, right about the time he reached for that cannonball, I thought I'd go out and find a big rock and bash his skull in just like Cain.

Maybe Kincaid saw my look, or maybe he thought it was a good idea, but whichever way it was, he said, "To make it up to you, I'll loan you a Union uniform and a musket this summer, and you can be assigned a spot on Cemetery Ridge and shoot me."

I thought I could just as easy do that from my front porch, but I said I'd think about it to get him out of my house. "You let me know when you have a mind to," he said, and he carried that cannonball away, having the good sense not to stop and let me handle it.

I put him off for three days, let him worry about that hole staying just the way he'd made it firing off his antique cannon like that was as normal as lighting a bottle rocket. Like maybe I'd found out the whole wall will have to be rebuilt and there was a bill waiting for him that included the word thousands.

On the third day, when I saw the wall, I had it out with my wife Rachel. "You patched it with cardboard," I started in.

"It's covered in Saran-Wrap," she said. "Don't you worry—it's taped heavy."

"That's not the problem," I said. "What to worry about is Kincaid thinking we're willing to live this way."

"We'll send him the bill when it's taken care of. We'll shame him."

"The fuck it will."

"Oh Harold," Rachel said. "Go do this pretend. It's better than holding a grudge. It might even be fun."

"Your birthday's the 2nd. You want Gettysburg for your forty-fourth?"

"I can wait," Rachel said. "Just don't you be bringing me back any souvenirs. Don't you dare."

That uniform looked hot for wearing at the beginning of July is what I told Kincaid. Running across an open field in July dressed like that was a way to take casualties without a shot being fired, and he frowned like my father used to instead of saying, "Shut the fuck up."

He told me the only reason he had the Union uniform was his friend from twenty years of re-enacting had died in a car accident during the winter and left it to him in his will for safekeeping and good use. "You can't just show up," he said, "but you can take his place if I pull some strings. You'll be stationed on Cemetery Ridge. The 69th Pennsylvania Brigade."

It felt like I was being punished, not rewarded, but Kincaid kept on with the history details and said, "Just wait, you'll see" so many times that I surrendered.

"Throw in a steak dinner and you're on," I said. "Some old-timey barbequed red meat and you have me."

"Your boys in the 69th stand tall," Kincaid said. "You'll be proud to be there." He held the uniform against my body for a moment. "It's a lucky thing you look to be the same size as Alex O'Donnell, that poor bastard." He hung it back up in the closet where he kept all the old stuff. "You'll meet Hancock," he said. "You'll be proud as all get out to serve under him."

Kincaid showed me a map and pointed to places like the Peach Orchard and such while I thought about my loaner antique musket aimed right where his lips opened and closed as he yammered on about the battle. "No wives," he suddenly said, getting my attention. "If you're thinking about making this a little vacation, shake that shit out of your head. This is a real re-enactment."

We were north of Scranton, over a hundred miles from Gettysburg. "Are we getting there on horseback?" I said.

"Once we wear the blue and gray. From then on, it's real." I looked forward to telling Rachel that Cynthia was bored by reruns, too.

It turned out there was a whole program that people paid money to see. Three day's worth, though thankfully Kincaid let us miss Day #1 and all the reminiscing about the skirmishes of July 1st, 1863 when I lied to him about Rachel's birthday, moving it up one day to delay my enlistment in the Union army. For July 2nd, which we saw from the opening gun, with a half hour off to check in at the motel, there was a mortar fire demonstration and speeches given by General Lee and General Longstreet, both of them full of confidence. Once I'd seen an hour's worth of explosions and the start of the re-enactment of the Battle of Hunterstown, complete with the thrill of whinnying horses and thundering hooves and men on horseback shouting in their best cavalry lingo, Kincaid let me go back to the motel early. He had friends to catch up with. I'd get my steak dinner tomorrow after he died.

The bar a block from our motel was crowded with uniforms. I stuck to myself like a draft dodger at a veteran's parade, and before I could do more than eat a cheeseburger and finish four beers, I thought I'd try turning in early to keep myself from staying there and expressing my thoughts on re-enactment out loud.

I lay in bed awake for three hours before Kincaid wobbled in. The first thing he did was shut off the air conditioning and open every window as wide as it would go. "You awake, hoss?" he said. "This here summer air will get us in the mood."

I didn't speak. I was afraid if I opened my mouth he'd remember to take out the screens or have us pitch a tent.

I woke up sweating. July 3rd was already sunny and hot. "No shower," Kincaid said. "We're in real mode now."

We drank coffee from tin cups Kincaid had brought with him.

He offered me some sort of fried dough that had grown warm and yeasty after a day in the trunk of his car. "I can hardly keep it down," he said, and for once I heartily agreed.

I didn't button up my uniform. I wasn't on the firing line yet. But there was another mortar fire demonstration, and I noticed some of the same people from the day before in the audience, all of them leaning forward to watch and listen as if they had some sort of short-term memory loss. We listened to General Lee talk some more about honor, duty and country; we spent an excruciating forty-five minutes listening to General Longstreet "reflect."

Mid-afternoon was when the action began. Kincaid set me up with the boys in blue and shook my hand like we'd just watched a coin flip on the fifty yard line. "Replacement for Private O'Donnell reporting," I said like Kincaid had instructed.

I shook a dozen outstretched hands. "Welcome to the 69th" each one of those bearded men repeated.

Up there on the hill, among men with beards, there wasn't the talk I expected about details of the battle. Everybody was serious, like this had never happened before, like the men in gray might overrun our position and run some of us through with bayonets. "You cherry?" a tall, skinny guy wearing sergeant's stripes said, and when I didn't deny it, he explained how I was to fire first, then he'd take my place while I reloaded so I could step back in and fire again. "Here's how you pour the powder," he said, so quick with getting me locked and loaded that I thought he was descended from General Hancock himself. "No live ammo," he added, "but you'll soon find out there's enough smoke and noise to get the juices flowing."

I clutched my musket with both hands and lifted it to my chest as a sign of solidarity. "Got it?" he said, and when I nodded, he retreated into the shade.

Private Gerald Jennings, the man posted beside me, rolled a cigarette with paper that looked to be yellowed from a hundred and fifty years in a dead man's pocket. "Smoke?" he said, and I shook my head.

I started to pay attention to the troops spread out and walking toward us when they reached what looked to be a quarter mile away. The sergeant peered over my shoulder, breathing on my neck, and I buttoned up my uniform like there was an inspection coming. He and I watched the men in gray uniforms until, when they must have been told they were in range, they began to run, their howls rolling up toward us like wind.

"Fuck yeah," Private Jennings muttered as he raised his rifle. "Firing right about fucking now."

I heard the small explosion from his gun, the powder bursting, and I leveled the barrel of my musket, sighted down its length, and pulled the trigger. Men were falling. Some of them yelled curses, all of the ones I could hear sounding church-related like Good Lord Jesus Christ and Mother of God.

The skinny sergeant pushed me aside and knelt. I had more powder, and I poured it where I'd been shown it belonged, so slow and clumsy that the sergeant was back beside me preparing another round before I finished. "Sorry," I said, keeping my head down. Half a minute later I fired again at Confederates who were so close now I could make out faces. I started to look for Kincaid among the upright.

I reloaded again, hearing Jennings muttering "Fuck yeah" as he scrambled back to shoot. The Confederates drew even closer, but they seemed disheartened now, their rebel yells diminished to near-yodels. More quickly than I expected, the firing became sporadic, then altogether stopped. The battle was condensed because we didn't have all day, but there were bodies all over, enough to simulate slaughter. When a few designated stragglers raised their hands, I made my way down the hill to look for Kincaid among the bodies.

It was like finding my car in an airport lot, but I managed.

Kincaid was lying off by himself, face up. I nudged him with my boot, but he didn't change his expression. Those open eyes had to be seeing me, but I didn't even catch him blinking.

I nudged him harder, more like a kick, and his head and arms flopped a bit. I admit I liked standing over him like that. Turning him onto his face with my boot was the best present Kincaid could have given me. It was better than money.

SOMEWHERE IN THERE,
THE TRUTH

Seventeen years buried, this story. Like the cicadas predicted for any day now. Enough time for me to be staring forty in the face and feeling like I'd like to shed some part of myself like those bugs can do. My wife Jeanie, she doesn't take to me coming round again to Dale Timmons' big birthday party gone wrong, the downslide to where Dwayne Reese, my friend since the third grade, ends up dead in the back seat of Eugene Cuff's Ford Mustang. But now, because the DA says there's witnesses willing to come forward after all these years, it's in the newspaper every day this past week and counting. And me? I'm looking at wearing a coat and tie today to testify against Eugene and Roy Mertz, boys, like Dwayne Reese, I ran with back then gone now to strangers. And they will surely squint my way like they mean me to die right there on the stand when I add my way of seeing things in among all the lies and excuses, hoping the jury can see somewhere in there, the truth.

Dwayne's been talked about like he's been dug up and getting the once over, but it's Eugene and Roy waiting to see if somebody on that jury won't believe they kicked and beat the life out of him during Dale Jr's. twenty-first birthday party. Work boots do that sort of fatality damage. And a ball bat, one of those metal ones they're thinking of banning because they put fielders in harm's way.

On top of things, there's one of those make-it-worse questions being asked—was there still hope for Dwayne after that ass-whipping? The jury's been hearing from more than one who was there that day that he got dumped in Roy's truck bed and laid along the Timber Creek Road to look like he'd been hit and run, what points to him being alive there for hours until he ended up somehow in the back seat of Eugene's Mustang.

I hadn't gone to watch any of it. I had to take a vacation day even to testify, but to tell the truth once would have been enough of Eugene and Roy eyeballing me and the other storytellers scattered around that room, and maybe myself sitting right in front of somebody who was there to swear my version a lie, somebody considering so hard on what I was taking an oath on that he'd begin to wish me serious harm.

Reading the paper each morning had shown me there'd been variations on peoples' stories, so many that it began to sound like Eugene and Roy might beat this thing and be able to pay visits to those, like me, who were giving a side that put them in a bad light. It was only the one thing everybody said they remembered the same way—Dwayne coming on to Rita Sue, Eugene's girl, and him knowing Eugene was the jealous type doubled down by drinking in the late afternoon sun. Particulars? Dwayne saying things with people around that you keep to yourself until you close a door behind you. Dwayne's hand on Rita Sue's arm, her sweating like everybody that day, even in her sleeveless, but turning heads with his hand running along her bare flesh like that, like he was fixing to move his fingers to where there was no going back. Rita Sue not squirming away, maybe even enjoying somebody paying attention to her instead of the beer. Dwayne acting like it could be his own self deciding just where on her body his hands might end up.

Eight kegs was what they had out there on what's still called the Heimbach Farm. Though my Aunt Gretel Timmons had given up her name these forty years, it was a matter of the name being passed down more than on a mailbox.

It's been the Heimbach Farm for more than a hundred years,

but for the last twenty-five there's only a patch of vegetables and a few chickens and the rows of raspberries Aunt Gretel loves during June and July. So farm isn't exactly the right word, and some call it the Timmons Place now because Dale Jr's. mowing a big-ass circle around the house once a month is as close to farming as anybody with a lawnmower back in town.

But back those seventeen years, even with Dale Sr. still alive, our family name was all over that land the day of the party. And surely it was Heimbach Farm where people were told to go, though Aunt Gretel regretted being so generous when the word spread so wide not everybody who parked both shoulders of the county road solid for a mile was on speaking terms.

It was a day my nearly brand new wife Jeanie stayed home and maybe that would have made all the difference from then on to today, her eyeballing everything too, but she had her migraine and the curtains all closed in every room an hour before I left. And it was a day my first wife Shelby left our Chrissie, almost three at the time, with her mother because she wasn't about to miss a chance to drink with boys who wished they could follow me into her bed.

Aunt Gretel had Dale Sr. mow a full five acres the day before, the stubs of milkweed and thistle and burdock reminding anybody dumb enough to go barefoot or in cheap sandals what the field would look like in a couple of weeks. That big swath took the clearing nearly to where a trailer set up on cinderblocks was rusting away back in the thickets. A cinderblock porch in front of it was split all to hell from two tree-of-heavens pushing up like they can do from what looks like nothing at all for roots to take.

Dale Jr., after he managed to graduate high school, said he had plans for that trailer, but all he did was pile up pizza boxes and beer cans and porn magazines inside where he'd set up an old mattress and a couple of scuffed up beanbag chairs like that would make it a place any not pass-out-drunk girl would enjoy for even half a minute. He'd hung an extension cord over the door, but when the party came around, it still led nowhere, leaving anyone walking there to take a piss to guess what he had in mind.

What there was most of near the trailer that day was shattered glass and rusty cans near the stumps of beech and pine that had been cleared when the trailer was new, all that debris from target shooting. Dale Jr., he was fond of betting on himself as some sort of Buffalo Bill, maybe seeing himself winning large enough to do more than pretend he could do something besides wait for his daddy to die in order to be the man of any house.

Another hundred years, I thought, and maybe all that shit would be broken down and erased for good by the wind and rain. And though I knew I was wrong with that guess, that was more than far enough in the future it didn't matter what happened to any of it. My way of thinking back then, and turning out wrong, because what mattered now was how every bit of that day and that place could lead to the truth, and me with my own small part in it testifying after all these years about just what I remembered about how and why Dwayne died that day.

The day I was scheduled, the morning paper gave me its last clues to what I was walking into. The day before, Marlin Sauer had said Dwayne didn't do anything others didn't do—flirting, what men do and women enjoy, the drinking helping things along out there by the Keister Road. A good start on Dwayne's behalf, but then, speaking for the prosecution no less, Marlin swore he didn't see Dwayne touched. "I seen everything" was his brag line, making the DA look the sap.

Todd Riggs, who I shared a few thirty packs with back in the day, had started off on the right foot, saying Dwayne took a few licks, but then he said, "It was just a little knock around, nobody falling down or like that." And Dwayne, he said, had all his senses after. "Lucid" is what the newspaper article quoted him as saying. "Dwayne was lucid. That's what he was—lucid," as if Todd had studied on that word like he might impress the jury more that way, like he'd looked straight at the jury and said "lucid" the way a witness makes his lie prettier with book words.

It didn't sound like the way to nail down an open-and-shut, not after the DA had decided to prosecute two men who weren't even suspects back when the case was new. But then Carla Rohl, half-sister to Eugene, ended the day in tears while she testified Dwayne was assaulted hard-core while people watched. A woman marking her half-brother as a killer is a powerful thing. "I feel bad for the guy not getting his justice" was how she explained her talking after so long, quick to add Eugene and Dwayne being best friends, words to surprise anybody I knew. The defense lawyer didn't question that. What he did do was get Carla to admit her old boyfriend Warren Shaner was an original suspect, getting that old news in front of a jury who might have long since forgotten or maybe never heard of at all.

I didn't need any sort of interpreter to tell me I might be risking myself for a case already pulled under and drowned, but the newspaper had its own mind made up. I could see that in the headline—Conspiracy of Silence. And down farther, in the pictures that ran each day, Eugene and Roy in hunting gear with the sort of scruffy beards and overgrown mustaches a man who's been in camp a week would carry when he posed with a trophy buck the paper cropped out. Dwayne, he was decked out in a coat and tie in his photo, and every day his name was underneath as Dwayne Reese IV, like he was from royalty instead of from Daddies who wanted their own names repeated for a hundred years.

My wife Jeanie, while she was helping me with my tie, said you tell the story three ways and each of them are lies to everybody while I was thinking all those looking at Rita Sue after seventeen years would be hard pressed to think a man would risk himself to flirt with her having turned to fat and not having the sense to give up her tank tops and tight jeans. But there she was married to Eugene for thirteen of these years, so he'd slept beside her night after night while every which way but the truth was going on.

"I can go late," I said. "There's Aunt Gretel and who knows who else before me. You think there's roll call for this?"

"I know what you're thinking," Jeanie said, "but don't you dare."

"You don't see me starting, do you?"

"And don't you stop anywhere along the way."

"I'm just nervous. Anybody would be."

"Nervous is ok. Nervous doesn't stick to you afterwards like beer on your breath or a slur in your words."

"I'm ok," I said, and I meant it. I knew testifying after all these years was more complicated than stocking shelves at Home Depot. I kept my promise. To make sure, I left the cooler in the garage.

I'll admit it gave me the shudders, that courthouse, its outside all made of stone turned so dark it looked like it had been built before Columbus sailed. Inside, though, there weren't any fancy chandeliers or tapestries or any of the things castles always have, just a men's room with fixtures old fashioned enough to prove how many years the guilty and the innocent had relieved themselves there.

The rest was the same offices I'd visited a few times about my own troubles in the next county over, that courthouse a less imposing place, one built by farmers who didn't foresee much more than deed and custody issues taking up a part-time judge's time. And surely, I was happy to go through a metal detector because I knew plenty of candidates for armed mayhem who had a curiosity about the goings-on inside the court room.

There were a few before me yet, but just two I still saw around sitting up by the judge and promising the truth. Roy's cousin, half-removed, said there was plenty of chaos, what's expected when up to a hundred set themselves into partying mode. And Ginny Waite, who announced herself a cousin of Eugene, something I'd never heard, said nobody raised a hand to stop anything, more an accusation against the rest of us than anything that would convict.

All in all, everybody I heard looked to be moving guilty into the red zone, leaving me and Aunt Gretel to take it across the goal line. I walked to the Stop 'n Go by myself for lunch, a bag of chips and a Slim Jim I washed down with a Cherry Coke. I saw some faces I knew in the aisles, but I kept moving, keeping a space between me and anybody. And then I spent the last hour of the ninety minute lunch break, a forever amount of time, sitting with a PA Sportsman magazine in the tiny town library where nobody I recognized would come in.

That is, for twenty minutes, when Aunt Gretel snuck up behind me and said, "Hey there, Keith—hiding out?" making me hold up the magazine like an excuse while she sat down beside me on the couch. "Sitting among all these books reminds me how much your grandma liked her fairy tales so much she thought the name of a smart little girl would help me along some day. Your daddy ever tell you that about me?"

I laughed like I thought I was supposed to. "The only way he'd tell me that would be if he was Hansel, and he had to explain how he had the worst name in Pennsylvania."

Aunt Gretel laid a hand on my thigh and patted it. "Your grandma had somebody else in mind for him. Your daddy got Jack from another one of those stories, but nobody's ever connected him to any sort of giant killer."

"What about Keith?" I said. "She ever tell my Dad about somebody she hoped I'd be?"

"I don't recollect Keith for good or bad," she said. "Maybe that's all you can ask for around here where people are scattered every which way, but still they get themselves tangled." She pushed off my thigh with her hand to help her stand. "I got to get back and think things over about the say-so I have to give, but you stop by when this is over, for sure, promise."

I waited another ten minutes before I walked the two blocks back to the courthouse, sweating the whole way and wishing I'd brought my cooler and had just enough Busch Light on ice to steady myself. What did I see but my girl Chrissie standing just outside the courtroom door showing more of herself than what was good for her and reminding me that Jerry Hoke, her stepfather, was on tap for the defense.

Chrissie was nearly twenty now, still a few years shy of my age that day when Dwayne died, and she hadn't visited with me since she turned fifteen, Jeanie telling me, "She's grown in more ways than one" back then, something I had agreed with. For sure, I was happy not to see first-hand her sneaking out to parties and such where men or boys who think they are would give her drinks and pills and calculate just when she was ready to be taken somewhere private so if something terrible happened, there would only be the suspicion of who was responsible but never the proof.

Coming up on her so close, I needed something to say, so I started in with "You have any cicadas out your way yet?"

"No," she said, all calm like, so I pressed on.

"Those bugs must be crazy from being underground for so long. They just make their sound, all of them playing the same note and keeping it up like they know there's no time for anything else."

"You'd be screaming too if you knew how things were," Chrissie said, and now she was putting on a pout that made me feel a son instead of a father..

"They're not screaming," I said, "and anyway, they don't know."

"That's where you're wrong," she said. "Of course they know. That's all they know. That, and how much they all want to get laid."

She said it straight out like I was supposed to know she had those thoughts and acted on them. Like it wasn't a new thing at all. And just then, there came Shelby all decked out for sunbathing too, like the two of them were competing with all that cleavage showing.

Jerry Hoke, in a maroon shirt and white tie, walked up beside them, and I gave him a nod. "What are you looking at?" Jerry said, and I turned away. "I thought so," he added as I walked through the metal detector as if it might keep them all from following, but what came after me was Chrissie's loud laugh.

A few minutes later Aunt Gretel started right in. "That boy was in such bad shape I remember the exact words I used on Eugene and Roy. 'You want to kill somebody, you move that body off my property.'"

I could see the jury trying to decide whether this damned Eugene and Roy or Aunt Gretel, but she never looked anywhere but at the DA. "I drove off to the convenience about the time it was looking to get dark. I needed bread and milk and the like, and I was wishing by then the whole lot of them would have drunk the place dry and left by the time I got back. And there was Dwayne Reese face down in the middle of the Beech Hollow Road. I didn't need anybody to tell me I should get right to the convenience and call 911."

"You didn't stop?" the DA prodded.

"Of course I did. Who wouldn't? I tugged on that boy's arm, and he opened his eyes and made a noise I hope I never hear again, a sound like worms make if we could hear them, like what you'd say if you was covered in slime. Not many drive along Beech Hollow. I figured he'd stay right there until the experts came to take care of him."

Aunt Gretel described the store. She described the 911 call. She even totaled up what she bought and paid for. But what got everybody's attention was her trip back home. "I was back on Beech Hollow, and there was Eugene and Roy about to lift that boy by the looks of it, and Eugene, he looked through me. I knew what that meant."

"Objection," the defense lawyer said, but it was too late to scratch out that small, good thing, from the jury's memory, so that lawyer, he got right up on Aunt Gretel the first chance he had. "Let's clear something up," he said. "You didn't tell this story to the police seventeen years ago, did you?"

"I was told by the police what they thought had happened, that it was another pair back then that done this to that boy. I didn't need to be told twice they'd leave me be about the shindig at my place if I let them tell the story their way."

Soon after it was my turn, and I told what I'd always known, that Eugene and Roy kicked and beat Dwayne maybe a hundred times before they stopped and Roy pissed on Dwayne laying there senseless in Aunt Gretel's new-mown field.

Eugene looked at me as if he was trying to identify somebody at our 20th class reunion, but I went through the details a second time, making sure the jury would know I was the bearer of the true story. "Why did you keep quiet back then?" the DA asked, and I took a breath and got ready to confess.

"Later that summer," I said, "when the police were sniffing around, Eugene punched me in the head." I said it twice, repeating it when the DA asked again in a tone that sounded like he expected my shame to show how honest I was. "A punch in the head, right above the temple like it was, is different than in the face. It was the punch of a man who was giving a lesson, and me, I had my three year-old daughter in my arms and had to settle for keeping my balance and not dropping her on the ground outside her mother's doublewide where I'd come to bring Chrissie back after she'd spent a weekend with me."

The defense lawyer walked up toward me slow, like I was somebody to size up. "That punch, if it occurred, was several months after the party, was it not, but the police spoke with you earlier, didn't they?" he said.

"Yes."

"How do you account for the story you gave them before that alleged punch?"

He smiled like he expected me to stammer. But I was ready. "I was on probation for a DUI. I was afraid I'd go to prison if I said I was at a party with alcohol."

"So you say you saw a man get beaten to death, but a driving while intoxicated conviction was more important to you?"

I took a breath and kept my eyes on him like Jeanie had told me. "I'm not proud of what I did," I said. "I'm here to fix that as best I can."

"One incident shouldn't have made you so afraid."

"I had three DUIs on my sheet."

The lawyer turned away and stared at the jury. "And you were drunk at a party that you would have to drive home from later in the day?"

"I was going slow. You know, pacing myself. I wasn't going to drive drunk."

He smiled again. Self-satisfied. Terrifying.

After I sat back down in the audience, I looked at the jury, but whatever their expressions had said while I was talking had been erased. Every last one of us was swearing to something we didn't swear to seventeen years ago. One thing was clear—one way or another, we were all afraid of the law. And if any of those jurors subscribed to once a liar, always a liar, we were in for it.

And I had time, while the lawyers pestered the judge about something or other, to consider on just how many times Shelby had told Chrissie that story about the day Eugene punched me, how she was standing so close by I could have passed Chrissie to her to free my hands. How Chrissie, by now, might believe she remembered that punch and my backing down rather than thinking she remembered it from hearing it second-hand.

I hurried out as soon as the judge adjourned us. I was happy to live fifteen miles from the trial, happy to get out of the lot before anybody else decided to give me the once-over.

What's worse? To be a killer or the one who lies for him? With all those secrets out in the open and recorded word for word, there was a buzz in my head like the one that was coming from the cicadas in a few days, frantic-like until I wanted to snap open a Busch Light right there and start pushing everything underground for another seventeen years, leaving just the everyday secret to deal with, the ones like everybody has, not these loud, swarming red-eyed ones with bodies so temporary they must be terrified to surface.

"You say your piece and bear up under what follows," Jeanie had said, and I'd agreed, but with eight miles under my wheels, I stopped at The Log Cabin, figuring nobody from that courthouse would be inside. Wearing my white shirt and blue tie made me feel like I was from another country, somebody who wouldn't be understood if I tried to talk. I tossed down three drafts and was ready to order a fourth when a voice I knew to be Jerry Hoke's spoke right into my ear from behind. "You know why you don't have to worry about having the shit kicked out of you?"

I was supposed to say "Why?" like his question was the start of a knock-knock joke, but I just looked at the bar until he said, "Because you're so afraid of everything nobody even knows you're there."

I took two breaths and turned, but Jerry, his tie already stripped, was on his way to a table where Shelby was sitting. I left a ten on the bar and walked out into a sun that surprised me with its low-slung glare, and I opened a Busch Light from the refrigerator as soon as I walked in, tugging that tie off.

"Bad?" Jeanie said.

"I said what I had to say."

She made her bitch face and said, "You made a stop already. You couldn't wait even that long? You know what could happen."

"I was in and out in half an hour. At the Cabin, practically in the driveway already. There's nothing to happen from that."

So there I was, back to myself, and when Jeanie switched to "You did what you could" and "It's not your fault" like she still had sorry in her, I let her talk without telling her to shut up with those lies.

Jeanie, she gets this magazine once a month like her period, and for a couple of days she reads me things while I drink my coffee. The day after I testified it was this: "As late as 1892, in Vermont, the body of Mercy Brown, thought to be a vampire, was exhumed for public autopsy."

Just like that is how she started in, expecting me to be all in for listening to a story with a vampire in the middle of it. "The father had to give permission, think of that," Jeanie said, "but he had a son coughing up blood from the same TB that had killed his daughter and his wife before her, so what was there to lose?"

Plenty, I thought, but I poured a second cup and sat back to let it cool.

"He had to watch his neighbors dig up his daughter," Jeanie said, sounding all worked up now, like she was talking about somebody she knew. "He had to agree to have her heart burned and his son eat the ashes."

"So did it work?" I said

"What? You trying to be funny? Of course it didn't work. The son died two months later."

"Maybe if they'd dug her up sooner, the heart thing would have worked."

"You're disgusting. Think about it. What father watches his child twice buried? What father lets a bunch of idiots burn his daughter's heart and feed it to his son?"

"How does anybody know this stuff is real after all these years?"

"Research. It says here Mercy left behind a quilt she stitched from scraps and remnants she expected some day to tuck under the chins of her children. Down at the end it gives the names of the people who have learned these things, but they're never anybody you ever heard of."

I sipped my coffee and waited for her to settle. "What do you really think?" she said at last, and something in her voice made me think it over instead of saying how fucking stupid people can be.

"Everything's worth a try," I said.

"I'm asking about the father—him forced to watch his girl eaten like an animal."

"Nobody's touching Dwayne, if that's what you're thinking, not after seventeen years."

Jeanie slapped the magazine shut and stood up so fast I thought she might roll it up and swat me. "Yes, they are," she said, but she walked away and left the magazine behind.

A minute later, when I read the account of my testimony, I felt as if I'd been caught in some filthy act, like I'd exposed myself to a young girl, everything good about myself lost from this single act. I called a guy I knew at Home Depot and got him to switch with me, something he was happy to do because I took his Saturday in exchange.

This time I had a six pack in the cooler, but I walked into the court room with just the coffee in me. I listened to four men, including Jerry Hoke, swear there was no fight. "Roy's truck never left," Jerry said. He was wearing the same get up as the day before. "I could pick his out from a hundred same make and model."

Just before lunch break, Todd Riggs' ex-wife swore Todd was drunk and sleeping it off in their truck when "that little bitty squabble came and went."

"Your lies will follow you," Dwayne's father yelled as she stepped down, and I knew he was right about that, something to say to any of us even if it got him strong-armed from the room..

I walked the cooler into the park that sat behind the courthouse and welcomed my first one. I sat at a picnic table, and it came to me that if Dwayne had been beaten this summer, the killing would have been recorded on a dozen phones, maybe more. There was no need for testimony anymore. Just watch the movie and see for your own self.

There's some, I'd bet, who'd say the camera angle lies, but there'd be plenty who wouldn't delete something like that. A jury would have that ball bat and those boots to think on. They'd have to figure out just when Dwayne was good as dead. Spooling back to see when that bat caught him flush on the skull or a boot caved in his ribs and something came apart inside, bleeding begun where nobody could see.

All somebody like me would have to do is turn my home movie over to the police. People would see there was no stopping them from doing harm. They'd look at that ass-whipping and look at me and know the only thing I could do was make sure I had backup for my story. But right then what I wanted to see was Aunt Gretel hovering over Dwayne still alive out Beech Hollow, maybe killing him twice.

I had the cooler back in the car with twenty minutes yet to fill, but I had such a need to piss I went back inside. When I came out of the men's room, there was Chrissie again like she was waiting to show me she knew to cover herself when her stepfather was there to say his piece.

With her in a buttoned-up blouse, I could smile and say, "Hard to tell who's telling the truth."

"It's fucked is what it is," she said, and I could tell she saw the beer in me, so sure of it I groped around for something smart to say.

"We used to know a bunch of words for terrible," I said. "Now we just have fucked."

"Fucked covers a lot of territory."

I locked my eyes on her, steady now. "It doesn't cover anything. It's just a noise."

"Who sent you off to college?"

"Horrible. Awful. Pathetic." I hesitated, scrambling to keep it up. "Beastly."

"Beastly?" Better to say fucked than a pussy word like that."

I wanted to say more, make a list so long she'd have to admit I was right about something, but I noticed Jerry Hoke closing in, and all I came up with was "Forget it."

"Fucking horrible. Fucking awful. Fucking pathetic. But you can't say fucking beastly without sounding like a fucking asshole."

I thought she'd been drinking for lunch like me. And then there was a moment when I thought she was softening, her grimace melting toward something like affection, or at least regret. Her eyes were watery, what I wanted to take for sadness, but looked, I decided, to be somewhere between excitement and fear, an expression I remembered her mother had tightened into during the early months of carrying Chrissie inside her.

But there was Jerry Hoke beside her now, looking on with nothing but pride, and I couldn't tell whether it was because he thought his testimony had helped free his friends or because he thought Chrissie was sexy, that he liked being seen as the father of a young woman whose body men turned to look at.

I felt the need to piss again, and by the time I was finished, Chrissie was gone, and I'd decided to use the rest of that day like the Saturday I would be missing.

I had half an hour and two beers to myself before Jeanie came home from grocery shopping and found the cooler with the empties where I'd left it on the front seat. I heard her slapping cupboards shut for a few minutes before she came out on the deck. "You gave up our Saturday to drive around half drunk?"

"There's no way they'll be convicted," I said. "I heard enough to make me think I lied up there yesterday." I stood, and when I didn't move straight toward the screen door on the way to the refrigerator, I hoped Jeanie would relax, maybe even sympathize.

Instead, she said, "You know what I hate?" starting in like she does with a question I couldn't possibly answer.

"What?"

"All these years and you never once said anything about what Dwayne must have thought."

"Getting beat like that, he wouldn't be thinking, not like you mean. He'd have been trying to curl himself up and cover where it hurt the most."

"When it stopped then. When he was still alive and being handled like a carcass."

"I'll give you he might have wondered how it all got out of hand."

She looked around the yard, and it came to me she was seeing if there was a weapon handy, something she could pick up and beat me with. "He would have wondered why nobody stepped in."

"Like me?"

"Like the good friend you and some others said they were."

"You weren't there. You don't know how it was."

"I'm an adult who's breathing. It doesn't take any more than that to know."

"Then you'll be just like that jury. They'll think what they want, but they'll never know."

She slapped me then, not my face, but against my chest. Both hands thumping up and down like a child. When she'd gone on longer than I would have guessed, I grabbed her wrists. "You know what I think?" she said, not struggling. "I think you're jealous of Dwayne."

I let her wrists go. "You got yourself so worked up, you're

talking crazy now. Nobody wants to be beat to death in front of a hundred people."

"I'm not talking the method," she said. "And you know in your heart I'm right."

By the time I got on the way to Aunt Gretel's on Sunday it was almost noon. I had the cooler in the trunk instead of beside me on the seat. If I had a mind to start, it needed to be on the way home. I didn't need Aunt Gretel looking at me like I was some beaten dog.

Aunt Gretel was out by the raspberry bushes when I pulled in. "It's too early," she said as I made my way toward her, "I know that, but I'm as bad as a little kid coming up to Christmas when it's barely December."

"I bet they'll be sweet and juicy when they're ready," I said, and then, fishing for words, I added, "The place looks smaller than it used to."

"It oughta. I have Dale Jr. mow less these days. Once a month I make him drive the tractor over just this patch, laying the cutter bar down low so for a week or two, at least, the land looks cared for from a car driving past. Just to keep all that shit from getting so close to the house it would start getting ideas about coming inside."

"I thought you might be swarming with cicadas by now, but I don't hear or see anything." I said. "You think the know-it-alls got it wrong?"

"We'll be invaded, don't you worry about that, like when Saddam woke up one morning and found out he was shit out of luck." As if she expected to hear a buzz explode like an air raid siren, she looked out toward where what was left of the apple orchard was being absorbed by the expanding growth of scrub trees. "Let me show you something," she said, and I followed her until we stood among the apple trees, what was left of them, but Aunt Gretel said, "Look over this way" as if she had a secret hidden among the nearby sumac.

142

"You remember the names of all this that takes over fast?"

"Tree of heaven," I said, playing along with one I recognized because I'd always been fascinated by the way they'd split that cinderblock porch in front of the old trailer.

As if my answer was incomplete, Aunt Gretel said, "From China. As if anybody here needed another kind of tree from so far away. It's like when a neighborhood changes, when after a while there's nobody left like you because the strangers have put down roots."

"Goldenrod," I said. "Lamb's ear, onion grass, Queen Anne's lace, skunk cabbage, Virginia creeper, poison ivy."

"So you do remember what I taught you," she said.

"The names of all the stuff you don't want."

"Can you find the cicadas?" She knelt down beside one of the apple trees. "Get yourself down here and take a look."

I bent over and squinted at the patchy weeds. "What am I supposed to see?"

"Look at the bare spots. See all those tiny little holes? See them? That means they're coming real soon."

"The cicadas?"

"None other. They've worked their way up from down by the roots. They're all around us here, waiting for whatever it is that tells them to crawl out and fly." She stood and brushed her hands together. "These old apples were worth a shit back when their Mamas laid their eggs in their branches, but now it doesn't matter if the whole lot of them decided to strip them bare."

I rubbed my foot over a bare patch of earth and stepped out into the mowed area. "I went back Friday. I traded off at work."

"I expect you found out there was a herd of them rounded up to say otherwise than us."

"Enough for doubt."

"For some folks," she said. "The rest of us have to live with the knowing. All that positivity about them boys getting what they deserve won't get far with a jury full of those that don't know them."

"It was like they could sling the truth into a truck bed and dump it so deep in the woods it would die there and nobody could ever prove anything ever again."

.Aunt Gretel nodded, but then she sniffed the air. "You smell that stink?" she said. "You can cut down all this shit if you have a mind to, but when the wind turns this way that stink you're smelling gets right after you and there's no getting rid of it."

"I hadn't noticed," I said.

"That makes you a liar. It's been what, five years since you've set foot on this place? Lucky you. These days we're surrounded by chicken farmers. There's so much dried shit scrambled up into the air, it's like pollen. Other people get their dust from blossoms, we get ours from a chicken's ass."

"Really," I said. "It's not that bad."

"Easy for you to say. If you lived here, you'd be wanting to set those barns on fire like the rest of us."

"It must be worth the smell," I said, and Aunt Gretel shrugged in a way that made me sad.

"I've been told my land could hold three of those barns. Cloyd Mays, you remember him down the road a piece? He's still at it with the farm but four years ago he mortgaged up again and built himself three barns. 60,000 chickens he's got there shitting up a storm. They get born and they're gone in five weeks, can you believe that? He can do almost half a million chickens a year as long as he can look the other way about the stink and the way those chickens get treated."

"You and me both ought to move away," I said.

Aunt Gretel spread her arms and rocked as if she intended to fly. "Where to?"

"Just away," I said. "Away from it all."

"That's no place," she said. "That takes you to nowhere."

I was home after work Monday, just into my second Busch Light, when the phone rang, a voice on the other end saying "Not guilty" followed by nothing but breaths as if those words formed an obscene slur. I counted seven breaths before I hung up.

"One-sided calls don't promise much but trouble," Jeanie said.

"Somebody letting me know Eugene and Roy got set free."

"A long time listening for that."

"The rest was breathing."

"A man's or a woman's?"

"A woman. She talked deep like a man and with just the two words it could have been anybody."

"Even Rita Sue Cuff?"

"Sure, it could have been. She had to sit and listen to me swear her husband beat Dwayne Reese to death."

I poured my next beer into a glass and took it outside where the cicadas had begun to swarm just like Aunt Gretel had promised. I got it now about them. Their natural defense was numbers. If some of them made their way into the light a year early, the birds ate every last one of them so fast they never got a chance to mate and keep things going. But it made me wonder what sort of weapons those cicadas carried a million years ago before hiding among a crowd so large that there weren't enough birds to eat all of them satisfied the ones that were left. Once that system worked so well they didn't have any other way of defending themselves except being on time and acting exactly like the rest of their kin.

Jeanie sat down beside me on the swing we had on the side of the deck by the house. She swatted a few cicadas away, but she didn't complain. "You know what I wish?" she said.

"No."

"I wish you were a storyteller." She paused in a way that made me think I'd never know what she meant unless I begged her to explain. At last, she stepped close and looped her arms around my back, looking up at me as if she'd just raised her head from my shoulder after we'd finished doing one of those slow shuffles we used to do when we were drinking together and maybe one song away from sex. "Then you could start the story that I want to hear straight out to the end, like one of those Jesus stories where everything bad means something good."

"A parable?" I said, and felt her press against me in a way that made my free hand slide under her shirt.

"Yes, like that."

SIGHT UNSEEN

This much was certain—because of the mess it left, the bear had been eating from a dumpster behind the Rib House just before it was electrocuted. The bus boys claimed it climbed the power pole because it was frightened by a dog. "The dog was still hanging around," they told me. "A black lab. What else could scare a bear up a pole like that and then not be run off by that bear tumbling down all scorched to hell and back."

I just wrote it down. I was there for rock radio WOOM, not the newspaper or the police, so I let them elaborate any way they wanted. The bear weighed one hundred and fifty pounds. The dog I saw looked to be about seventy-five, so it seemed to me the bear lacked spirit. And now it lacked everything, charred the way it was from crawling onto the cross bar and taking however many volts run through those power lines.

It was a better story to cover than most in Moorefield, but I admit a good reporter would fact check something like that, put the number of volts in his story, but WOOM's listeners didn't care. They wanted to hear the voices of people they recognized and details about the burned body of the bear during the three minutes of news we snuck in, as much as we could risk at one time without having them switch to the rock station they could pick up from Altoona if it was a good reception day.

Those bus boys had a story to tell, and I had them on tape. "First the lights flickered," they said, "something you can't have in a restaurant, and second, we were going out back to smoke no matter if it was World War III starting up because we got our break about then. And there's no missing any kind of bear, don't need to be no grizzly, when it's laying at the bottom of the electric pole at the edge of your parking lot and all charred like he'd walked slowly through fire."

"Fuck us both if we didn't think this was one mess we were getting stuck with," the other guy, older than my thirty-five, a bad age to be a bus boy, said. "We just walked up to that bear like guys who believed dead was dead and there wasn't anything like resurrection or second chances in this world."

So they were on our newscast for two days, minus the expletives, something Rob Gerlach, the college intern who worked the news for broadcasting credits and saved the station a few more dollars, did for me so I could let them do the talking. I knew they'd be telling everybody they were on the radio. It was better than a hundred dollar jackpot phone-in promo to jack up the ratings, and I talked that bear up as long as I could.

Besides, by now my listeners knew I'd get that bear into my patter between rock blocks, something about how Rib House patrons might think twice about parking behind the restaurant without checking over their heads. What's more, I milked that bear's misfortune because I felt the need to run with something I could call mine since WOOM had been purchased a month before by a company that had a chain of stations across the country, and the new manager had handed out a shortened playlist that said, at the bottom, No Exceptions.

The newspaper version, it turned out, got picked up by the wire service and started appearing in city papers, and then, in the middle of November, Dennis Miller used the story on Saturday Night Live's Weekend Update. I was watching, half asleep, and suddenly there was a picture of that bear behind Miller as he solemnly reported on its demise. "Apparently," Miller said, "there's a college located in

Moorefield, but no one seems to know why. The town is so rural that the residents weren't surprised to hear about the accident. However, the bear population is clamoring for increased safety measures around dumpsters."

Miller smiled sardonically and moved on, but Moorefield, I thought, was going to be located on thousands of viewers' maps, looking it up myself when the show was over. I was going to tell my listeners on Monday night that there was another town just five miles from here, and a second one just three miles from that one, but I had to admit the school in town was the only college within a seventy-five mile radius, the only such college in the state that far from another. And on Monday, knowing this was going to be a week's worth of patter, I lifted a catalogue from the Admissions Office and used it for statistics: There are 1600 students and 32 majors," I said, "half of them connected to education." I paused for dramatic effect before I added, "Just in case Dennis Miller is driving nearby." I didn't say a word about what a long shot that was, the station reaching maybe half way to that nearest college, and the interstate set another ten miles farther away. If Miller was actually tuned in on the highway, my voice would sound as clear as the ones broadcast by aliens from another galaxy.

Like I always did, I kept quiet about my own college days. How badly can a college graduate be doing? How about one with a master's degree? It sounds like the stuff of tragedy, Willy Loman, et al, but it's the familiar story everybody yawns at when it's told.

And it truly was a boring story. By the time I had an MFA in fiction writing, Vietnam was three years over and so was the glut of baby boomers going to any college where I hoped to land a faculty position. I couldn't even get a job teaching high school because the first question was where did you student teach and my answer was "I didn't."

"I don't understand" was the polite but telling response each time, and I'd explain that I wasn't an education major, that I hadn't taken education classes. "Not even media training?" someone would say, implying that I wouldn't know how to turn on all of the projectors—slide, movie, overhead—that high school teachers were expected to use in 1977.

The interviews didn't end well is the long and short of it. There were jobs in inner city schools where administrators looked the other way while they had candidates' credentials on the table, but I told myself I had more time to write with a graveyard shift radio job, thinking a novel was in the making, maybe two, and there was a college library in Moorefield, however average, where I could read literary magazines and new novels to keep myself fresh. And here I was, ten years later, the seven p.m. to midnight deejay on WOOM, the promotion I'd received rescuing me from midnight to six a.m. five years before.

My mother got a kick out of that bear fiasco when I told her during my Thanksgiving visit, but I needed more than one story to nurse us through the buffet special at the motel dining room near her home in Butler. "It's too much trouble to cook anymore," she explained. "And all those leftovers. Turkeys should come in smaller sizes."

"A chicken would do," I said, but she'd looked horrified.

"It's turkey or it isn't Thanksgiving," she said, and there we were eating in an enormous, quarter-filled room, every one of the patrons over sixty except me and one man my age who I tried not to stare at because he was eating alone.

Worse, the music piped from the ceiling was all big bands— Glenn Miller, the Dorsey Brothers, the outfits advertised on television with white-haired smiling couples sitting on porch swings. "Doesn't that sound like Guy Lombardo and the Royal Canadians?" my mother said while I forked up bites of pumpkin pie slathered with Cool Whip.

"I don't know, Mom," I said. "All I remember is "Auld Lang Syne." Hasn't he been dead for a while?"

"These ten years," she said. "New Year's Eve hasn't been the same since he went off the air."

The song, something I didn't recognize, ended. "Oh," my mother said, "there's 'Lisbon Antigua,'" and I smiled like I'd called in a request to the tape loop before we'd arrived. "It's strange, isn't it," she went on. "Guy Lombardo disappeared every year, yet there he was again every December 31st at 11:30 p.m., first on radio and then on television. Like clockwork. And always you could count on "Auld Lang Syne." I thought he wrote the song when I was growing up. There was always one big cheer with noisemaker toots, and then there was that song and everybody got sentimental and kissed and such. I bet there was more making up while that song played than any other song in history. It just made you want to be better."

I watched her drink her coffee, the dreadful canned gravy coagulating on her plate where she'd left a slice of white meat and a small mound of bread stuffing. Suddenly, she smiled. "I want you to play your trombone when you come home for the holidays," she said. "I have it in your old bedroom closet. You know. All these years, it's never been touched."

"I quit when I was fifteen, Mom. The trombone wasn't cool."

"What a thing to say. There were men on Guy Lombardo older than I am now who played trombone, and they were doing just fine. The trombone doesn't change the way that rock and roll you play does. Don't you get tired of it at your age? And that name— WOOM. What a thing. It sounds like it's pregnant—WOMB."

"It's pronounced WUMM, Mom, you know that. It's supposed to remind you of a fastball zipping by. WUMM—coming at you, fast and furious and right over the heart of rock's home plate."

"I'm sorry. Radio is just fine. For the time being, of course. I just want you to get your feet under yourself before too much more water goes over the dam."

I'd been out of school exactly ten years, but my mother thought it was thirteen because she didn't believe there was such a thing as graduate school for just writing stories. Truthfully, I hadn't gone to graduation or sent her an announcement, a set of circumstances that confirmed her doubts.

"Why not get your teaching credits?" she said. "There you are right beside a perfectly good college. I know they train a lot of teachers there. You could get accredited or whatever it's called in a jiffy."

I told her I had the first chapter of a novel written, which was true, though it was finished only in my head. "What's it about?" she asked at once, and when I said, "It's hard to explain," she gave me the look of pity she used on the poor and the crippled, the one that said "It's sad, but you'll have to learn to deal with it."

Just as promised, she dragged the black case out of the closet as soon as we returned to her house. "Here," she said. "It's yours. You open it."

I sat on the bed and laid the case across my knees, unsnapping the latches and unfolding it. The bell and slide looked so well preserved I thought my mother had cleaned and polished them. "Here's a bunch of your old music books," she said, dropping them on the bed beside me. "Now I'll let you be."

She closed the door behind her, but then opened it again. "You take your time," she said. "I won't listen until you want me to hear."

My mother had found five of the books of simple songs I'd learned in grade school, and I thumbed through them with the open case resting in front of me. I came to "Abide With Me," a hymn I'd played at the old folks home when I was ten, the year after I'd started playing "Auld Lang Syne" in our front yard right after Guy Lombardo was finished on television. There was a book of peppy marches, including the ones from each branch of the military—"The Marine

Hymn," "Anchors Aweigh," "The Air Force Song," and the one from the Army I remembered my father singing: "And the caissons go rolling along."

My father, in fact, had loved those fight songs, bellowing "From the halls of Montezuma," "Anchors aweigh, my boys," and "Off we go, into the wild blue yonder" in his bass voice as I played them, swinging one arm as if he was about to give in and march. He was an age that had two chances at combat—World War II and Korea, but he'd failed the physical, and so had I when Vietnam called, both of us with blood pressure higher than the maximum.

He was supposed to keep his weight down, but didn't. At thirty-five, I was as thin as I was in high school, and I was supposed to drink in moderation, but didn't. I dropped the music books inside the case and snapped the locks shut. A moment later my mother knocked on the door and opened it. "It's ok," she said. "You take it to Moorefield now. Practice up. You come home at New Year's and play out in the front yard like old times."

Dennis Miller had been right about the rural life. I wasn't an outdoorsman, so living in Moorefield was something of a trial. The two days after Thanksgiving weekend were holidays from school, everybody, even the teachers, out deer hunting. For two weeks the newspaper was full of pictures of men and women and boys and girls kneeling beside their trophies, all of which looked tame after the earlier run of men posed beside their trophy bears, all of them killed conventionally by bullets. The largest animals rated the front page, the photos that fall running alongside the benign, puzzled face of Ronald Reagan looking like he'd just been asked who the President was.

Yet there I was, thirty-five years old with just three stories in literary magazines, and those right out of my thesis portfolio. I missed the discipline the old workshops had given me, for without the threat of deadlines and public humiliation, I didn't seem capable of beginning a story, let alone finishing one. And there were other problems. After two months of sticking to WOOM's new short playlist, I was reassessing. Half of the heavy rotation songs got played twice during my five hour shift. By the beginning of December I didn't want to turn on the radio in my car or in the apartment because I'd already heard those songs so often, and in the silence I created I began to see the apartment I'd moved into in June differently as well.

My apartment was above a garage, and as winter set in I started listening to the owner's cars idling below, the couple that rented to me letting them warm up before they drove off to work. "Nothing to worry about," they said, but they lived in a separate house and my car had to sit outside and collect snow and ice.

I opened the window when I heard the motors turn over, and I could never get back to sleep even with fresh air pouring in, already frigid and guaranteed to turn punishing. I shivered and heard Guns n' Roses, who were getting forty-two spins a week, wailing in my head. And there I pushed myself out of bed and began working at the simplicity of making ends meet, what provided a routine for the day. A five hour shift, the on-call for promotions on Saturday afternoons, filling the air with live broadcasts from a car dealer's parking lot, a new fitness center, or a hardware store like the one I was scheduled to do in a couple of days.

I had Saturday nights and all day Sunday to find trouble for myself if I cared to look, but the college kids filled the bars at ten o'clock, and the locals headed to the two places on the outskirts of town where the kids didn't go—one a country and western bar for all ages, the other a dim, no juke box, one television place for the over fifty crowd. I hated country and western, and the other place promoted the slow suicide of sit on your ass silent drinking.

I was trying to avoid that, holding myself to beer and keeping only six cans cold in my refrigerator at a time to slow me down. My father's high blood pressure had brought him a stroke that left his right side paralyzed last winter at fifty-nine. Three months later, it had brought him a second stroke that killed him.

Above all, my reading had slowed from sporadic to rare. The only magazines in the college library with stories in them were The Atlantic and The New Yorker, and I was having trouble finishing anything printed in them until I saw a story in The New Yorker by Rachel Wright, who'd been in three workshops with me. "A brilliant young writer," an endorsement read. "Thirty-three years-old and writing with the assurance of Flannery O'Connor." Her story was about a masochistic young woman who let herself be tied and abused by men she barely knew. All of the men were intimidated when she asked them to put a plastic bag over her head and hold it there while they counted to fifty. None of them held that bag past twenty-five, not even the one she thought she loved.

I imagined Rachel Wright in situations like that, what her naked body would look like as she begged me to bag her. Her bio line said she had a novel about to be published by Random House. I thought of Cheryl, the girl friend I'd had for the first half of the year. She'd told me that if she found out a man she slept with watched porn, she'd never touch him again. "It's filthy," she said. "Somebody ought to burn that video store at the edge of town." And when I hadn't volunteered to do it or at least said, "Yes, they should," she'd looked at me as if she believed I was a veteran of XXX videos even though I didn't own a VCR.

It took another month, but that failure to rubber-stamp seemed to start the arc of our relationship descending. Two months later, in September, Cheryl was living with another man when that store burned, and I thought of her excitement when the news reached her, that man giving himself up to the rewards for righteous arson.

"Serves them right," I heard Cheryl saying between bouts of sex, sounding like my mother assessing the bear's death.

Not only didn't I have a VCR, my television was one my mother had given me after my father died and she'd bought a new one. It would lose its horizontal after fifteen minutes or sometimes, on a good day, half an hour. If I turned it off and back on again, it would last another twenty minutes or so. But mine had gone entirely blank during the summer, and even a hundred dollars for the cheapest of new sets was currently out of reach.

"It takes some getting used to," my mother had admitted on the phone in October, "but your father wouldn't part with it because it wasn't all the way broken. 'We'll get new when it doesn't come on at all,' he kept saying, but now you can have it until it gets you so mad you pitch it out the window. I knew I couldn't stand it when it went kerflooey three times during Lawrence Welk, and don't say why are you watching because I do it now for your father who loved him."

I left the trombone sit beside the television. Knowing my mother expected "Auld Lang Syne" in less than a month kept reminding me of Guy Lombardo, and what I remembered most was his band looked better on television than Lawrence Welk's, my father's favorite, because Welk had his band change blazers with the times, going to pastels in the seventies while Guy Lombardo stuck with black tuxedos. The old men in his band looked like old men in a dance band should look, classy in black and white, like Mr. Lucky and Peter Gunn and all the detectives my mother watched on that old television when its horizontal still held. With a little practice I learned Henry Mancini's heavy bass-line theme song to Peter Gunn. "You can play for his orchestra," my mother said. "He's from around here somewhere," but by the time I could sound anything like a real trombone player, those shows were off the air, replaced by Ben Casey and Dr. Kildare, shows about surgeons my mother watched with awe.

All along my father didn't seem to notice that Lawrence Welk had his band change haircuts and dress up in ugly coats until my mother, one Saturday night when I was in college, said, "That Larry Hooper looks pathetic with sideburns and his hair like that, and in lavender, of all colors, the poor man. It's a wonder he can still hit those low notes."

My father had stayed quiet, like he was concentrating on Hooper's performance because Welk's bass man was his favorite. Hooper looked worse than pathetic, I thought. He looked like a man who knew he was going to look like this in reruns, that people were going to see him in that hideous outfit after he was dead, singing "Old Man River" in a deep voice made hilarious by lavender.

And now Hooper was on my mind again because I was supposed to say, "The new WOOM—just born to be your juke box" every half hour. For three months this was to go on. "We're newborn until 1988," the manager said, but every time I said "just born" my mother's pronunciation came back to me, and the itch to drop my voice into a great Larry Hooper bass station ID for WOMB was seeping up around me like carbon monoxide from a two-car garage.

The truth is I was having a problem with that printed play list— heavy rotation, moderate rotation, light rotation—arriving every Tuesday. "We're part of a chain that stretches across the country," the manager said. "You're a link in something strong. A hundred miles from here is another link."

I'd received that lecture twice already because I'd been so used to playing what I wanted to that it was hard to limit myself to thirty songs plus that week's designated "classics." "It's a request line," I explained to the general manager, "but you're saying I can't play it unless it's on the play list?"

"Who requests it?" the boss said.

"I don't know."

"That's right. You just say 'I'll try to get to it,' and then you play something like it from the list and say, "Sorry, hope this one gets you off."

"Gets you off?"

The manager smiled. "It's rock and roll, isn't it?" he said.

"My friends tell me your bear was on television," my mother said the first time she called after Thanksgiving. "Why didn't you tell me? And there they were making light of him."

"I saw the show, Mom," I said, and it sounded so much like a confession I wanted to hang up.

"How's the trombone coming along?" she said then. "I was thinking about poor Guy Lombardo. He died right about the time you told me you were finished with the writing school. Bing Crosby died that year, too, you know, and your father with his troubles just beginning."

"And Elvis," I said.

"Elvis Presley? That young man? You know I don't follow the papers or your music, but when 1977 was ready to wind itself up, there wasn't any Guy Lombardo, and everything seemed out of kilter. That year didn't end the way it should. He wasn't there at midnight, and it was as if 1977 just kept going."

"Dick Clark was on another channel, Mom. I don't think too many people missed Guy Lombardo."

"Dick Clark? That disc jockey? Why would anybody wait for a disc jockey to tell them it was next year?" There was a long pause, the sound of her rummaging through the drawer full of coupons and small tools that opened just under where her phone was located. "Well," she finally said. "You write about that poor bear," she said. "It's a tearjerker. People love a good cry. More people would read the Bible if Jesus hadn't risen from the dead. That John the Baptist is a better story—he doesn't get a second chance. I never understood why he doesn't get more publicity."

"People want happy endings, Mom. I think you're wrong."

"Angels? Rescue? That's so boring. If that bear falls off the pole and is still alive and nursed back to health it's an anecdote. That bear frying like a murderer on the hot seat is something. Afraid of a dog, you say? Why would a bear be afraid of a dog? Now that's a story."

After she hung up, I dug up the three magazines with my stories in them and stacked them beside the bed. It was a way to start, I thought, reading those stories and getting back in the mood.

For Bradley's Hardware Buy-For-Dad's-Christmas, I was supposed to give away a barbecue grill to a lucky customer. Randomly. You know, pulling a name-and-address slip of paper from a red and green striped box. But to be honest here, when I saw a woman who I believed would make me forget Cheryl and her assaults on porn filling out an entry blank, I went over to shake the box a little and read her name, Wendy Salter, where she'd printed it on the top line.

I watched, with joy, her tight jeans disappear into the Walden's bookstore, and I printed her name on a fresh entry blank and stuffed it in my pocket. If Wendy came back before the end of the "hair squared half hour," meaning four songs each by Poison and Motley Crue, I was going to cheat and bring some small measure of pleasure to firm-breasted, book buying Wendy Salter and myself.

And she did, walking back at 4:45 so punctual it was like there was a time clock to punch. I reached down into that festive box and fumbled around for fifteen seconds, keeping up the patter about the good times waiting to happen by the grill, and then I pulled my hand out holding Wendy Salter's name.

When she didn't squeal or jump or clap, I knew I'd made a good call. She smiled and walked up to receive the gift certificate to redeem any time before December 24th, and I asked her, as soon as I cued up Van Halen, if she'd like to have a beer with me in exactly eleven minutes when the promotion ended. It was only after she said "Sure thing" with gusto that I noticed she wasn't carrying a

Walden's bag, but I was willing to put that down to her dismay at the lousy selection.

"What do you really listen to when you listen to music?" Wendy said two hours and four beers later, the last of which I'd handed her from among the six cold ones I had lined up in my refrigerator.

"Stuff that I don't play, I guess."

"Like what?"

She sounded so eager, I thought she was miraculously star struck in the company of a small-town disc jockey. "Garage bands," I said. "The Sonics, the Seeds, stuff like that."

"I never heard of them. Were they popular a long time ago?"

The price of honesty. Wendy suddenly had such a look of dubiousness I imagined her adding ten years to my age. "They were never popular," I said. "It wasn't so long ago. Mid to late 60s. The same time serious music was getting out there. I was into that, too, people like Phil Ochs, the poor man's Bob Dylan."

Wendy perked up when she heard Dylan's name, but she had the look of a dog coming to attention when Rover surfaces from the deep water of language.

"It's usually what you get into in high school, isn't it? I mean, after that you don't seem to get into music as much so you end up with what you loved when you were sixteen—like the Bee Gees for me, like disco." She grinned at me. "That and sex," she said. "That's what I loved."

You chose well, I said to myself, stifling every other bit of more than ten year-old music trivia as I moved toward her and her beautifully-shaped acid-washed jeans.

After an hour in bed, I was back at the refrigerator to find another pair of Rolling Rocks, slipping two warm cans into the freezer before I shuffled back, naked and happy, into the bedroom. Wendy was holding up my contributor's copy of Thought Provoker Magazine. "Is this you in this magazine?" she said, the sheet slipping down over her breasts in such a way I was ready to forgive her for letting the pages fall open in such a way I thought the staples would pull loose.

"Yeah, those magazines are like yearbooks. I was trying to remember what it was like to be a writer."

"You don't love being a disc jockey?"

"When I talk, the words disappear," I said. "The ones on the page stay forever."

"You mean in a book?" Wendy said. "If I was you I'd be happy being on the radio. I don't know anybody who reads."

I'd heard myself say it before and knew Wendy's answer by heart, but hearing those words from a woman who was naked in my bed made me think of that bear getting spooked by something he could kill if he had a mind to.

There were two more magazines, but she didn't open them. She slipped my shirt on and carried her beer to the TV and pushed the power button, running through the five channels I could get with a cheap antenna before leaving it tuned to the Golden Girls. "What's this here?" she said.

"A trombone."

"Whatever for?" she asked. "Do you play it?" And when she spun around for emphasis, the shirt opened so widely I felt myself begin to stir again.

"My mother's fantasy," I said, staring at the way that shirt barely draped itself over her breasts.

"Stand up," she said, and when I hesitated, glancing down, she smiled. "It looks better that way than just hanging there."

I stood up, beginning to go soft. "Let me look at you," she said. "I'm seeing you in one of those high school band uniforms. You look funny."

The apartment seemed so cold I felt myself shriveling to child size. The words "I quit in tenth grade" sounded so weak I kept them to myself. "You might have liked the white bucks we wore," I said.

"What?"

"Like Pat Boone."

"You're a funny guy," she said. "Do you want the barbecue thing I won? I don't even cook on a real stove. I just signed up because I sign up for everything and I never win."

"I love barbecue."

"There," she said. "I knew we had something in common, but I just go up to the Rib House and pig out when I'm in the mood. That stupid bear had good taste at least. They must have the best dumpster in town. I always see people leaving meat on the bones. What's wrong with that television set? It's all diagonals."

It turned out that Wendy Salter wasn't in the phone book. I imagined her living with a stepfather, so I had to rely on her calling and there weren't any messages for three straight days. Meanwhile, I put an ad in the Penny Saver—trombone, $75; television, $25. Maybe Wendy would see it and call.

I'd promised to do Sunday night, 8-12, for Larry Alsop, who had a job interview in Scranton first thing Monday morning. "This might get me out of here," he said. Alsop was twenty-three; he'd been working at WOOM for six months, but I wished him well and followed the playlist from top to bottom until the phone rang at 11:30.

"You sound cool," a woman's voice said.

"Thanks."

"Can you play 'If You See Kay'? You remember that one?"

"April Wine. Sure," I said, and when she laughed, I asked, "Is this Wendy?"

I looked at the playlist and found "Pour Some Sugar on Me,"

the closest innuendo I could find. "Def Leppard for the sexiest voice in Moorefield," I said, putting it on for the second time that night. "Hope this gets you off."

The phone flashed before the first chorus. The same voice was on the line. "What's this shit?" she said. "Is that what Wendy likes? Is she retarded or is she just fifteen years old?"

"I'm still looking. There's a bunch of vinyl in the back. It's all out of order."

"There's still time to make this work."

"Yes, there is," I agreed.

The old records we weren't allowed to play were shelved in badly arranged alphabetical order—a shelf of T-Z, one of G-J, and then what looked to be A-C. Sure enough, there was April Wine's Power Play, and in my happiness, I added Adam Ant, Pat Benatar, and the B-52s so I could proclaim "a square of the rare" to resurrect 1982. And the BeeGees. After all, somebody had played them every day on this station the year I finished my MFA. Maybe Wendy was listening, too. Maybe she'd put her friend up to calling.

As soon as I put on "If You See Kay," the phone flashed, but I didn't answer. When I followed it with "Goody Two Shoes," it flashed as soon as Adam Ant opened his mouth, but I wasn't taking any more requests because I had enough old records to keep me going until my shift ended and I signed WOOM off the air because we shut down for six hours every Sunday night.

After I shut the door behind me, I saw a car pull into the lot. The station manager, I thought, but it was a Camaro and the driver, when she opened the door, looked like Kay herself in a leather jacket and deep red tight skirt. "Hey there," I said, conjuring my store-promotion voice. "Are you the mystery caller?"

It was so quiet in the parking lot I could hear her stockings rub together as she shifted her weight and stood up. "You don't sound like yourself," she said. "It's funny how the radio does that to people. I heard myself once and I thought they were rolling the wrong tape."

The woman wore heavy makeup, but she was beautiful, as young as Larry Alsop, maybe younger, and suddenly, as she stayed beside her car, leaning slightly on the open door, I was sure she was working toward telling me I was way too old to have my voice. "I'm not the disc jockey," I said. "I'm the engineer."

"Mr. Engineer," she said. "You're staring."

"The deejay will be out in a few minutes."

She looked past me. "There's only one car in the lot."

"I walk," I said. "It's over a mile to town, but I do it every night."

Only a voice, she would think, when no one came out. She would have me pegged then, a man who was embarrassed or afraid. "Well, that surely doesn't sound like anything a deejay would do," she said. "You take care you don't get sideswiped this time of night."

I started the hike toward town, looking behind me for a quarter mile until I saw her headlights come on, and then I veered off into a driveway, followed it for fifty feet, and stood behind a tree until her car passed. I waited a minute to see if she turned around before I turned back toward the station and got in my car.

There were two messages on my machine when I made it home. Two men wanted to buy my trombone. One was lowballing, offering $50. The other said he'd buy it for the $75 asking price, sight unseen. "Unless I can't move the slide," he added like a footnote, chuckling. Both of them left numbers, but nobody had called about the television. Now that I thought about it, why would anyone want a twenty-five dollar television? It couldn't possibly work worth a damn.

Sight unseen? After I called that guy the next morning, he said he'd be over during his lunch hour, that he couldn't wait to get his hands on a cheap trombone, and at 12:30 I heard somebody knocking on the door that opened onto the stairs behind the garage. I hesitated, the thought coming to me that maybe this was going to be the station manager come to fire me in person, so when I looked out the window, I was relieved to see a stranger, a guy my age, maybe a little older.

Ok, I said to myself, but he had the same haircut as Larry Alsop, long with tight curls down the back of his neck like the one-armed drummer from Def Leppard. If he hadn't been wearing pegged acid-washed jeans, the bottoms rolled up tight against his ankles exactly like Wendy Salter's, I could have imagined him launching into "Pour Some Sugar on Me."

I stepped back from the window, sat in a chair, and saw poor old Larry Hooper with his tentative sideburns and hideous blazer, the camera panning in on his hang-dog face as he took "Old Man River" way down low before it flashed over to a beaming Lawrence Welk. The would-be buyer knocked again, louder this time, and I knew that about now he'd be looking up at the windows because my car, with its WOOM bumper sticker, was parked right there in the driveway.

I waited another minute, listening until I heard a car door slam and an engine turn over. I didn't have to check from the window. I could just sit in the chair and look at that trombone case standing beside the television until any reasonable lunch hour was over. And no, I didn't think about getting that trombone out and playing it, but I wondered whether my high school band still wore those blue uniforms with gold stripes, whether they still applied polish to their white bucks so every show began without a scuff mark. And then I hoped that was true.

ARE YOU STILL THERE?

My son answered the phone before the second ring. "Yeah," Alex said, so I knew he'd been expecting one of his friends to call. He held the phone against his ear for a minute without saying another word, and then, without speaking, he hung up.

"What's that supposed to mean?" I said.

"I don't know."

"What do you mean, you don't know?"

Alex edged toward the stairs, but when he had one foot on the first step, he said, "Some weird guy, ok?"

I thought about the details my twelve year-old might mention. "What do you mean, weird?"

"Some guy named Beaver." He didn't start climbing the stairs, and I crossed out half the perversions on my list, waiting, then, to have one or two of the remaining items confirmed. "It was stupid," Alex said. "It was nothing but some stupid guy. All he said was `You know who I am, you know why I'm calling.'"

"It took him a minute to say that?" I was ready to take guard duty. I was ready to sit by my phone until Beaver got the urge again.

"He said, `You have something to tell me. You better say it.'"

"And?"

"You heard. I didn't say it. I waited a while and then I hung up."

"Great," I said, but when Beaver called again, a half hour later, Alex slammed the phone down before I could reach him.

"Same thing," he said. "Exactly."

I was taking this personally now. I wanted to discover what Beaver was so sure of, but I'd made a double appointment with a podiatrist—Alex's pronation syndrome, my ingrown toenail—so Beaver, when he called a third time to a house with no answering machine, would have to listen to however many rings he was willing to sweat through in order to get a child's voice on the line.

"Thick, yellow, discolored," the doctor said when I was settled on the stool beside the foot bath. I looked at him like someone learning a foreign language's racial slurs. "Thick, yellow, discolored," he repeated, and I had to retaliate or answer.

"I don't think so," I said.

He seemed confused. "I have it wrong, perhaps?"

"It's ingrown," I said, working out the code. "It's trying to burrow into my big toe."

The doctor stared into the placid, shallow water of the foot bath. "I have you confused with someone else. I haven't seen you in so long, I've forgotten why you're here."

He flipped a switch and the water began to churn. Before we had separated, my wife had taken Alex to every appointment, and now I wanted to keep my shoe and sock on because I didn't want this fool I'd never met before to amputate my foot because he remembered me as a diabetic with gangrene. "Well, you put your foot in here for a few minutes while I take care of your son and his footpads. Then we'll see what the problem is."

I wondered how many patients had used this water; I wondered if Alex would be crippled for life because my wife had chosen a podiatrist by how close his office was to our house. Instead of doing anything sensible, I stripped my left foot and plunged it into the warm whirlpool.

"Don't move the stool," a sign above the foot bath warned. "One patient damaged the wall behind you." The lettering looked as if it had been printed by a committee of third graders, and I reached back and felt for the hole in the fake oak paneling. Either the destruction had been repaired or it was out of reach of someone stuck in shallow water. I'll check later, I told myself, after I get both feet on the ground, but when the doctor returned, I was as hypnotized as Cinderella when he dried my foot and slid a Saran-Wrap slipper over it, asking me to follow him to an examination room where Alex was sitting like someone recalling the comfort of the womb.

"Well," the podiatrist said, squinting at my toe, "why do you think it's going in like that?"

"No idea."

"They usually don't do that," he said.

"No, they don't," I had to agree.

The whole toenail had turned black after I'd jammed it playing basketball. A month later it had lifted off. I'd lost half a dozen toenails that way, and all of the replacements had grown in just fine. Now this one had gotten half way formed and started to curve down as if my ex-wife, just twelve miles away, had been perfecting the witchcraft of minor medical nuisances since the day she had moved out three months ago, telling me to keep Alex until she decided which way things were headed. "For now," she'd said. "At least to keep him in the same school."

The doctor started to wave his hands over my foot. A spell, I concluded. Next he would begin to chant sounds he'd mastered in the jungles of New Guinea. "I love this woodwind cadenza," he said, and I heard the music in the ceiling. "Mozart was a miracle worker," he went on. Alex, when I looked his way, was still sedated.

"Well," the doctor said during a pause in the series of breathy flourishes, "we can halve this toenail and give it a second chance, or we can file it back a bit and try to coax it to straighten up."

"Is that likely?"

"That it will straighten? Oh, I don't know. Perhaps. Sawing the nail is surer, but you'd want to avoid that probably." His hands dropped back to my foot. The woodwinds had blended back into the orchestra. "Let's file," he said, reaching for what looked like a power drill. "You'll get a little warmth now."

I saw Alex snap out of it and sit forward to gauge how much pain I could handle, whether or not I'd disappoint him by screaming or cheer him up by kicking this quack and leaving before he could permanently damage us.

In fifteen seconds, however, the doctor was finished. He'd sanded my nail smooth and round, and though it still curled inward, it wasn't pressing on the skin, and I had at least a month before I'd know for sure that I'd been duped.

"There," he declared, "now you can keep at it with a file and see how things go."

"And?"

"There's a chance. If not, well, off with the crooked part one of these days." He handed me my sock and shoe.

"Your son, you know, has sweaty feet," he said. I tugged on the sock to give myself something to do besides answer. "I've given him some things to think about. Some remedies. The pads he has, by the way, still fit, but I've shown him some exercises to strengthen the muscles in and around his feet. They'll help eliminate the need for those pads. Here, let me show you."

I slipped my shoe on while he grabbed a medical book off his desk. He tossed it on the floor, and it flopped open to diagrams of ankles. "Here," he said, standing and kicking the cover shut. He propped his feet against the book, his toes over the edge of the front cover. For a few seconds he pressed down, then he lifted. "Of course," he said, stopping and sitting back down, "the exercises are more effective if they're done with the shoes off. Your son saw me perform them the proper way, so he won't have a problem."

In the car I said, "Were his feet sweaty?"

"What a dork," Alex said. "I'm supposed to spray PAM in my

shoes."

"The frying pan stuff?"

"Less friction," Alex said. "Less sweat."

I dropped him off and waited until he let himself inside. I had to interview the mayor of the town where the newspaper I worked for was located, but he could wait a few minutes while I checked for loiterers named Beaver. I wasn't looking forward to the assignment anyway, having to put an objective face on The Sidewalk Mayor, who'd replaced, during his first twenty months in office, all of the walkways in the town's business section. Ten blocks, both sides, of concrete. "Uniform sidewalks attract people to the downtown area," he'd told me a year ago when I'd interviewed him about the stirrings of citizen outrage. "The same people who complain now will be thankful later. They need to understand revitalization."

Now he'd purchased new chairs for each member of the town council, which met once a month. The chairs were padded; they had arms and swiveled and cost five times the price of the plastic ones they'd replaced. "You can't have volunteers breaking their asses on those lousy hardbacks," he said after I arrived and got to the questions I'd come to ask.

"Look," he added, "the same fellow who bought these chairs puts dimes in parking meters to keep them from running out on people who shop downtown." He reached in his pocket and pulled out a handful of change. He had the same stricken look my wife wore like a mask the last six months before she left, somewhere between sadness and anger where misery lies. "A dollar a day," he said. "I stuff expired meters during lunch until I've spent a dollar. And nobody knows."

I wrote it down. I needed something to avoid the feel of bias. A few more quotes and I had all I could use for a third-page story on frivolous spending, but he followed me outside, his expression shifting to something like triumphant. "The Sidewalk Mayor my ass," he said. "Wait until next term. I'm going to be the Johnny Appleseed of mayors. All along this street, all the way down, I'm yanking the parking meters and planting fruit trees in every hole. Apple, peach, pear, plum—you name it. You put that in your story and see how people vote. No more meters. All that fruit just hanging there for the picking. In five years this street will look like the Garden of Eden. You'll be working in the Orchard City."

I kept quiet about the mayor's vision, and my son didn't get any more calls from Beaver, but a week later, when I picked up the phone, I heard Anne, my ex-wife, on the line. "What's going on with Alex?" she said.

"I'm stumped," I answered. "What do you have in mind?"

"The police called. They said there was a problem with Alex."

"They had the wrong number."

"Sure they did, Greg. But I got them on track." I listened to see if I could tell what household chore she was finishing while she talked to me, the phone tucked under her chin.

"Nobody's called. I don't know anything."

"The police call about Alex, and you can't think of any reason why?"

"No."

"Great. So there you are, Greg, right on top of things. Have you seen Alex lately? Does he still live there?" I thought I heard her shoving a set of old newspapers into a bag for recycling, stuffing the words of The Sidewalk Mayor and a thousand other local newsmakers into a paper sack.

"He's at arm's length. You want to ask him about his crimes?"

"Do your homework, Greg. That's all I'm saying."

I needed to be that old comic book hero Plastic Man to reach Alex, but I knew where he was, upstairs getting dressed to go to the Renaissance Faire, something he'd been asking about half the summer. The investigation, I thought, could wait until later. Maybe it would dissolve like Beaver's harassment, initiating a long series of easy solutions.

Though I didn't have much faith in the handiwork of probabilities. A year ago Anne had staked out Bag-a-Bug to kill a horde of Japanese Beetles that had settled in her garden. By the end of the first day, there were hundreds of them lying inert in the sack. She'd dumped them into the honeysuckle that covered the hill behind our lot. "There," she'd said, "enough of them for a while," but the bag had swollen the following day with ecstatic beetles drawn to their death by the simulated smell of insect sex. How far does lust travel? I'd thought. How many beetles can one yard support? And after three days of dumping, Anne had seen that the beetles were reviving, that they were passed out, not dead, small miracles of the back yard returning like men willing to risk AIDS for moments of bliss. She'd outsmarted them, then. She'd dumped the bugs from one bag into another, closed them tight in a sort of premature mass burial.

It was beetle season again, I knew. Anne would have, for certain, a new Bag-a-Bug tied to a stick. This year she'd be anticipating rather than reacting.

An hour later, Alex and I were trudging among the booths. I'd already finished a medieval turkey leg and an Olde Scotch breaded egg. Alex had washed down two slices of pizza with a Childe's Grog. "Mom would love this," Alex said.

I wanted to say that was just one more problem, but Alex grabbed my arm. "Look," he said, "there's Doctor Mozart, and he has a wife."

Sure enough, the podiatrist was crossing between booths about thirty feet from us. The woman was holding the foot doctor's hand, both of them wearing sunglasses. She was slim and pretty, with red hair that caught the sun in a way that made me ache with a desire to touch it.

"It's so weird," Alex said. "They look normal."

"You think they should be dressed up like peasants?"

"They wouldn't be peasants. He's a doctor."

"What would we be then?"

"What?" Alex said. "Besides a son and his father? I don't know. Was there a newspaper back then?"

"I don't think so. Most people couldn't read. There wasn't even a printing press."

"So you'd have to be somebody else?"

"Yes. And there'd be nobody to fix your feet."

"Nobody knew how to do anything back then. Everybody was stupid, but this place acts like it was fun."

"The Renaissance," I said. "It was one big happy family."

The podiatrist veered away from us, his arm around the woman's shoulder now. She leaned into him as they stopped near the group of traveling minstrels. For a moment, I thought he might begin conducting, but Alex stepped into my line of vision and said, "Do you remember when Mom stopped loving you?"

"No," I said. "Not at all." I thought Alex wanted to talk about unhappiness and loneliness, something serious, but all he said was "Oh," as if my answer surprised him.

"Hail, good fellow," a woman called from the booth the foot doctor and his wife had just left. She wanted to show us a pendulum with a knob on the end shaped like a heart or, maybe, a turnip. Nearby, one ornately carved peg stood on the counter. All someone had to do, she made us understand, was push the pendulum and knock the peg down, one swing for a dollar, winner takes home a knight or gentlewoman doll.

Although the woman was wearing a peasant dress, I thought I'd seen this game being run by men with tattoos at county fairs. "Prithee," she said, "take a free swing."

"Why not, Dad?" Alex said, and I had to agree, so I lined it up and let it go, brushing the peg, which teetered, then tumbled.

"Hark, a winner," the woman warbled. And then she added, "Thou canst have a prize on a free swing, but thou can have a special—five swings for three dollars. Thou hast earned it."

It sounded like a good deal, even in Neo-Dark Age. I slapped down three dollars, took aim, and though I brushed the peg once out of five tries, barely missing on the other four, I didn't win Alex a chance to choose between lords and ladies. "Bad fortune," the woman murmured each time I missed, and then, "Thou wantest more?"

I shook my head and turned away before she could laugh. After we'd distanced ourselves, Alex said, "I think it was rigged."

"No, it wasn't."

"She suckered you in."

"I knew what I was doing. I just got tense. They count on people getting tense."

I told him to choose the next booth. We walked past jugglers and a slow-roasting boar. We passed the minstrels, the doctor and the beautiful woman nowhere in sight, and stopped in front of a stall with a sign that said the woman inside could tell your fortune from whatever was on the bottom of your foot. Calluses. Tiny bumps. Strange whorls. "This one," Alex said. "You know why."

My toenail didn't count, I thought. I hadn't examined the bottoms of my feet since high school, the last time I'd had athlete's foot. I never went without shoes; I hadn't had a blister in twenty years. I'd never heard of foot reading. This old woman was wearing a peasant dress that looked to be identical to the one worn by the shyster with the swinging heart. All I could think of, as I watched her handle Alex's foot, was "This little piggy went wee-wee-wee all the way home."

But just as Alex was learning he could expect a long life, success after disappointment, and one important journey, I noticed the naked woman. She was full frontal, anatomically correct, her blue body standing the length of the right arm of the man wearing a sleeveless t-shirt on the opposite side of the foot reader's booth. The man lifted a cigarette to his mouth, and she folded into a surrealistic suggestion. He dropped his arm and she unfurled again.

Before he took another drag, a woman and two small boys walked up to stand beside him, a family, obviously, which was willing to be seen with a man sporting an inked nude. And what struck me at once was the unmistakable similarity of the mother to the naked woman. The same hair style. The same face. I was sure she'd posed, that she'd allowed some tattoo artist to reproduce her breasts and crotch on her husband's arm.

I looked back and forth from her blouse to those breasts, getting a fix on the artist's talent. When the man flexed his arm, signaling to his sons, his wife performed a sort of sit-up, and then she vanished, the cigarette back at his lips, the family turning toward the minstrel and the jugglers and the smoking pig.

I heard from the police the next evening. "Your boy's been making obscene calls," the voice on the line said.

"I doubt it," I said. "Alex is pretty naive for twelve, let alone mastering enough phrases to manage an obscene call."

"Mr. Beaver says it's your boy. He has him on tape. We need you to come in and listen to the tape. Bring your boy, let him listen to himself."

"I don't understand," I said, but I felt the sticky film of foolishness adhering to the entire length of my body.

"Your boy's been making obscene calls to Mr. Beaver," the policeman said, and I expected him to add, "You know who that is; you know who I'm calling about."

"How do you know it's my son?"

"He leaves his name at the end. He tells Mr. Beaver who he is."

I was relieved. "Nobody does that," I burbled.

"That's what I thought while I was listening to what your boy

176

was saying to the answering machine. You'll be shocked Mr. Foss, I guarantee it."

"Nobody leaves his name."

"And his phone number. His name and his phone number. It's a plea for help, Mr. Foss. It's like a failed suicide. Wait till you hear these tapes."

"It's a friend. It's somebody my son knows trying to be funny."

"Nobody's friend talks like this."

"I think you're mistaken here."

"Wait till you bring your boy in. You'll see who's mistaken."

I wasn't driving twenty miles to Bradyburg, the little town where Beaver and the idiot policeman lived, but I told Alex the answer to the Beaver Riddle and asked him which of his classmates liked or hated him enough to say, "This is Alex Foss, 555-4887" after they'd run out of sex combinations and positions.

"You don't need their names, Dad," he said. "That cop will get a handle on this. Those calls would be on our phone bill. Beaver lives too far away to be a local call."

"So there it is," I said, relieved that I had a detective for a son.

Alex looked around the living room as if he was taking inventory now that this issue had been settled. His eyes fixed on the two shelves of family photographs, four of which included all of us, three of which were only of Anne. "You going to put these all away," he said, keeping his eyes on the photos.

"You think it's weird?"

"No," he said, and then he turned back toward me. "Are you filing your toenail, Dad?"

"Sometimes."

"I'm not doing my exercises either."

I tried to put Beaver and the learning disability of the policeman out of my mind. I had enough to do calling school board presidents and writing copy about teacher unrest, the possibilities of strikes in the fall. I looked at the lines of copy on the screen in front of me each morning, attempting to read my articles like someone on a fixed income who was worried about teacher salaries and rising taxes. I tried to see those articles folded in on themselves by conscientious paperboys, tossed onto the porches of seventeen thousand houses, but each time I had seven column inches or ten or thirteen, never enough room to elaborate or improvise after somebody like Nevin Hartlett, from the taxpayers' association in the town where the newspaper was printed, said, "You know what our organization wants to know? Where will it all end?"

When Anne called again the following day, she said, "I bet I know those boys. I bet I know their mothers."

"What," I said. "You want me to cold call the mothers of suspects?"

"What are you planning on doing?" she said. "You're the father here. Or are you just hoping it will go away?"

I could hear dishes being moved. Anne, like she did when she talked on the phone, was staying busy. Filling the dishwasher, I thought, and I tried to picture her moving through rooms as she talked, straightening a towel in the bathroom or replacing a book on a shelf to make herself useful while she wasted her time with me. "It's just boys, Anne. It's better than Alex being beaten up."

"Jesus Christ," Anne said, and I heard her close a door. I flexed my arm and imagined her naked body inked on its surface, one version of her sitting up, then lying down, her bare legs running the length of my extended forearm. I imagined the man she might be fucking, someone who was happy as hell she hadn't dragged along her son like just about any other mother would have done.

And then I heard the sound of urine splashing into a toilet, the soft tearing of toilet paper. "Are you still there?" she said, and I waited for her to flush before I hung up.

The next day the policeman called back. "You haven't brought your boy in," he said.

"That's right."

"I'm disappointed. The boy needs counseling. Mr. Beaver is willing to forget this if the boy gets counseling."

"My son is fine. And I'd feel a notch or two better if you figured out that somebody else left his name and number."

"Maybe his mother knows him better. Maybe I should talk to her and see what she thinks."

"She doesn't live here."

"Well, then," the policeman said as if he'd made a decision. "I want to tell you a story, Mr. Foss. I want you to know about this."

"Sure," I said, fighting off the urge to yammer, "Go screw yourself."

"In Washington, last spring, somebody vandalized Lincoln's tomb. Somebody spray-painted it with filth. And this is the part I want you to hear: The teenagers who did the damage spray-painted their own names on the monument, and that's how they got caught. What do you think of that, Mr. Foss?"

I read the papers from New York and Washington every day and hadn't seen that story. I thought the policeman was making it up, that he was counting on me being someone who would take his word and not fact check. "My son hasn't called Mr. Beaver," I said.

"I bet you didn't know that, Mr. Foss," the policeman said, "but it was in the newspapers for everybody to read."

"If you say so."

"I'm not going to let this go, Mr. Foss. Your boy has a serious problem. Mr. Beaver is recording all his calls now; he needs to be satisfied. You have twenty-four hours to comply voluntarily."

I went outside to walk a couple of miles. I needed something to wear me out, but a half mile down the road I had to stop because my toe insisted on it. By the time I'd made my way back to the apartment, I was limping.

I sat down in the kitchen and pulled off my running shoe and my sweat sock. The skin above the curled nail was swollen and red. When I tried to lift the nail, I winced and cursed. The day's mail was on the table. Alex had opened the phone bill and circled all six of the long distance calls, each of which was to a different number in a different area code. "Porn line," he'd written beside the first one, "Hot sex" beside the second. And then "All Male," "Girl/Girl," "Threesomes," and "Underage."

I opened the phone book. I ran my finger down the Bradyburg listings to see how many Beavers lived in a town that small. There were four of them, more than I would have thought. Maybe they were all related, but I wasn't interested in sorting. Any adult male voice answering to Beaver would do.

"Hello," a man said.

"Hi," I started. "Is this Mr. Beaver?"

"Yes."

I tried to decipher whether it was the voice of a man recording his calls, and as soon as I let the first moment go by, I was stuck. How did someone recite a list of obscene proposals out loud, even if he planned to end his hard-core want-ad with the name and phone number of the only full-time police officer in a town so small it had no crime to speak of?

Just having the line open made me expect the doorbell to ring, the policeman to be standing there, Alex bounding downstairs while I explained the details of my own investigation in the living room where he could examine every one of our family photographs, the ones of Alex as a small child, the ones of my absent wife. I would tell him I was a reporter, after all. I was responsible for getting both sides of every story. And didn't he see that Alex was right? The phone bills were all the proof anybody could need. The cop would see that, even though Alex would understand I was incapable of even the smallest of solutions.

PROOFREADING

After we left Burger King, Steve Crandall said he wanted to switch seats because he was tired of sitting in between stacks of horn cases, and there was still an hour's drive along the Pennsylvania Turnpike before we reached Pittsburgh and home. "No big deal," I said, climbing in ahead of him, but he stood between the open double doors as if he expected me to change my mind and jump out if he wasn't guarding it.

He didn't step aside until Don Kohler, the other first horn who'd been riding in back of the equipment van, shuffled up. Steve didn't say anything as Don climbed in, but I knew enough to stay wedged between the cases across from Don while Steve swung the doors shut behind him and settled back with a wink. I drew my knees up and so did Don, and Steve stretched out with his hands behind his head, grinning like he'd just put his feet up on a teacher's desk.

So it was Steve who had his weight against the door as we accelerated into traffic from the on-ramp, Mr. Kohler, who was driving, swinging between two trucks that were spaced far enough apart for him to fit in if he floored it. When the door popped open at fifty-five or sixty miles per hour, Steve's legs flew up and he was gone without a sound.

The doors flapped, leaving Don and me alone with a van full of trumpets, the two of us staring out like you see animals doing from trailers, like you know something awful was happening but couldn't get a handle on it. And then Don started pounding on the glass between us and Mr. Kohler, and everything slowed down.

We never got to see Steve. We sat in the van and neither of us talked, our chins on our knees until a state trooper looked inside, running his hands along the doors while he asked us to step down and follow him to where we could sit on a patch of crown vetch that covered a slope. From there we could see the ambulance and the patrol car and the flares a quarter mile back the highway.

"You think he's dead?" Don finally said.

I shook my head, but Don didn't do anything but start to gnaw on his thumb nail. "Probably," I finally said, the first word I'd managed since Steve had vanished.

Mr. Kohler was Don's father. I remember he'd closed the doors and rapped on them twice when I'd climbed in after our show in Altoona and propped myself against them still wearing my visored hat, but he hadn't rapped on them before we'd left the Greensburg Burger King. Steve had swung them shut himself because Mr. Kohler was having a cigarette before he climbed into the driver's seat.

Steve had a skull fracture and massive head trauma. He had other broken things, too, but that's what killed him, my father explained on the way to the funeral. "It's why people wear helmets on motorcycles," he said. "And bicycles," he added, as if now I was supposed to buy one after riding a bike for almost ten years without dying.

"All right," I said, but that's as far as I could get.

"Not now, Jack," my mother said.

My father looked across the seat at her, taking his eyes off the road in a way that made me stare into the oncoming traffic. "What better time?" he asked, and she rapped her knuckles on the dashboard like a judge.

"Rex Kohler says he thought it was you who fell out," Mrs. Crandall told me at the reception before the funeral service. In the back of the room where there were 200 chairs set up, Mr. Kohler and Don were sitting by themselves four rows behind where anyone else was sitting. They'd taken those seats five minutes after I walked in and hadn't moved.

Mr. Crandall put his arm around his wife before he spoke. "To the police, he said that. Now he has to live with himself."

"There's no telling if he's at fault," Mrs. Crandall said.

Mr. Crandall raised his other arm and draped it over the shoulders of his daughter. I knew her name was Sharon, and I remembered, because Steve had told me, that she was a year behind me in school. "Yes," Mr. Crandall said. "No telling whatsoever."

Mrs. Crandall looked over at her daughter as if she expected her to duck out from under the arm and run. "Don't you ever feel guilty," Mrs. Crandall said to me. "Don't you ever."

I was glad it was the end of July. During the summer I hardly ever saw anybody from school except guys who were in drum and bugle. I'd been working just over a year for my father, who published a weekly newspaper. My mother sold ads, my father did the lay out and personally delivered those papers to every store that carried them and every mailbox that belonged to a subscriber. He had costs down to minimum, and my job was to get everything into the same font style and size, no matter how the writing came to us, some of it handwritten, even in pencil, and nearly all of it badly done. I proof-read and rewrote because, my father said on the day I started, I'd gone farther in school now than he had. "You can't count my last year," he said. "I was just there to play football, and then I quit after I tore up my knee during my junior year. Besides, you take after your mother. You're in love with details, so I'm giving them all to you to take care of."

Details meant mistakes, and they were easy to find. The people who sent in articles wrote like they'd all quit school when they'd turned sixteen. It wasn't just punctuation and spelling; those were obvious and simple. Nobody, for instance, ever used a semi-colon, but I wanted my father's paper to be better, so I began to change the sentences. It didn't take any more time to rewrite those stories about vacations, Boy Scout awards, and baseball games than it did to simply type them, but when a customer complained and then a second called as well, to say that what had been published was not what they had submitted, my father told me I couldn't change the words. "Only the punctuation," he said. "Only the spelling and the grammar," and I allowed paragraphs of nothing but simple sentences to run down a column, the same adjective to be used in five consecutive sentences, each of which had ten words or less.

Over Labor Day weekend, on Saturday, the corps put on its last show of the summer. We hadn't practiced for three weeks after the accident, and the routines were ragged, but the bleachers were packed, and everybody cheered, especially when there was a song dedicated to Steve near the end. The Crandalls were there with Sharon, and I thought they'd been invited, but it turned out that nobody had called them and asked. "It must have been awful to watch and listen," my mother said. "You'd think it would be the last place you'd want to be." I thought of worse places right away, ending with on the shoulder of the turnpike beside Steve's body. "We need to be happy in this house of ours now," my mother said. "Don't you think so?"

"Yes," I said at once, but even then I knew she meant that things had changed in a way she hadn't anticipated. She looked at me as if I was different, too, and I suppose I had to be even though I believed I wasn't.

"What does a man like Rex Kohler do with himself now?" my mother said.

"He's like Nixon," my father said. "He lives with it or he doesn't."

"You need to take such care," my mother said. "There's no end of it."

"Yes there is, Darlene," he said, "and the boy will get through this better with less hubbub."

My mother wiped her mouth with her napkin. My father's, like it always was, lay beside his plate unused, and right then it looked like something that belonged to a man who didn't know better than to use his sleeve.

"Hubbub, Frank? Hubbub?" She dropped her napkin onto her half-eaten roast beef and watched as it began to absorb gravy, turning brown along its edges the way paper does when it's burning yet there aren't any flames.

"We've been fortunate is all," my father said. "This isn't the end of the world for us. This isn't the Watergate business coming to a head. We're not thinking of resigning."

My mother picked up her plate, carried it across the kitchen, and scraped her food and the napkin into the wastebasket beside the sink, slapping the lid down in a way that reminded me how that meat and gravy would smell in there by the next day if neither my father nor I emptied it. "What do you think?" my mother said to me. "You think your mother worrying about you is hubbub?"

"No," I said, though at that moment, to tell the truth, I wanted her to shut up.

My father, the day of the funeral, had told me a story about when he was drafted into World War II. "I went down to where the draft board gave its physicals," he said. "Me and another guy who played football with me in high school. His name was Al Kopniski. He went through the line and he passed. I got taken aside because of my bum ear. We didn't talk about it afterwards. Al went and I didn't. And then he didn't make it back."

I'd stood in the shade made by the overhang of the funeral home, but my father had stood in his suit and tie in the full sun of late July. He didn't say anything else, and I thought he meant for me to understand his story without asking a question, so I nodded like I thought he expected me to, like Al Kopniski would have nodded as they got home from the draft physical.

He pushed the knot of his tie up tighter against his throat, a signal he was going back inside where the service was scheduled to begin in a few minutes, but as I stepped into the sunlight, he said, "So much of our lives is chance, Jay. It's a thing you know now."

School began the next day. I didn't see Don much because instead of playing in the marching band, I ran cross country, a sport I loved. Like always, there were no more than twenty people watching at our first meet—a few girlfriends, a couple of parents—so it was easy to spot Mrs. Crandall standing behind the fence along the track. Since Steve had never run cross country, I thought she was there to pick up Sharon from whatever she might be doing after school, and had walked across the street to the track to pass the time. We were stripping off our warm-ups when she waved, fluttering her hand, and I waved back.

A minute later, as we lined up for the lap we took around the track before we left the stadium for the next two and a half miles, I saw Sharon Crandall step up beside her. Just as the starter said, "Take your marks," her mother pointed my way.

I finished seventh, fourth on our team, one place higher than I usually did, and the Crandalls were still standing there as I crossed the finish line. Dressed in a skirt that was cut a few inches above her knees, Sharon looked different than she had at the funeral in her long dark dress.

"That was exciting," Mrs. Crandall said. "You're very good. Wasn't he, Sharon?"

Sharon smiled and nodded. I wanted to tell both of them they didn't have to wait around all that time to see how things turned out. They had time to walk to the corner and get a Coke while everybody struggled through the woods and the back road of the nearby park. "Well, Jay, we had something on our minds here besides your race,

I'll own up to that. We'd like for you and your parents to come to dinner sometime very soon. Mention it to your mother. I'll call her this evening."

"We can't say no," my mother said an hour later. "You have to do whatever someone wants when tragedy comes calling."

"Like hell," my father said, what he always uttered when it was inevitable he'd surrender.

Steve and I had been band buddies, but other than that, we didn't hang out. I'd never been to his house, and he hadn't been to mine. He'd told me his father was ten years younger than my father, but Mr. Crandall looked to be six inches shorter when they stood side by side in the Crandall's living room. And Mr. Crandall was bald, something I hadn't paid attention to at the funeral home, but now made him seem older than my father, who was fifty-four, the same age as my mother, yet acting as if he was shaking hands with the Governor of Pennsylvania.

Mr. Crandall was wearing a coat and tie, and my father looked uneasy in his open shirt. I thought about manners, how my father read the paper at the table when he ate. I saw my father look at the two forks, and I thought he was searching his memory for whether it was the outside or the inside fork for the salad. My mother picked up the outside fork and then replaced it like a signal. She smiled at me, but it was my father who touched his fork when Mrs. Crandall set the salads in front of us, picking his up first.

My mother and Mrs. Crandall did nearly all the talking at the table. Sitting beside Sharon, I had an excuse to glance at her breasts each time my mother asked her a question about school. I was happy with that arrangement, but Mrs. Crandall, once she'd cleared the salad plates, didn't ask me anything, and by the time everyone had a chance to help themselves to seconds if they wanted, I thought a stranger would think only women and girls could talk during dinner.

I tried to remember what country I'd read about where only the men talked at the table, but all I could picture was women wearing full length dresses and veils. For all I knew those women chattered away through the cloth that covered their faces, but it didn't seem likely.

I was nearly finished when Sharon said something about geometry, taking a breath that lifted her breasts between sentences. "Cat got your tongue, Jay?" Mrs. Crandall said.

"No," I said, but it was one of those questions that didn't encourage more than a one-word answer, and I felt myself swallowing as if I'd played a wrong note. My mother peered my way, examining me, I thought, wondering who I'd become. I reached for my water glass, trying to keep from freezing up the way I did when I waited to be photographed, but when I lifted it I realized she was evaluating herself, how she looked to the Crandalls because of me, and I replaced the glass without drinking and looked to the side at Sharon and smiled.

"Well," my father said in the car. "That was interesting."

We lived only half a mile from the Crandalls, but my mother, even though the weather was perfect, had insisted we'd drive because "that's what needs to be done."

"We can do our part," my mother said. "Our little bit can be all for the best in the long run. You just have to wait and see."

My father didn't answer. It was as if my mother was talking about heaven. No matter how hard it was to believe in God, there was always "the long run" to dangle like bait.

The trip was short, and my father got out of the car immediately and went in the house. "Stay out for a minute," my mother said. I saw the lights come on in the kitchen, my father disappear into the living room where another light came on. "It's such a warm evening, it feels like a lie," my mother said. "And in the dark you can't see how the green is going out of the trees."

"I think Dad is pissed because he didn't know how to act at dinner."

I thought my mother would agree, but instead, as if I hadn't spoken, she said, "I've always thought the quality in a man I couldn't abide was his not being trustworthy."

"That makes sense," I said, but I thought at once she meant to tell me I was becoming that sort of man.

"Do you think so, too?" she said. "That's good. She put her hand on mine and squeezed.

I didn't say anything else. I saw my father return to the kitchen and open the refrigerator as if we hadn't finished a long dinner an hour earlier. All I had to do was let her get around to being more specific if she needed to. "Consider on that, then," she said. "You're nearly who you're going to be."

"I will," I said at once, though I thought who I was going to be seemed a long way off. That my mother, fifty-four years old like my father, might be dead before anything like that had happened to me.

"You were a gift," she said, and she let go of my hand and walked into the house.

The next day, as I stood at my locker, Sharon walked toward me as if we were friends. She said "Hi," and handed me an envelope. Inside was a note on stationery, a light purple flower I didn't recognize in the top left and lower right hand corners. "Jay," it read, "would you go to the Turning of the Leaves Dance with me next Saturday?" All of the letters were printed, but even the i was curved. There was a real invitation inside the envelope, one of those kind that's made at a print shop and says RSVP on the bottom. The Hidden Valley Country Club, it said. The letters were raised, and I ran my fingers over them from left to right.

I slid it between the pages of my chemistry book, but when I saw Sharon standing by the track while we practiced after school,

I decided that even if he'd never know, saying "Yes" was one thing I could do for Steve. "Sure," I said, getting the word out before I even got close.

"Thank you," Sharon said, and I tried to figure what came next.

"Maier," Coach Brazleton shouted. "The track goes this way." I heard guys laughing, but I was happy to be singled out. All I had to say was "See you."

The next day, a Saturday, Sharon watched our meet with her mother again. I ran a time two seconds slower than the meet before, but the other team was weak, so when I finished fourth, there were only three guys from my team ahead of me.

"You nearly won," Mrs. Crandall said, although I'd seen Greg Linkinfelter, our best runner, standing on the infield as I entered the track for the last quarter mile. She reached over and held Sharon's hand. "I'm so looking forward to seeing the two of you all dressed up," she said.

My mother looked puzzled when I asked her on Sunday whether or not she thought I needed to buy a corsage for a dance like the one described on the invitation. "How strange," she said. "Maybe you just made a good impression the other night."

I wanted to tell her about the cross country meet, but I said, "Her parents will be there, too. It's mostly for old people, I think."

"Yes, I think you're right about that. Unless other parents encourage their teenagers to go to something like this."

I handed the corsage to Sharon as I walked in the door the next Saturday night. Mrs. Crandall ooohed and aaahed for a full minute, pinning it on the strap of Sharon's dress so close to her breast that I could stare without worrying. "You look so nice together," Mrs. Crandall said, taking our picture five times before she said, "Well, I have to go make myself presentable," and disappeared down the hall.

From where we were standing as she took our picture, I could see Mr. Crandall sitting at the kitchen table. He was having a drink, his hand not leaving the glass even when it was resting on the table, but he was facing away from us, so it was like Sharon and I were alone when her mother closed her bedroom door.

I hadn't paid any attention to the Crandall's house when we'd come to dinner, but now I noticed, as we stood in the living room, that there wasn't a television. I'd never seen a living room without one. There were bookshelves along three walls. There were magazines arranged so thickly on a coffee table that I thought of a doctor's office waiting room. It was as if Mr. Crandall sat in some other room in the house keeping appointments with people who read to keep their minds off what they might hear in a few minutes.

Across from the green couch was a place where a television belonged, the carpet bright where no one walked. That spot, unused, looked like a room nobody entered. "How old are you?" Sharon said.

"Almost sixteen." As soon as I said it, I thought I was an asshole for not saying fifteen.

"Be more exact," she said. "When's your birthday?"

"In six weeks and two days."

I could tell she was calculating something. "Steve was fifty-three days older than you. When he was your age, he was still alive."

And had less than a week to live, I thought, the numbers taking the blood out of my groin. I thought if I spoke the words would show what a shit head I was. I moved farther from where Mr. Crandall was sitting, and she followed me, standing close to me now, the corsage nearly glowing in the soft light of one shaded lamp. "Our birthdays are only a day apart. Did you know that?" she said.

"No."

"When you were one year old, I was being born. We'd have the same birthday if everything happened quicker. I came out at 12:13—isn't that something?"

"I think I was born late at night," I said.

"Why don't you know?"

I shrugged. I'd tried to make her story better by pretending our birthdays were even closer, but I had no idea what time of day I was born. "You should ask. It's something everybody should know."

"So you're almost fifteen?"

She smiled. "You could say that."

The Crandalls were already sitting in the front seat by the time I closed Sharon's door and slid into the back of their Lincoln. Mrs. Crandall reached back and pushed the lock button down on my door. Mr. Crandall didn't turn around, but Sharon, before Mrs. Crandall faced forward, touched her lock even though it was already down.

Mr. Crandall stopped to greet two men in dark suits that looked exactly like his, and I fumbled with the buttons on my sport coat, trying to decide which one should be hooked. "Don't worry, Jay," Mrs. Crandall said. "Young people aren't required to be up tight." She guided me and Sharon to a huge window. Hidden Valley, it turned out, was what you could see from the clubhouse behind the eighteenth green of the private golf course. The hillside ran down to the thick woods of what she told me was a state game preserve. "It's so nice to know that property can't be developed," she said.

"I've never seen this," I said, and she patted my shoulder.

"Now you have, Jay. It's beautiful, isn't it?"

After we were introduced to a dozen old couples, all of the men in those dark suits, Sharon and I walked away from the Crandalls. There wasn't anything to do but circle the room until we had to stop on the opposite side, but Sharon smiled. "Ok," she said. "We're safe now."

The band was playing a slow song, but it was too soon to be dancing. Only three couples were on the floor, all of them older looking than my parents. "We can sit down," I said. "We can talk for a while."

"Do you think so?" she said, the sound of that question putting me off.

"I'm not your brother," I said, right off, and she pressed her hand over my arm the way I'd seen my mother do with Mrs. Crandall at the funeral home.

"My parents are watching us," she said, taking her hand away. "I feel like a tree they've just planted, like they're watching to see if the leaves will fall off."

"We can dance," I said. "We can act like old people."

She smiled and things skidded back into normal. "Ok," she said. "Let's get old together," and when her expression didn't change, I slipped my arm around her and shuffled my feet.

After a few seconds Sharon moved close to me, and when her breasts pressed against my chest, I felt myself getting hard. "Oh" she said, backing away a bit and looking down.

"Sorry."

"It's nice," she said. "I'm glad dancing with me makes you feel that way."

Monday morning, Don Kohler was standing beside my locker holding his trumpet case as if he was ready to use it as defense against getting kicked in the balls. "They tested that door," he said. "It took fifty tries, but it popped open again." He stared at me, his free hand clenching.

"All right," I said.

"My father wants you to know," Don said, but his eyes shifted away, and I turned to see Sharon standing five feet behind me with three girls I didn't know. Because tenth grade was where you started in our high school, they had to be her age, but she looked older than all of them. My eyes went right to her chest, how the blouse she wore stretched tight over those breasts that had pressed against me the Saturday before. "Hi there," she said at once. The other girls looked at me like I'd just moved there, evaluating me. They were ordinary looking girls, and so, I knew, was Sharon, but until that dance I'd never had a girl press against me, even the three girls I'd kissed had all held back a little as if they were thinking about what we were doing. I'd kissed Sharon in the hallway of the country club after two songs, and she'd pushed against me the way I imagined girls doing when I was masturbating in my room.

"Hi," I said, but my voice cracked, and when one of the girls giggled, I thought Sharon had told her every detail about my reaction to her body.

On Tuesday, Mrs. Crandall and Sharon were at our meet, but they didn't stand together. I looked from one to the other as I took off my warm-ups, and both of them appeared to be memorizing how I slid my sweatpants over my running shoes. I took off in a near sprint when the gun sounded, and by the time we left the track to enter the woods, I'd opened up twenty yards on the nearest runner. "Rabbit," I heard a guy from the other team shout, but I didn't slow down.

A half mile later, when the narrow path broadened and began to climb a grassy hill, I slowed down, letting five guys pass me, but instead of falling into my usual spot, I slowed even more until fourteen other runners passed me, even Rob Coyle, our weakest runner, who was gasping as if he'd just fallen out of a boat. When he crested the hill, I stopped altogether and began to walk. At the top of the hill I could see everybody loop back into where the woods thickened again and there were two judges stationed to keep guys from cheating, and then I doubled back and sat down against a tree until I knew enough time had passed for even Rob Coyle to finish.

I headed toward where the course went into the woods for the first time, and just as I stepped out, I saw Mrs. Crandall enter the woods where runners came out before they returned to the track. I didn't see Sharon. If she was looking for me, she was already in those woods. There wasn't anybody left on the track but Coach Brazleton, but I'd already started to limp before I crossed the infield toward him. "Maier," he said, "I figured you for throwing up out there. You went out so fast, I thought I was watching fox and hounds."

He looked down at my feet as I hesitated, keeping my weight on one foot. "There's three guys out there right now. We sent out a posse, but it looks like they'll come back empty-handed."

"Sorry."

"And your mother's out there, too. She was all wound up."

"I saw her."

"She'll be relieved, but who knows how long a mother will search before she checks back to see what's up."

I nodded and limped toward the locker room. The other team's bus was pulling away, and I knew we'd won or else Coach Brazleton would have been nasty with me for running like an idiot.

I asked the student manager for ice. "It's not too bad," he said. "It's hardly even swollen."

Rob Coyle looked me over. "I thought you made yourself sick," he said. "I thought you quit."

"I stepped in a hole. I thought I broke my ankle for a minute."

"It's ok," he said. "I stopped to puke when I got back into the woods. I didn't feel so bad when I knew you were barfing too. I waited for a while to see if you were coming."

A half hour later Sharon and her mother were still waiting on the sidewalk. I limped toward them so heavily my knee began to ache. "You poor thing," Mrs. Crandall said at once. "And Sharon was so beside herself she went to the car."

Sharon crossed one bare calf over the other, and for a moment I thought of ballet. "I stepped in a hole," I said, and she put her weight back on both legs.

"Come to dinner Friday night," Mrs. Crandall said. "You won't be dancing, but some comfort food will do you good."

"All right," I said, though what I wanted to do just then was sprint across the stretch of grass that separated the school from the street.

When Friday arrived, I told my mother I was going out for pizza with friends from cross country. "There's no meet tomorrow," I said. "It's the only empty Saturday all season, so we're splurging."

"Enjoy," she said. "And it's nice to see you in a sweater and collared shirt instead of those t-shirts."

"It's getting cold at night now."

"Good. If that makes you dress better, I can't wait for winter." She fussed with my collar, tugging it up in the back. "The Crandalls aren't suing Rex Kohler," she said, letting go of my shirt and stepping back to recheck me. "Isn't that a surprise these days? That there are people who actually know money can't buy back what's been lost?"

"Dad says we should sue Nixon," I said, and she laughed.

"Your father's being facetious," she said, "and he doesn't know it."

"How's that ankle of yours?" Mr. Crandall asked as I stepped through the door. "You looked just fine coming up the walk."

"It's better."

"You young people. You heal right up."

"You make yourself at home," Mrs. Crandall said from the kitchen. She had the oven open, peering inside at a piece of meat that looked large enough for Thanksgiving. "Sharon went back to her room when she saw you. Girl things. Go tell that daughter of mine she has five minutes to get out here. Just knock on her door."

Mr. Crandall walked into the living room and sat on the couch. With his left hand, he picked up a magazine, spread it open, then lifted a drink off the small table beside the arm rest with his right. Mrs. Crandall shooed me down the hall with the baster she was holding. "Go ahead," she said. "Don't be bashful. The two of you can have time to yourselves while I'm finishing up here. The second door on your right."

Besides the one to the bathroom at the end of the hall, there were three other doors, one of which was open, letting me see into an enormous bedroom that I knew belonged to Sharon's parents because the wall above the bed was covered with photographs of golf outings and business meetings. Since I knew which closed door was Sharon's, the one next to hers had to be Steve's.

I knocked on Sharon's door to give my hand something to do besides try the doorknob to Steve's room, and she opened it so quickly, catching me still looking at Steve's door, I thought she'd been listening to my footsteps. "I still go in there at night," she said.

"Sorry," I said. "It just made me think, you know."

"Sure. Come on in." She backpedaled, and I followed her inside. "I could always hear him through the wall," Sharon said. "Just moving around, you know. The littlest things. Sometimes I think I hear him now, but I know it can't be, and I'm always surprised when I go in and it hasn't changed."

I'd never been in a girl's bedroom before. I didn't have a sister or even a cousin who was a girl who lived nearby. What I noticed first was an edge of lace that was caught in one of her dresser drawers. It was beige and Sharon saw where I was looking before I could turn away. "Oh," she said, "that shouldn't be there," and she opened the drawer and smoothed what I knew was a slip back into place. Before she could close the drawer again, I saw her bras lying beside the slip.

"I like things neat," she said. "My dad says my bed would pass inspection in the army."

The spread was pulled so tight, I believed her, but with all the furniture she had, a desk and two bookshelves, there wasn't much room to stand except close to each other, and I stood so awkwardly Sharon pushed the door shut to make more room. "There," she said, but as soon as that door shut I felt myself going hard, and there was no place to sit and hide myself except on her perfectly made bed. I turned as if I wanted to look out the window, but the drapes were pulled shut, and she stepped up beside me. "It's ok," she said, and though I didn't know what she meant by that I kissed her then and moved my hand onto her breast. She stepped back, but she didn't turn away, and she undid three buttons on her blouse and let me stare at her white bra.

"Dinner's ready," her father called from down the hall. I looked at the door and then back at Sharon, but she hadn't touched the buttons of her blouse. "He never opens it," she said.

"It's on the table, you two," he said, his voice sounding closer.

"We're coming," she shouted, her hands moving to the lowest button, but she still had two to go when the door opened, her father looking from her to me, his face flushed.

"Under my roof," Mr. Crandall said. "You little prick."

"Sorry," I said.

"Don't say that. You're not sorry. What were you going to do if that door was locked like you thought it was?"

I brushed past, ducking because I half-expected him to club me with his fist. Mrs. Crandall was at the end of the hall, potholders on both hands like Betty Crocker in my mother's old cookbooks. I couldn't look at her as I passed, but I paused at the front door, listening for Sharon's voice. "God damn you to hell," Mr. Crandall shouted while I fumbled the door open.

I hurried down the Crandall's driveway, but I slowed when Mr. Crandall didn't follow. I looked back and saw Mrs. Crandall in the kitchen window, and I told myself this was all for the best in the long run, and as soon as I formed the words, I was sorry they'd surfaced, that there was a terrible thing in me to imagine such a lie.

I crossed the street, but when I turned again, somebody had switched off the kitchen light. I had enough distance between me and the Crandall's house to stop. A few seconds later, the light in the living room went off, so there were two windows from which somebody could be watching, but it was impossible to know who. What I did know was that from where I was standing, I could wait however long it took for all of the lights in that house to go dark.

SUBSIDENCE

I promised my wife Joyce the sort of vacation she wanted when she was going in for her operation. "You fight this thing," I said. "You let the doctors do their work, and we'll go on that cruise." She smiled because she knew I hadn't taken as much as a week off in thirty years from the two pizza shops I own, so fifteen days was a promise I didn't make lightly. It was an act of faith in my managers and in the doctors who said Joyce would be ok as long as she took it easy. What else do you do on a cruise except take it easy? I thought, but now, coming home after so much sitting around, the first thing we see as we enter the housing plan is sawhorses with reflectors and so many stretched strips of crime-scene tape that it looks as if a bunch of middle-school boys have gotten their hands on it and used it like toilet paper at Halloween.

"What's happened?" Joyce wants to know. "A gas leak?" She's sitting up and holding her purse against her chest, but I shake my head and slow down to take a good look before I answer.

A hundred yards from our house, the street that crosses the one we live on is blocked completely on the downhill side by sawhorses with blinking lights. ROAD CLOSED is repeated on three signs that stretch across the street as it drops into the darkness. We see mailboxes tipped toward sunken yards, houses with heavy equipment parked near the shrubbery. "Oh my," Joyce says. "It's everywhere," and I don't ask her to be more specific. The lights are out in every house leading to the next parallel street below us. I keep driving, coming through the curve just before our house turns visible. The Reiger's yard and the Neumann's and the Erdley's—they all have those sawhorses across their driveways, but their mailboxes are standing up straight, and there's nothing in the yards but grass and bushes and trees, an arrangement that gives me hope.

I see that there isn't a light on in those three houses closest to us and across the street. It's exactly 9:20. Nobody we know goes to bed then, not all three of those families on the same night at least, the Reigers and the Neumanns twenty years younger, the women teachers, so they're not on vacation like Joyce and me in the middle of September.

"They've all left over there," I say. "Something's happened to their houses."

Joyce hunches down to get a better look at our own house as we turn into the driveway, and we sit there for a minute without talking until she says, "The Jaworski's have a light on. That's got to be a good sign."

A better sign, I think, but not necessarily good, the Jaworskis our neighbors on just the one side. I take the flashlight from the glove compartment, and Joyce clutches my arm. "You go on in the house," I say. "I'm only having a look is all." I flick the switch, and the light comes on in the car as if we're about to search for something small and missing. "And don't you be lifting even one of those suitcases while I'm gone," I add, pulling my arm away before she can ask to walk along.

I cross the street and step into Ed Erdley's yard, seeing at once that someone has dug a ditch along the side of his house and around the back corner. There is a crack running through the cinderblock the length of the side, and it branches near the corner into ten feet of something that looks like fangs.

Out back there's a sinkhole in Ed's yard so deep I'm afraid to get near its edge. A truck would be in over its roof. Even one of those ones jacked up on top of oversized tires. The Reiger's yard is level, but I don't have to get close to see that one corner of the frame has slid off the foundation. The old coal mines, I think. We'd been living here more than fifty years and knew they'd closed up ten years before that, but subsidence hadn't been a problem, not then and not ever, and nobody had thought about it since Ed Erdley and Tom Neumann had built the last houses on our street thirty years ago.

"It looks bad for those folks," I tell Joyce after I haul her suitcases inside. "It looks like their places took a beating."

"You can't tell something like that for sure from just looking," Joyce says, and I give her that, but my mind's not changed one bit. I empty my suitcase, scattering everything across the bed, so I have a reason to go downstairs without worrying her. I check every wall in the basement. I slip outside and walk the perimeter of our house before I go out in the dark to my tennis court, what fills half the lot next door to our house on the side away from the Jaworskis, and check, by moonlight, to see if any cracks have opened up on the surface. It's no different than tending to a house, one more thing to worry about.

Joyce sleeps in, but I drive to both pizza shops first thing in the morning. You find things out before nine a.m. Whether people clean up the way they should. Whether they're careful. Tables, counters, ovens, the floor where people might not notice but they could if they were looking.

At eleven o'clock, I call Joyce to see how she's feeling. I call again at one, and she tells me to stop. "You think I'm all of a sudden going to fall apart because the cruise is over?" she says. "You think it was like 'Make-a-Wish' where the kids are as good as dead by the time they go to Disneyworld?"

I'm driving through the plan by five-twenty, counting just over thirty houses closed, not including the ones across the street from us on the shortest road in Hillside View because the houses there end almost before they start, the road winding up the hill to the old Miller place that's still surrounded by so much forested land you can't see it from our porch. Only the one street is closed, but there's damage creeping out two blocks from it on either side by the looks of the sawhorses.

The loop takes five minutes, and still I'm home earlier than I ever am, surprising Joyce by bringing her a pie with broccoli and mushrooms, her favorite, before she starts fussing around the kitchen and has something on the stove. "Nobody answers the phone across the street," she says as we eat, "but Janet Jaworski says it all happened overnight, that for three days now she's been holding her breath."

I finish a second slice, the first pizza I've had in sixteen days. I'm thinking about starting in on a third when I see Ed Erdley drive across his front lawn so he can park right up close to his garage on the other side of the sawhorses. "Look at that, would you?" I say. "Don't be surprised if Ed and Anne are gone for good before long." Joyce doesn't finish the crust from her one slice, but she drops it into the box and slides what's left over into the refrigerator. "I'm going over there," I say.

"Hurry then," Joyce says, "before it gets worse."

The closest tunnels, according to the map Ed shows me a few minutes later, spreading it out on the roof of his car, run along the back yards of the houses on his side of the street. "According to this here, our lot is just inside the safe zone," he says, "but somebody missed their distances a bit."

"A few feet," I say.

Ed nods. "That's all it takes." He folds the map so many times it nearly disappears into his hand. "Come on in and take a look," and I follow him as if he's offered a beer from his refrigerator.

"You can't tell, can you?" Erdley says. The light is starting to fade, September half over, but Ed doesn't hit any of the switches when he leads me into the house. Disconnected, I think, but I'm not about to ask.

"What?" I say, though I know he means the way the house feels under my feet, whether I can sense it isn't exactly level now.

"If you woke up in here and didn't look outside, you'd think the world was just fine and dandy."

"It doesn't feel like it's tilted or anything, if that's what you mean."

"But it's wounded. You know, like a ship with a hole torn in its side. Like the goddamned Titanic. You can stand on the deck and pretend everything's ok for a while, but it's just a matter of time before you're in the ocean."

"Houses don't go under."

"That's what you think. Wait until you wake up one morning and wonder where this here one has gone."

I walk through the back door onto his porch. I expect to feel safer outside, but now I can see the sinkhole up close, and it feels like the world could open beneath us and drop us straight down to China.

Erdley hurries past me and into the yard, and for a moment I think he's going to lower himself over the edge and ask me to climb down inside with him. Instead, he turns left and disappears around the corner of the house as if he's heard somebody calling his name.

It takes less than a minute before I feel like that house is about to collapse. No matter how far-fetched it is to think that way. No matter that there is room enough, three feet or thereabouts, between the house and the sinkhole, a place to walk like Erdley has just done. No matter for any of the common sense things I come up with, because when I turn and try the back door and find it locked, my heart begins to beat like it does after a long rally on my court, and I have to work at keeping my eyes open so I won't imagine the floor going out from under me or begin to pound on the door like a boy scared out of his back yard tent by rustling in the shrubbery.

I take a breath and count to ten before I take another. A minute of that and I'm settled enough to step off the porch and allow the earth to hold me up. Out front, when I get there, Ed's by his car. I see he has boxes on the back seat—dishes, I think, clothes, photographs. He's carried them out of the kitchen or the bedroom while I worried about nothing on the porch. "Not one sign of trouble over your way," Ed says. "Even that tennis court of yours. It's perfect by the looks of it."

"It takes work," I say, and when he doesn't react, I add, "Like everything."

"Up until this past week, I always thought if you ever needed the money, you could sell that lot for a pretty penny, the only one left up here with just the Leckeys on the upper side there, and then all those trees like we live next to a state park."

I'd bought that extra lot for another $850 in 1953, six weeks after I'd married Joyce when she graduated from high school. I'd always wanted a tennis court, a real one made of clay, not just a parking lot with lines, and I'd had it built fifteen years later when the boys were growing up, but they didn't take to the game, so all the grounds keeping duties fell to me after they put their rackets away in high school. You water it and you roll it and it's beautiful to play on, easy on the knees. It's the surface that keeps you busy, getting the nicks and scratches healed. And it's the boundary tape you worry about when it shows signs of not lying flat or curling a bit, tugging loose. You see the smallest part of it go wrong, and there's a problem that needs attending or you can count on trouble.

"You know, when I looked at lots and wanted to be up here on the short street," Erdley says, "there were the two on my side and that one of yours. We would have been next-door neighbors if you were selling. You have a better view over here."

206

"Neumeyer," I say. "He held on to two lots on your side. That's why they were still there for the taking when you came by. He bought three when he built. He was an investor, and then he died and all of it went with the estate. It was George Reiger buying Neumeyer's and selling the lots for the windfall. I was just lucky."

"Tennis." Ed says the word like the name of a rival high school when you're about to play football against them. "All these years I've been wondering how you come by something like that? Nobody around here plays it."

"My mother thought it would help me get along in the world. We couldn't afford golf."

"I only ever see that fellow in the Saab with the college sticker on the bumper swinging a racket out there. There's plenty of courts up that way."

"The college has asphalt. I have Hard-Tru."

"That powder of yours has a name?"

"Yes."

"Of course it does."

Erdley looks up past Neumann's to where the last two houses are still open for business. I think he's going to tell me how one of them was for sale when he moved in, that he could have bought one of them and still have a roof over his head, but he says, "I used to help deliver coal. Isn't that a kick in the pants?"

"Yes," I say right off, and he explains how when the truck came, the driver dumped the coal in the alley behind the houses on the street where he lived as a boy. "People forget how coal was still burned in furnaces right after the war," he says. "The families who lived in those houses would hire me and my brother. A lot of places had basement windows that were under the back porch. One of us shoveled the coal into bushel baskets, and the other had to get under that porch, take the basket, and hand it down to whoever lived there. You wanted to be using the shovel if you could. There's not much worse than breathing coal dust."

I think of Joyce, what might be worse, but I keep that to myself.

"You ever been in a mine?" Ed says.

"No."

"It's right next door to hell. My brother ended up there."

Because I can't remember ever meeting Erdley's brother, I imagine he's dead, that Erdley is about to tell me how coal killed that brother and has a leg up on doing the same to him. "I'm not supposed to go into my own goddamned house," Ed says. "Can you imagine?"

"I haven't seen either Reiger or Neumann since we got back."

"I don't know about Neumann, but George Reiger emptied his place. He had a mover haul everything away the second day after. You go over and take a look inside. Next there'll be kids in there doing God knows what."

I look at Reiger's house and wish I didn't know it was hollow. "Taking care is supposed to matter," Ed says. "God damn it to hell anyway."

My doubles partner Larry, the guy in the Saab, drives down from the college that sits twelve miles up the road. He's seventy-one and still teaching. Here I am seventy-four with the pizza shops still going while Ed Erdley, sixty-eight now, has been praising his retirement for three years, sitting in front of his television on that back porch where there's something else to watch now besides detective shows.

Larry's kept his legs under him like I have, and last year we were doubles champs at the Pennsylvania senior Olympics, seventy and over. We didn't practice against anybody all summer, or this summer, for that matter, because nobody in my neighborhood plays the game. But this year, the week before the cruise, we'd lost in the finals, "A step back, partner," Larry said as we left the court. Both members of the other team were barely seventy years old.

A few months before that, he said he wanted to be called Laurence. "It's his name," Joyce said when I complained. "What's wrong with wanting to be called by your name?"

"Because it's Laurence," I said. "Nobody is Laurence except guys who are afraid to get their hands dirty."

"He's not that bad," Joyce said, sounding like the President supporting another dictator so a Socialist or a Fundamentalist doesn't take power, but she wasn't considering how, two years ago when we'd started playing together, just before his 70th birthday made him eligible to become my partner for our first Senior Olympics, Larry had swept the court with the wide broom after we finished, hung it up, and told me I should hire some neighbor boys to clean up after us. Since then, he brings sports drinks in a cooler. And one light beer for afterwards when he acts as if I've taken his advice and the boys will show up to do maintenance. "The refreshment committee," Joyce calls him, because he acts as if he's volunteered, that he is being generous.

Those sports drinks are the color of toilet bowl cleaner. I sip mine to be polite, and he takes large swallows while he reminds me to stay hydrated. The beer I finish in a minute, holding the bottle while he drains his so slowly I think he is waiting for it to get warm so he can drink like the British.

I called him Larry until I stopped calling him anything. I can't say "Laurence" any more than I can say words like "cleanse" and "intercourse."

Or a phrase like "My time in the hospital," how Joyce puts her problems rather than mention any of the parts of her that have been removed.

·

Larry shows up at 6:30 the third day we're home and wonders about the disaster across the street each time we switch sides of the court. "Have you investigated your options?" he says as we finish, each of us holding that one light beer.

"Insurance?"

"Liability. Reparations."

There it is, I think, noticing Ed Erdley pull across his lawn. Reparations. As if you could ever manage to be paid enough to get back to even.

Ed surprises me by walking right up to the court and looking through the fence as if he expects us to put our beer down and play. "My doubles partner," I say to him, and turning to Larry, "my neighbor Ed."

Larry takes my empty bottle and replaces it in his cooler for recycling. "You read about something like this environmental disaster, and it doesn't make an impression until you witness it for yourself," he says. "This could make for a modern day Molly Maguire scenario."

Erdley grips the fence with both hands. "The Molly Maguires had it goddamned right," he says. "People need to be heard, or else the world ought to duck its head."

"I'd wager that the township commissioners had an inkling," Larry says. "I'd expect they'd been told about this possibility a generation or more ago."

"Yeah?" Erdley says. He's never approached the court before Larry leaves, but now he leans into the fence as if he's being pushed from behind. "Why didn't I ever hear about it?"

Larry slips his empty bottle into his cooler and looks at Erdley for a moment as if he's spoken up without raising his hand. "People privy to such things don't live here," he says.

Ed glances my way and steps back from the fence. Laurence, I want to say. Of course. As I open the gate, Ed retreats two steps. "So many mines," he says. "So many things under the ground we don't know what we have down there anymore."

I agree, but in front of Larry I don't bring up nuclear refuse, toxic medical waste, all of the plastic and such that will outlast us by thousands of years. For now, the residents of our housing plan have had their fortunes told by coal: Here, it formed. There, it did not.

In the weekly newspaper that carries all our local news is a notice about a meeting of home owners affected by "the major subsidence incident." I park in front of the fire hall, where a meeting has already begun with township officials and a set of engineering and mining experts. The hall is packed, every chair taken, a row of people, all men, jammed along both side walls. I stand in the back as one by one, seventeen in all while I watch, homeowners walk to the microphone in the center aisle and voice their anger. After each speech, limited, apparently, to two minutes, there's a round of applause, whether the speaker is loud or soft, profane or polite. Every one of them cites damage to his house or property, and because I recognize a face or two, I know how far down the hill behind Erdley's the subsidence goes.

When the first engineer begins to deliver his assurances, Erdley taps me on the shoulder. "You curious?" he says.

"I want to know as much as the next man."

"The lucky ones don't get to speak," which doesn't explain why he hasn't gone to the microphone.

I don't see Leckey or Jaworski, but by the numbers in the room I know there are families here whose houses haven't been mortally wounded. "Luckier than some doesn't make me lucky," I say, the words of the engineer drowned out by a chorus of protests from the crowd.

Erdley throws one hand out toward the center of the room. "It must be like driving past a wreck every day. You take a look and keep driving."

"I never paid any attention to where those mines were located," I say. "We were kids when we moved in. When you're a kid you don't pay attention to something like this. I thought the closest shaft was at the end of the street. Back when we had sewers put in forty years ago, I thought old man Miller was kidding when he said he didn't need to tap in because he dumped everything down a mine shaft. I thought he was cheap. You know how the rich can be, but I always thought if I took it on myself to take a look back there I'd see a green spot somewhere, the kind that gives a septic tank away."

"Listen to that," Ed says. I think he's making fun of me, but he's staring down the center aisle, and I realize I haven't heard a word the engineer's been saying.

Friday evening Larry calls to worry about us losing light in the early evening now that September's starting to wind down. He's anxious to play, but how about in the afternoon because he can manage any one of four days during the week. "What kind of job is professor that Larry can play tennis at two o'clock?" I ask Joyce.

"Like yours," Joyce says. "You could make time, too, if you wanted to."

"I could sleep in and let Frank and Vince run everything like we're on another cruise."

"You could."

"And then what would I do with myself?"

"Relax."

"Relax comes after work, not in place of it," but when Joyce sighs, I give in and tell Larry next Tuesday at four, just about splitting the difference. I tell him it's a trial run, that playing before dinner might not work out for me with the shops. First thing in the morning we drive the seventy miles to spend the weekend at our older son's. His daughter is pregnant and visiting, and Joyce is anxious for the child to be born. "I want to see her," she says. "I want to hold my great-granddaughter and know she's real."

"It's just three months now," I say. "She'll be here before you know it."

"Three months is longer than you think."

"You're doing fine," I say.

"So far."

"So far is good. So far is all anyone can count on."

I don't notice the holes in the court until Monday morning. "Who would do such a thing?" Joyce says, coming out to look after she hears me cursing. When I don't answer right off, she says, "Kids, I'll bet. "Who else could climb that fence so high all the way around with the gate locked like it is?"

Four holes. Somebody with a shovel digging a foot deep in three by five foot rectangles just inside the service line in each box. The soil and the gray Hard-Tru powder are all mixed up in piles inside and around the holes. What's remarkable is that the vandals have swept the court behind them. I can see how they'd dragged the broom right up to the gate, something I can't imagine kids bothering to do unless they somehow thought the soles of their shoes would leave distinctive marks. "It looks like somebody who could pick a lock maybe."

"If you can pick a lock," Joyce says, "you make sure you get yourself something worthwhile for your trouble. Whoever did this isn't a lock-picker. They could have climbed right there. The gate has an extra place to put your feet."

"Does a lock look damaged when it's picked?" I say. "Can you tell?"

Joyce looks at me as I examine the lock again. "What? You think one of our neighbors did that damage?" she says, and I nod at the holes as if they prove something. "Like Ed Erdley?" she says then. "My God, Harold. He's been our neighbor for thirty years."

"Until this happened, he was. Now he's a refugee."

"That's crazy talk. He knows we didn't make his foundation crack."

"You look at that sinkhole in your yard long enough, and pretty soon you don't think the way you used to."

"So he decides to dig us a bunch of holes? Think about that. It's like the terrorists who want to give us diseases because they're sick of their own lives."

I don't answer. "You can't think that way," she says, "or you'll be over there burning down his house some night."

"He'll feel better then," I say. "He'll know he was right to dig these holes."

"It can be fixed, Harold."

"Somehow."

"And next year you'll be seventy-five and young again for the next age group in the Olympics."

"But Larry will only be seventy-two. I win a set from him now and then, but he already thinks the three years is making a difference."

"He was just upset about losing this time."

"You'll see. I'll be playing out of my age group, and he knows that. And now this."

"Laurence wouldn't dump you like that."

"I don't know anybody close to my age who plays," I say. "I'll never find a new partner."

"There's the singles," Joyce says. "There's bound to be just a few playing that at seventy-five."

"Eight," I say. "I checked. And every one of them was paired with another for the doubles. It was like incest."

For my whole life I've always imagined myself a carrier of justice, someone who would at least attempt to square things that didn't sit right. I've fired maybe ten men on the spot for drinking and twice that, equally between men and women, for stealing. I've waited until the end of the shift to fire thirty or more men and women for habitually being late. I told all of them I needed to trust people in order to run two pizza shops. It's my risk, not theirs, I said, and though exactly eight of the men cursed me, that was the end of it.

I've defended my sons against the petty wrongs of adolescence. I fought a man, once, a father like myself, who'd allowed his boy to drive his car at fourteen with my older son as a passenger, a trip that ended against two trees.

That one man I'd hit in the face, taking him by surprise before we'd wrestled each other to the ground and exhausted ourselves with expletives and holding each other at bay.

But now Erdley has done this digging. I'm sure of it. Neumann barely knows me; Reiger has been gone since the beginning. There's no one else to think I'm responsible for his house. To think my tennis court has cracked his foundation. I send Larry an e-mail. I tell him we're off for a week because the court is damaged.

It was Ray Neumann who'd told me once that the doctor who'd bought the Miller place still piped his sewage into a mine shaft. He'd taken a hike, new to the street, to get the lay of the land, and discovered where the pipe peeked out of the ground before it turned down into a space carved into a heavy wooden cover "out a ways from the house like you'd expect."

I've never walked back to verify that story. What did I care if Miller and the doctor I've never met piped their shit into a hole in the ground? It was their smell and a long way to anything that was mine, but with no tennis to be played, I follow the street past Leckey's to where the asphalt ends and the stretch of crushed stone begins. It's another hundred yards to the house where old man Miller lived when I purchased the lots from him. "Those mines come right up close," Miller told me when I bought, "but they've never been a problem for anybody who's bought from me."

A few years later Miller sold off all the lots to a developer. He kept twelve acres for himself, refusing the township services. His road was private, he said. He had his own well. He could take care of himself, and that included not hooking on to the sewer.

It was the sort of arrangement some men can always make. Miller died just after Erdley built, and that doctor who bought the property is an old man now who owns three antique cars and drives an SUV so large it could pass for one of those small buses that haul the crippled and the retarded to school. Years ago he'd hired professional landscapers to work on all twelve acres, and they'd turned them into a park where nobody walked.

As soon as I step off the road and drift into the trees, I feel like I'm a thousand miles from home. There's fifty feet of forest, but then, nearer the house, the trees have been planted by design. Nothing is out of place. Hundreds of blue spruce in rows that allow for thin walkways and one broad path wide enough for a tractor to be driven among these trees to do maintenance.

Near the house the trees give way to rhododendrons, azalea, and holly, all of it in thick patches bordered by paths just wide enough for one person at a time. It reminds me of a nursery, a place where people browse until they choose half a dozen plants in pots, hoping their houses will soon look more like a picture they've seen in a magazine.

I stop before I get to the wide sweep of lawn, a hundred feet of it that looks to be without weeds, even clover. I know I can be seen from the house now, that somebody like the doctor with his antique cars might have an alarm system or at least a couple of well-trained dogs.

I don't need to go farther. What I've come for is to find the mine shaft that gets filled with sewage, but there's no sign of it among the bushes or the early rows of trees as I circle the house. It could be so well-concealed among a tangle of holly that I don't see it, but I guess that it's closed now, that there isn't a pipe at all anymore, the doctor hooked to the sewer system, the well long abandoned, filled and planted over. Some day, I think, more than vandals will come here in the night because these people have arranged things to bring them. If anyone deserves Erdley's envy and bitterness, it's this doctor.

When I return to the house, Joyce has flowers on the kitchen table, the largest vase she has filled with a bouquet. She's beaming. "From Laurence," she says. "Doesn't that make you want to take back your words?"

"What are they for? Because the court's been injured?"

"For me, Harold. It's been one hundred days since my operation." She hands me the card that reads, For your good fortune during the next "century."

"Isn't that thoughtful?"

Those flowers tower over us as we eat. The kitchen feels like a hospital room.

After dinner I get to work on the court, sifting the Hard-Tru from the soil, packing down that dirt and spreading the salvaged gray powder over the top. When Erdley comes by to carry away another load of household items, he walks straight to the court. "Somebody lead-footed at Wimbledon?" he says, all innocent with ignorance.

"That would be grass to grow back and repair," I say, "a rich man's problem."

As if he needs to inspect my misery to gauge his satisfaction, Erdley comes closer. "Some job you have there," he says.

"It will be good as new before you know it."

Erdley spreads his feet apart in the space left by the open gate. "I know enough to not walk out there in these clodhoppers," he says.

"Good." I mean it. I've reworked all four holes, but anyone, if they took a second look, could see that the levels were off a bit, too shallow and so soft that a ball won't come up properly. It will take professionals to finish this job, people I don't want because Erdley will see that I can't fix the damage.

'You got your shovel out, you want to start filling in my back yard?" Erdley says.

There's an edge to that question that pokes out between funny and bitter. For a moment it teeters as if something might be settled. "A hole that big makes people want to even the score if they can," I say.

"There's no doing that. You can never get things back to even."

"People try though. They do damage to others and expect to feel better."

"Like this court?" Ed says. "Like that would make up for what I have? Is that what you think?"

"It's come to me like that from time to time."

"Why Jesus Christ on the goddamned cross if you're not crazy then from time to time."

I turn back to the holes, smoothing them with the broom, giving Erdley time to say more if he chooses to, or leave, which is what he does, already disappeared into his house by the time I look up. When I leave the court, I don't bother to lock the gate. Anybody coming to wreck the court would move on when they saw the job had already been done.

The following Tuesday I'm working in the office we made out of the boys' old room, and I hear a car pull up. Larry, I think, remembering how I'd postponed our tennis and then forgotten about postponing again. I watch him from the window. He doesn't put his bag down when he opens the gate. He moves from one hole to the other, and after he's made the circuit, he returns to his car and places his bag on the back seat. "Who's responsible?" he says when I walk out. He doesn't move away from the car even though I stand twenty feet from him on the patch of mulch near the court's gate.

"I don't know for sure."

His hand is already on the door to his Saab. "It looks like you did the work yourself, but you need to call someone for that," he says.

"We'll see."

"You'll ruin it even more."

"It's mine to ruin."

"It's yours to be repaired," he says. "You've wasted a week already, and the weather will go bad before you know it. The country club in Allendale has Hard-Tru. Call their pro. He'll have a contact."

"Maybe I will."

"What do you think?" he says. "A week? You have my number. And my e-mail."

When Joyce asks me why Larry has left so quickly, I tell her he thinks we should give the court another week before we use it. "So it's nearly fixed?" she says, and I nod. "That's one less thing to worry about then," she goes on, and I tell her it's fixed but not fixed, that it will be fine, that it will take time for the fill to settle, and then it will be topped again and rolled until the edges of those holes are seamless.

"Like being stitched up after surgery," she says. "You're different inside, but you look the same to others."

"Like that," I say. "Yes."

I go back to my business in the office. An hour later, when I look for Joyce in the kitchen, the side door is open, and I see her standing on the court.

In her bare feet, it turns out, when I go out to see what she's up to. "I took my shoes off," she says. "I know they make a mess if they're the wrong kind. I thought it would feel like the beach, but it doesn't. It's more like carpet over cement." She has a ball in each hand, and I can see she's holding them in front of her face, dropping them in a way that I know is meant to test how consistent the bounce is on the repaired part compared to the undisturbed. "I've seen you do this before," she says. "No wonder Laurence went home."

"It will work itself out."

"How? You already did everything you could. Four big holes. Somebody will hit these almost every point."

I take the balls from her before she can move to the next spot. "You don't have to check the others," I say.

"Laurence won't be back as long as it stays like this."

"Yes, he will."

"When it's fixed right. When it's good as new."

Larry sends an e-mail on Monday. "What do you say to my bringing along a new fellow to join us? He's just turned seventy—we've decided to partner up for the Olympics. Find us a fourth."

He's doesn't ask if the court is ready. When I show it to Joyce, saying "See?" she says, "It won't be tomorrow, Harold. I told him a few more days."

"What difference does that make?"

"Somebody's coming in the morning."

"You called the country club?"

"It takes more than your wishing. And there's a policeman on his way over with some news you need to hear right from his mouth."

"Some teenagers dug up a green at the golf course," the policeman says as soon as he gets out of his car. "It sounded like your problem."

"Yes," Joyce replies at once, and I know she's had the police here when I was at the shops. "If those boys think they're Robin Hoods or something, harassing the rich, they have us wrong."

"It's not like that," the cop says. "They broke into a school; they burned down a garage. There's no sign they're thinking about anything but amusing themselves at somebody else's expense."

"They're not even from around here," Joyce says, after he tells us the town they're from. "They don't even know us." I let her do the talking. It wasn't any idea of mine to bring in the police when I was sure Ed Erdley had done the digging, and I'm willing, now, to let her have the floor.

"This court looks like it's back in the game," the cop says, and I wait for Joyce to speak, but she doesn't.

"Close," I say, "but not quite."

The cop squints a bit and shakes his head. "I guess you'd know better than me." He looks up the street past Leckey's, and I know he's imagining who might live at the end of that road snaking through the trees, whether somebody like that would regularly join me for tennis on a court that looks like it belongs at a country club. "Ok then," he says. "You'll hear from us before too long. Those boys owe you."

"Aren't you happy?" Joyce says to me. "Now you know what I've known all along—it's not your friend and neighbor digging up the court like a monster?"

With that cop standing there, "yes" doesn't come to me like she expects. What comes to me is that it would be better for those holes to have a purpose. I understand the need to square things, but those boys acted out of nothing more than boredom or malice. "There's plenty more where they came from," the cop says. "After a while you just get used to it. Nothing surprises you on this job."

With that, he finally leaves, and Joyce smiles as if having the crime solved makes the world just dandy. The patrol car disappears, and here we are in our yard where we can see Erdley's ruined house and my damaged court at the same time, Joyce telling me, "You go over there now and apologize to your friend." as if everything could be repaired, as if she can't see that even though he's come out of his house with a box in his hands to find out our news, he's already gone. As if she doesn't understand that Erdley's house coming down means I'm the one holding the bag, sooner or maybe, just a little later, showing buyers that miner's map with its maze of veins, but knowing nobody, with those lots sitting vacant across the street, will believe what it says is true.

Other Titles from Elixir Press

Poetry Titles from Elixir Press

Circassian Girl by Michelle Mitchell-Foust
Imago Mundi by Michelle Mitchell-Foust
Distance From Birth by Tracy Philpot
Original White Animals by Tracy Philpot
Flow Blue by Sarah Kennedy
A Witch's Dictionary by Sarah Kennedy
The Gold Thread by Sarah Kennedy
Rapture by Sarah Kennedy
Monster Zero by Jay Snodgrass
Drag by Duriel E. Harris
Running the Voodoo Down by Jim McGarrah
Assignation at Vanishing Point by Jane Satterfield
Her Familiars by Jane Satterfield
The Jewish Fake Book by Sima Rabinowitz
Recital by Samn Stockwell
Murder Ballads by Jake Adam York
Floating Girl (Angel of War) by Robert Randolph
Puritan Spectacle by Robert Strong
X-testaments by Karen Zealand
Keeping the Tigers Behind Us by Glenn J. Freeman
Bonneville by Jenny Mueller
State Park by Jenny Mueller
Cities of Flesh and the Dead by Diann Blakely
Green Ink Wings by Sherre Myers
Orange Reminds You Of Listening by Kristin Abraham
In What I Have Done & What I Have Failed To Do
     by Joseph P. Wood
Bray by Paul Gibbons
The Halo Rule by Teresa Leo
Perpetual Care by Katie Cappello
*The Raindrop's Gospel: The Trials of St. Jerome
     and St. Paula* by Maurya Simon

Prelude to Air from Water by Sandy Florian
Let Me Open You A Swan by Deborah Bogen
Cargo by Kristin Kelly
Spit by Esther Lee
Rag & Bone by Kathryn Nuernberger
Kingdom of Throat-stuck Luck by George Kalamaras
Mormon Boy by Seth Brady Tucker
Nostalgia for the Criminal Past by Kathleen Winter
Little Oblivion by Susan Allspaw
Quelled Communiqués by Chloe Joan Lopez
Stupor by David Ray Vance
Curio by John A. Nieves
The Rub by Ariana-Sophia Kartsonis
Visiting Indira Gandhi's Palmist by Kirun Kapur
Freaked by Liz Robbins
Looming by Jennifer Franklin
Flammable Matter by Jacob Victorine
Prayer Book of the Anxious by Josephine Yu
flicker by Lisa Bickmore
Sure Extinction by John Estes
State Park by Jenny Mueller
Selected Proverbs by Michael Cryer

Fiction Titles

How Things Break by Kerala Goodkin
Juju by Judy Moffat
Grass by Sean Aden Lovelace
Hymn of Ash by George Looney
Nine Ten Again by Phil Condon
Memory Sickness by Phong Nguyen
Troglodyte by Tracy DeBrincat
The Loss of All Lost Things by Amina Gautier
The Killer's Dog by Gary Fincke
Everyone Was There by Anthony Varallo